Nobody Cries At BINGO

dawn dumont

thistledown press

Thistledown Press Ltd.
410 2nd Avenue North
Saskatoon, Saskatchewan, S7K 2C3
www.thistledownpress.com

Library and Archives Canada Cataloguing in Publication

Dumont, Dawn, 1978–
Nobody cries at bingo / Dawn Dumont.
Issued in print and electronic formats.
ISBN 978-1-897235-84-3 (pbk).—ISBN 978-1-927068-11-3 (html).

I. Title.
PS8607.U445N63 2011   C813'.6   C2011-901709-1

Cover painting *Neighbourhood Watch* by Jim Logan
Cover and book design by Jackie Forrie
Printed and bound in Canada

Thistledown Press gratefully acknowledges the financial assistance of the Canada
Council for the Arts, the Saskatchewan Arts Board, and the Government of Canada
through the Canada Book Fund for its publishing program.

dawn dumont

For Nancy and Rose

Young's Point

I was born in a small Saskatchewan town called Balcarres. The town had given itself the nickname, the "Pride of the Prairies," which is a pretty bold statement for a community that boasts more boarded up stores and businesses than regular ones.

Shortly after my debut, I was relocated to the Okanese reserve via a ride in our grandparents' car. Okanese is Cree for Rosebud. The reserve doesn't really have a nickname although many people have called it the "armpit of the universe," usually after they lost an election.

We lived on the Okanese reserve in our green house on the hill with our mom and, sometimes, our dad, until our parents broke up for the 6,945th time. As they say, the 6,945th time is always the charm and Mom really committed herself to this breakup. She packed up our belongings in black garbage bags and moved me and my three siblings — my older sister Tabitha, my younger sister Celeste, and my younger brother David — six hours away from our home to The Pas, Manitoba.

The Pas calls itself the "Gateway to the North," as though that was something people were actively seeking. The word Gateway is a misnomer. The Pas, with its movie theatre that showed only one movie at a time, its grocery stores that didn't sell ripe vegetables, and community centres devoted to the holy religion of hockey, closed off more opportunities than it opened. Of course, The Pas had plenty of other stuff; it was abundant in opportunities to wear toques, balaclavas, and long underwear.

When we first got to Manitoba, we stayed with my aunts and their kids. They provided us with a single bedroom where we slept together in the same bed, all of us arranged around our mom to get maximum contact with her body. When Mom managed to find a house to rent, our aunts helped us move in their big pickup trucks. Moving day was quick because we had so many helping hands and because we had so little.

Our new home was located in Young's Point, a small community about ten minutes outside of The Pas. Young's Point had a square shape, with a skinny dirt road encircling it like a running track. In the centre, facing outwards, were tiny homes with one or two bedrooms. Some had running water; some did not. The sign that led into the housing complex read, "Young's Point, God Lives Here." Despite all evidence to the contrary, we took this as a good sign-sign.

All of our cousins declared that our two-bedroom bungalow was "cool," though most adults would generally agree that it was a dump. One of our older cousins, Norman, showed us how our kitchen window would serve us. "You could see a tornado coming through this window and then you could run out the back door!" He demonstrated by screaming and running out the door.

Norman was one of our favourite cousins because he liked to wrestle and he made us laugh all the time. He lived with my aunt and uncle as a foster child. He was with them for so long that he felt like a full cousin.

"Norman is so silly. Everyone knows the only place you can hide from a tornado is in the basement!" I told Celeste.

Celeste looked thoughtful. "Where is the basement?"

We went through the house opening and closing doors. Finally we went to our expert on everything housing and non-housing related. "Tabitha, where's the basement?"

"There isn't any."

"Where do we go when there's a tornado, then?"

It was Tabitha's turn to look thoughtful. "I could always tie you to a tree."

I suspected she was kidding. She didn't smile so it was possible she was telling the truth. I would have tattled on her but a part of me wanted to be tied to a tree. Then I could see the tornado and be safe. Celeste agreed.

Our fear of tornados was not unfounded. Even though we were living in northern Manitoba and there hadn't been a tornado in about a hundred years, we were originally from Saskatchewan where they were a regular occurrence. Mom brought her fear of tornadoes everywhere she went. "Look at the cloud, look how it's turning black and making a funnel. That's how they start. Next thing you know, your house is flying through the air."

Celeste's eyes lit up. "Like *The Wizard of Oz*?"

"No! Like . . . like . . . a horrible, bloody car crash." Mom wanted her kids to share her fears.

Every week a water truck drove onto Young's Point and pulled up in front of the houses to fill the tanks sitting at the back. My siblings and I were small and watched the water truck from our kitchen window, our cereal-smeared faces lit with glee to see any vehicle larger than the two door beaters that dominated our neighbourhood.

Tabitha and I went to school every day on a big yellow bus that roared through the complex every morning. It dropped us off at the Opasquayak School located on the south end of town. As a Kindergarten student, I wasn't allowed to play with the big kids at recess. We had our own place to play, a small fenced off yard with two half-full sand pits that reeked of urine and boredom, and one set of swings — if you were lucky enough to get one of the swings, you stayed on it until recess was over, no matter that your legs went dead. On the other side of the chain link fence was the big kids' area. They had multiple swing sets, slides, a merry-go- round and ball diamonds. Older kids ran through the area screaming with an exuberance not seen since ancient Greece banned bacchanalia. I yearned to be on the other side of the fence. But I was mindful of the rules and even when my older sister commanded me to crawl through a hole in the fence separating the big kids from the little kids, I shook my head and yelled, "I can't. I'll get in trouble!"

She called back, "Quit being a brownnoser and just come!" I stared at the hole and willed my body to move. It was no use; I sincerely believed the sky would fall on me if I broke the school's rules. So instead, I stood there on my side of the chain link fence staring at my sister while she and her friends watched me from the other side, with a "What the hell is she doing?" look on their faces until the bell rang. The worst part was seeing the disappointment written into the chubby cheeks of my sister's face — I hated letting her down.

Kindergarten was a confusing time. I spent most of my day trying to figure out ways to please the teacher but always ended up annoying her. She asked us to rotate our way through the toys, rather than hogging one to ourselves. I did what she asked with enthusiasm, even going to the point of prying toys out of other kids' hands when I felt they had played with them long enough.

The teacher laughed when another girl's lisp made her say "shit" instead of "sit." She didn't think it was funny at all when I said, "hell" instead of "hello." As a result of my failures to impress my teacher, I spent many afternoons sitting in "The Corner," which had its own cubicle walls so that you could enjoy your punishment in privacy.

At the end of every Kindergarten day, I rode the bus home with my sister. The seats were huge and my feet would dangle freely. I enjoyed looking at the reflection of myself in the driver's oversized mirror. Here I was sitting and kicking my legs and there I was, much smaller and off to an angle doing the same thing. "Stop kicking," Tabitha said.

The small girl in the mirror stopped kicking and looked sad.

To distract me, Tabitha asked me about my day.

"Today Teacher . . . ," I began.

"Did you forget your teacher's name again?'

"Yes. Today Teacher gave us all cookies and Casey's cookie got broken in half and she started crying."

"Over a cookie?" Tabitha rolled her eyes.

"Casey cries a lot. So Teacher says, 'look Casey it's like you have two cookies now.' And Casey stopped crying. So then I took my cookie and broke it into lots of pieces. And I said, 'Teacher, I have lots of cookies too.'"

"And what did she say?"

"Stop making a mess."

"Did you tie your shoes yourself today?"

I nodded my head. And the little girl in the mirror nodded her head too. Both of us were lying. Learning to tie shoes was turning out to be a nightmare. I had discovered it was easier to loosen the knot and slip off my shoes. Then at the end of the school day, I'd slip them back on and tighten up the knot again.

To distract her from my lie, I asked the question that was always guaranteed to generate an answer. "Where is Dad?"

"I already told you. He's in Saskatchewan at our other house."

"When is he coming here?"

"I don't know. Stop asking everyone, especially Mom. Okay?"

"Okay." I made my mouth big when I said it so that the girl in the mirror agreed with me.

You could see everyone else on the bus in the mirror. I made a face at myself. Then I saw an older boy staring at me through it. Caught, I quickly looked out the window. When I dared to look again, the older boy was making faces at me.

I tapped Tabitha on the shoulder. "There's someone staring at me."

"Where?"

"In the mirror."

Tabitha looked in the mirror. Little kids picked their noses. Some boys bullied another boy. Girls sat backwards and flipped their hair as they talked to their friends. The older boy in the mirror was gone.

"What did he look like?"

"Big. Like he's too old for this bus."

"Well, I don't see him."

He had ruined the mirror game for me. Now all I had left was the window. I could barely see the little girl there.

I tapped my sister on the shoulder again.

"I need to go to the bathroom."

"Why didn't you go in school?"

"Teacher wouldn't let me."

Bathroom breaks were orderly ventures in Kindergarten. Like a short, co-dependent football team, we did everything together. When it was time to empty our bladders, we stood in straight lines and marched down the hallway.

That afternoon our teacher had read us a book about a little boy who was adventurous. "Little boys are always so naughty. I wish I had a little boy!" she had commented to our class, thus kicking off every little girl's journey to self-hate in the room.

Inspired by the naughty boy, I climbed onto the sink and looked over the side of the cubicle. Casey was in there, doing her thing.

"Surprise!" I called down.

Casey looked up, screamed and — predictably — began to cry. She pulled up her panties and stalked out of the bathroom. Before I even had time to climb off the sink, the teacher was there waving her finger at me. I found myself back in "the corner" before I remembered that I still hadn't used the toilet.

Tabitha rolled her eyes at my stupidity. "It's only two minutes to our house. You can last two minutes, can't you?"

I shook my head. I knew without looking at the little girl in the mirror that panic had spread across my face.

"Too bad cuz you have to wait."

Tabitha was my guide to the world and as such was infallible. This time, however, she was dead wrong. I did not have to wait. The bus hit a bump in the grid road and the decision was made for me. My bladder released its heavy load. I felt sweet relief and my first thought was, "That's not so bad. Actually it's sort of warm and pleasant."

The good feeling was quickly swept aside as my sister's proclamations of "Gross!" informed the rest of the bus's occupants to my accident. Soon, the kids were echoing my sister's comment and adding new ones: "What a baby," "that kindergarten baby peed herself," and "I wish I hadn't waited until now to eat my peanut butter sandwich."

Fortunately it happened right outside our house. The bus door opened and Tabitha ran inside and announced my shame to everyone. I followed at a much soggier pace. Mom led me into the bathroom and sat me on the slop pail. The slop pail — if you need any further explanation — was a metal pail about three feet high that served the same function as a toilet, except of course, it did not flush.

"What's the point of that?" Tabitha asked. "She already peed all over me!"

As it turned out, there was more detritus that needed voiding. My bowels relaxed as their burden was unloaded.

"See? There was a point," Mom laughed and David and Celeste joined in. Even I laughed.

"This is the grossest house ever!" Tabitha stalked away.

The slop pail was uncomfortable but Mom claimed we were lucky to have it. "Hell of a lot better than when I was kid. Back then you had to freeze your bum off outside."

"You peed outside? Like a dog?" I asked.

"No! In the outhouse. We weren't animals, for God's sake."

"What's an outhouse?"

"A little building that's outside the house where you go to the bathroom. You kids don't know anything about roughing it, that's for sure."

The slop pail was the next step up on the bathroom evolutionary ladder. While never a pleasure to use, it was even more difficult to operate if you were short. My hands would have to go down first, on either side of the slop pail, and then I'd have to jump a little and get my butt on. But very carefully because when it comes to slop pails, failure is not an option. If you slip, you might fall in the murky waste — bum first — or, much worse, tip it over and decorate the bathroom with the contents. That's a mistake you only make once in your life. (Or if you are my brother David, every single day for a month until Mom decided to move him *back* into diapers.)

Despite the slop pail challenges, our cousins loved coming to visit us. Young's Point was off the reserve; it was undiscovered territory and they were eager to make their mark. The highlight of every visit was walking through the woods to a convenience store so small it was basically amounted to an enterprising hippie couple who sold chocolate bars and potato chips out of their kitchen.

"We could get mugged," Norman said, peering into the trees. "Up in the city, people get mugged all the time." Then he etched his name into a fir tree with his knife.

I stared into the dark woods trying to discern the muggers. On a walk with Tabitha, she dismissed my concerns. "As if. There aren't any muggers here, just bears," she said as she practiced smoking with a twig.

Tabitha not only knew everything, she was willing to try anything. Her long legs discovered a stream running through the woods and she immediately began to wade into it. "What about polio?" I asked her, even as I scratched the huge polio vaccine scar on my arm.

"There's no such thing," she said. "Now get in here and wet your feet."

I moved slowly, entering only one foot at a time, sucking in my breath as the cold water found its way through my runner,

through my sock to my foot. "I got a booter! I got a booter!"
I cried.

Tabitha shook her head. "I told you to take your shoes off!"
she said, as she ushered me and my wet feet home, sloshing all
the way down the muddy path.

Walks with Tabitha were important for figuring out the
world.

"You know Tabitha, I can't tie my shoes. Other kids can do
it, but I can't," I said, on another trip to the junk food store.

"Did you try the Bunny ears?"

"Yes, I tried the Bunny years."

"E-ears."

"I thought you said, Y-Years."

She kneeled down. "You make two loops, each one looks
like a Bunny ear. You see?" she explained.

I sighed in relief. "Oh right. I thought I was going crazy."

"You're not crazy."

"I have another question. How come I can't ride my bike
yet?"

"Cuz your legs are too short," she said.

"So when they grow, I can do it?"

Tabitha lingered on her answer for a few seconds. I
waited — my heart clenched. Oh please don't say I won't ever
ride my bike, I have to ride my bike! Please don't say there's
something wrong with me that can't ever be fixed.

"When your legs grow, you'll do it."

"Thank goodness." I let out my breath. "I have another
question. How come the priests take our money?"

"I think they . . . use it for God."

That didn't answer my question exactly. I figured there was
some stuff people had to figure out on their own. So I thought
about it that night and by morning I had my answer.

I decided the big sister thing would be to share my newfound information with my younger sister, Celeste, who was badly in need of some world knowledge. Over our cereal bowls the next morning, I pontificated on the subject of priests and our money. "You see, Celeste, priests take our money because they are stupid."

Mom dropped a pot in the sink with a loud clang and spun around. "What did you say?"

"Priests take our money?"

"The other part," she growled.

"I love you?"

"What did you call priests?"

I looked at Celeste for help. She was smiling into her cereal. "Uh . . . stupid," I replied in a small voice.

"How dare you! They are good and holy men who help spread the word of God."

"How come they can't use their own money?"

"Hush! God is listening to everything you say and he will be angry at you for insulting his workers. And you don't want God to be mad at you." Mom was understandably upset. Her parents, graduates of the residential school system, had grown up with a healthy fear of the clergy and it had been passed on to their children.

My mom's anger was the reason I ended my religious teachings. I wasn't scared of God's anger. If he was like Santa, he never listened when I asked for things, so why would he listen to anything bad I had to say about him?

I was annoyed at Mom for interrupting my lesson because it undermined my credibility with my younger sister. Celeste had had a smirk on her face during the exchange. Although to be fair to Celeste, I think her face was just like that.

Mom was going through a stressful time. She was attempting to re-make her life. She was in her early thirties and she'd wasted enough years on a dead-end marriage. She had moved to The Pas to start over, and although it was hard, things were starting to work out for her. She had her kids in school, a welfare check coming in every month and a good job cleaning motel rooms that paid under the table. She had two sisters who had married guys on the nearby Big Eddy Reserve who were also willing to help out when needed. Mom felt like life was finally moving forward. It was the longest time that she had ever left my dad.

Mom was a new woman, an independent woman. And why shouldn't she be? Times were a' changing. It wasn't the seventies anymore when women took shit. It was the eighties. Women didn't need to stick around and get beaten by their husbands; they had choices. Hadn't Mary Tyler Moore proven this? Sure Mary wasn't a single mother burdened by the demands of looking after four children under the age of eleven, and true, she didn't have to contend with racism, but the message was the same: women could do things on their own.

Our next-door neighbour was also a Mary but she wasn't a spunky go-getter like the television Mary. She was a shy, thin Cree woman who was too timid to even knock on our door. When she was in the mood for gossip, she opened her door and lingered on her front steps until Mom noticed her and invited her in for coffee.

Then Mary would smile and gather her children around her. Her kids were like her, thin and shy. They were shadows next to our pudgy shapes. They crept along behind us as we played in the centre of Young's Point in our "playground."

The playground consisted of one piece of equipment — a huge slide. Nothing else, just an empty field and a giant wooden slide rising out of the earth like Ayers Rock. No one knew where it came from or how long it had been there.

I overheard my mom and her sisters discussing it. "I didn't even notice it when I rented the place. I just opened my curtains one day and there it was," Mom said.

"Looks dangerous," one of my aunts commented.

"I might as well forget about keeping the kids away from it. I could scream myself silly and they'd still run over to it. Look around, there's nothing else to play on for miles."

It was true. The slide was the only thing in Young's Point that looked like it might have been built with kids in mind, although there was no evidence that kids were supposed to enjoy it. For one thing it was at least three storeys high, a height that was challenging even to teenagers. My aunt's teenage boys had to dare each other to climb it.

"Go on Norm, try it out."

"Why me? You're the one who wants to do it," Norman replied.

"Cuz if you don't, we'll tell Dad we saw you smoking."

"Assholes. Here, hold my smokes."

Also, the slide was made completely out of a raw, unvarnished wood, and reinforced potato sacks were necessary to its enjoyment. We had none so we slid down on our bums and jackets. Each time you went down, you crossed your fingers that you wouldn't get a sliver in your hand or worse, your butt. Prayer doesn't always work and more than once I would find myself next to Tabitha as she gently pushed a sliver out of my palm.

"Stand still!" she ordered.

"I'm trying!" I said even as I stamped my feet in a hypnotic dance of pain and pleasure. It was scary to have a piece of wood in your hand but it also felt good to have her hands pressing it out. A sliver was so easily healed that it was the best of childhood hurts. In the hands only; a sliver in the butt was not so easily cured. Tabitha refused to work on those ones. Those were Mom's realm and saved for bath day.

Our quiet neighbours followed along beside us and did whatever we did with far less enthusiasm.

"How come they're so quiet?" I asked Tabitha.

"It's cuz they're from the north," Tabitha explained.

I couldn't wrap my head around that completely. "We're already north."

"More north."

"Like the North Pole?"

"No. Just north."

Mary laughed at everything my mom said, which made her mom's best friend. She would laugh into her hand like a little kid, her laugh escaping in a squeak. "*Eek, eek, eek.*" She laughed especially hard when my mom would say something naughty . . . like about men.

"Go play!" Mom yelled at us as we stood at the doorway from the living room.

In the kitchen they would talk, my mom's bossy confidence slowly overtaking the woman. Soon Mary was opening up to my mom. She talked about how she wanted to move back to her reserve in the north. She said her husband had come down here for work but he had changed. He was no longer nice to her. She felt the need to say these things even though her bruised face and timid manner had already told everyone the story.

"Well, if it happens again, you can come here," Mom said.

I shuddered as I listened around the corner. Mary's husband was the size of a bear. Our dad's anger was a scary sight to behold but Mary's husband was terrifying even when he was smiling.

Mary laughed at Mom's bold words. It wasn't the "*eek, eek,*" it was a full laugh that came from her gut. "No," she said still laughing, "I couldn't come here." Her eyes climbed up the walls of the house, lingering on the narrow beams and thin drywall, the windows and the door with only one lock.

Every day before five o'clock rolled around, she packed her kids up and rushed back to her house. Mom stood at the door and watched her go. She turned to Tabitha — who sat in as Mom's confidante when there were no other friends or sisters around. "If I hear about that man hitting Mary again, I'm gonna rush over there and knock his head off. I swear I will."

"How will you know if he hits Mary?" I asked from around the corner.

"Was I talking to you? Go play."

I took a step backwards into the living room and pretended that I couldn't hear my mom's conversation. Adult conversation was interesting, if confusing. How come women always got mad when men hit them? Yet when David hit Celeste or me, Mom never got angry. She'd say, "Let him play with you and he won't get so mad."

Celeste and I had already agreed that David was no fun and that was that. He would *never* play with us.

※

Dad showed up one day. There was no phone call to warn us, but Mom didn't seem surprised when he filled the doorway with his broad shoulders.

His arrival was like Christmas to us kids and not just because he arrived on Christmas Day. Without hesitation, Celeste and I launched ourselves onto his lap. We were his girls, his pony-tailed bookends of love.

We also sat there because we were able to push David away with our feet when he tried to get close to Dad. David toddled up to Dad with his chubby hands held expectantly over his head, his tight striped T-shirt slowly working its way up his big belly. He stopped at the base of Dad's chair, and looked up, baring his big dimples and deep soulful eyes rimmed with dark eyelashes only to find himself facing the business end of a stocking foot.

"What a suck David is," I told Dad, as David's cry rang out.

"He is always crying," Celeste added, her eyes crazy with delight. It was hard for her to hide her love of making David cry, especially since she was so good at it.

Tabitha and Dad had a different relationship than the rest of us. Their relationship was one of going places. Tabitha's small head looked even smaller next to his as they pulled away in the truck.

"Chips and a drink! Chips and a drink!" Celeste and I sang from the doorway. We were unable to cross the barrier of the doorframe and we yelled our orders by leaning our heads out like flowers straining for the sun. We were confident that Tabitha would deliver our requested goods and we stood at the front door waiting until they returned.

It was in the kitchen that Mom and Dad negotiated their relationship. Neither was good at words so they used silences instead. My mother's long pause as she took a sip of her coffee and stared out the window told him that she would not go back to being hit whenever he felt like it. And he better lay off his damn drinking, too. Dad stirred milk into his coffee cup. The gentle turn of his spoon told her that he was a different man.

Back in the living room, we played happily, as if our toys were brand new. Celeste and I barely fought and we allowed David to sit next to us. Having Dad around made us feel like we were complete. Everything before he came had been an experiment and now our lives were real. We didn't know our new family was built on insecure promises and assurances. To our way of thinking, if Dad was here, then he was staying and now everything would be perfect forever and ever.

Except for one thing; I still couldn't ride my bike. Mom had explained the mechanics of it. "Get on and drive it." Since she didn't know how to ride a bike herself- that was the extent of her advice.

Tabitha was a pro and had demonstrated the basic maneuvers. "Peddle like this. Push down, pull up. Keep moving and you won't fall over." She would ride past me, turn around, and ride back and brake in front of me. "See?"

My dad added his sage wisdom. "You gotta just do it."

"Uh, huh." I nodded as I took in all their bicycling tips. I also examined my palms, which were pockmarked with gravel from the last spill I had taken. Every fall made me question my desire. "Is it really necessary to know how to ride a bike?" Why couldn't I just run everywhere? Or get Mom to drive me?

Watching Tabitha fly by, I knew it would be impossible to keep up with her if I didn't learn. And too, I could feel a pair of brown eyes watching from the steps. I didn't have to turn to know what I would see there: a pudgy little girl with golden hair. Celeste's eyes told me that she was determined to do whatever I could do, and preferably better. When we weren't working together to thwart David, Celeste and I were competing with one another to be the cutest, most loveable girl in the world. I knew this without knowing this and it was a powerful motivator. I could not give up.

I grabbed my green bike with its banana seat and began my journey. I pushed it beside me around Young's Point. I jumped on the bike, and rolled forward with it for a few seconds. It began to sway to the left so I jumped off. "Crap," I said.

I ran beside it for a few seconds before jumping on again. I went around the Young's Point circle a full time without pedaling a single complete revolution. I imagined that everyone in the little houses was watching me and noting my failure.

"How you doing?" Tabitha called from the front yard where she was pumping up her tires. They were covered with patches but they still went flat every twenty minutes.

"Almost there," I answered, as I jogged past.

I glanced at the kitchen window. Celeste sat cross-legged on the kitchen table watching me like an envious Buddha. Her eyes gave me a jolt of energy and I ran a little faster.

I tried again, the bike swayed heavily to the right and I jumped off. This was hard. My face felt red and sweaty and I was on the verge of giving up when I felt it: a warm hand on my shoulder. I looked behind me. There was no one there. I didn't feel scared because I knew what it was. A guardian angel. I had learned about these in my catechism class held in the church basement. Everyone had one and they were there to protect us, and, in my case, to teach me how to a ride a bike.

A few seconds later, I jumped on my bike . . . and didn't fall off. One moment, I was running beside my bike and the next, I was riding it. I could feel the wind in my face and the gravel being crushed beneath my tires. I whispered my thanks to God and then added a small apology for calling his helpers stupid. I had every reason to be magnanimous; I had my bike, my family, and Young's Point. I was unstoppable now.

I Slept There

F OR MOST OF MY YOUTH, MY FAMILY and I were nomads wandering from province to province. My siblings and I were experienced road travelers before the age of five. We knew what to pack for a trip, and what snack to bring. We knew how to balance our pop intake with bathroom breaks, though we were kids and the odd accident sometimes occurred, which is why David wasn't allowed to sit in the middle of the seat. We could play all day in the car, sleep in it all night without ever, not even once, getting carsick.

It's our destiny to travel; we're Nehewin, more commonly known as Cree. It was the French who started calling us Cree, which meant big mouth. I'm going out on a limb and assuming it was meant as an insult. The name caught on and everyone started using it, including us. There are a few Native organizations that still use the word "Cree." That's like the French calling their government, the Association of Frogs. The Nehewin weren't exactly innocent when it comes to name-calling. Eskimo is a Nehewin word, which means raw meat eaters. This name also caught on, for many years much to the chagrin of the Inuit.

Traditionally, the Nehewin had no cities or towns, just places they visited depending on the season. Our territory stretched from the centre of Canada up into the early arctic, south into the Dakotas, east to Quebec and west to the mountains of British Columbia.

The tribe members were not random wanderers; their travels had a point. They were following the buffalo herds. This animal was our tribe's primary source of sustenance, shelter and fashion. The Nehewin's travelling habits were curtailed when the buffalo population, once an ocean of brown on the plains, withered to a few hundred. The Canadian government stepped in and created protected reserves for the buffalo where they now grow fat but remain wild. Then they created reserves for the Native people where they grew also fat and remain a little wild.

The travel agent for all our childhood excursions was a fun-loving young woman with a wild laugh; some may have called her daring, others reckless; we called her Mom. She followed no buffalo herd; only a desire for a better life that she felt was a hundred miles in the other direction. Mom was also a nomad for another reason; sometimes it is the only way to leave a man — this man being our dad.

"Shhh . . . get your shoes on. We have to go." Mom would shake us awake. We would climb out of our warm bunk beds, without complaining.

From an early age, my siblings and I were practiced in the art of getting dressed in the dark. We'd pull on our jeans and t-shirts discarded the night before beside our beds, and stealthily slip on our jackets, like pudgy ninjas. We were a well-oiled machine . . . except when it came to our shoes. They were always the hardest to find. They would wander from the sides of the bed into the laundry hamper or find their way to the porch. Too many times I spent rummaging through the shoebox with my mom's angry whisper behind me, "C'mon, c'mon!"

We'd tiptoe through the dark hallway past the tall man snoring with his head on the dinner table. We'd head for the side door, still half asleep, and find our way to the car, warming up outside.

While we slept, the car transported us through time and space in the blink of an eye. The last sound we heard was the clicking of the turning signal as Mom turned off the reserve onto the main road. And the next sound we heard would be the dinging of the car door as my mom reached inside the car and carried each of us to our temporary home.

On one of our trips, Mom ran out of steam between Manitoba and Saskatchewan. She had driven ten hours straight and needed sleep so she pulled into a farmer's field. In the back of the car we bounced along as the car drove over deep ruts and potholes hidden by the grass. Then my brother's body bounced high enough to hit the ceiling. He cried as all of his older sisters laughed at him. We were enjoying the ride a little too much and Mom threatened us with *lick'ens* until we stopped laughing.

She drove the car deep into the field behind a bale of hay. The bale was twice the size of the car and I told David that it fed giant horses. "And little boys," I added. This comment elicited a cuff to the side of the head, Mom's arm unerringly finding her target from the front seat.

We felt lucky to be in that field. We never went camping, as my mom feared the woods and everything in them. Camping also meant planning, something at odds with her spontaneous nature. It meant finding a tent, with poles. It meant reserving a spot and bringing sleeping bags or at least blankets. It meant packing food for three or four days. It meant knowing where you wanted to go and how long you wanted to stay there.

The pasture was more Saskatchewan than Manitoba with its flat land and sparse trees. The sky was full of sleeping sun when my mom set the car into park and turned off the motor.

"Wait till I tell our cousins," I told my sister Celeste as we ran to another bale to pee before bed. "They will be so jealous."

Our cousins led sedentary lives compared to us. They went to bed at night and when they woke up, they were in the same place. Their lives were not marked with any extended visits to Manitoba or midnight runs back to Saskatchewan. Mom blamed my dad's drinking for our travels but her sisters had also married alcoholics.

Mom said the difference between herself and her sisters was that she wouldn't take a *lick'en*, definitely not in front of her children. It seemed like we had two dads: the funny guy who loved to spoil us with trips to Chinese buffets and KFC, and the other, a stranger with explosive anger and hooded eyes who showed up after midnight.

We kept going back to him or he kept coming back to us. We would be on our own for a few months and then we'd hear a knock on the door. He'd be standing on the threshold with a sheepish, hopeful look on his face. Mom would invite him in to talk and before we knew it, Dad was back in his place at the head of the table.

Other times their re-attachment had a different pattern. Mom would go out with one of her friends to blow off some steam. Inevitably, they would run into Dad at a party. She would mock him with her independence. Intrigued, he would offer her a drink. She would ignore him and talk with her friends, pretending not to notice when his hand slipped around her waist. The next morning Dad would be home and we would celebrate with a trip to the local KFC where he would regale us with his adventures. This is probably why the smell of fried chicken reminds me of my dad's laugh . . . and vice versa.

I didn't mind the leaving or the returning. My only frustration was the lack of good reading material. There was nothing worse than arriving at a relative's house and finding that their library consisted of heavy metal magazines featuring stories like "The Inspiration Behind Motley Crue's 'Smoking in the Boyz Room'".

At home we had books everywhere. My mother was a voracious reader and finished a novel every two days. I followed in her wake, picking up her books and sneaking them back into my lair, the bed that I shared with my younger sister, which pissed her off. Celeste was always complaining about the hardcovers left in our bed. "I slept on this stupid book and now my spine is broken!"

I couldn't stop myself. Reading was my addiction and I read from the moment I woke up until I fell asleep at night. There was that moment before I learned to read when I used to trace my hand under the words, understanding that this symbol meant this thing in the picture above. And then there was that next moment, when the code was broken and everything was clear.

Books inspired me, which was easy since I was impressionable, to an unhealthy degree. After a spending a few minutes around a person with an accent, lisp or other affectation, I began to mimic it.

"Stop that," Mom said, after we left the grocery store.

"Stop . . . doing . . . wwwhhhat?" (The cashier had had a stutter.)

"Keep it up and I'll make it permanent."

Characters in books also inspired me. While reading *Anne of Green Gables*, my personality underwent a dramatic change. My normally pouty outlook became perky and personable. My natural tendency to stay inside, avoid chores and read while sprawled out on my bed, was replaced by an inclination towards singing made-up songs and improvising dances while I dusted the living room. My family noticed and said nothing; they didn't want to jinx it.

I read that my red-haired doppelganger gave fantastic names to local sights like the Avenue of Shining Lights. So I took my sister Celeste on a high-energy jaunt through the woods where I named all of our favourite haunts. The garbage pit became the Mountain of Lost Dreams, the local cesspool became the Lake of Smiling Waters, and our playhouse became the Mansion Over-Looking the Smiling Waters. Being Anne was tiring, and inevitably I returned to being myself.

We loved our orange and brown wood paneled station wagon. It wasn't just a mode of transportation: it was a bedroom, kitchen and playground. As Mom drove down the highway, my siblings and I would hang backwards over the seats until the blood rushed into our heads. From this view the world rushed towards us upside down. Sadly, like most fun things, if you did it too long, you'd end up throwing up.

Mom gossiped with her friend or if no friend was available, Tabitha, in the front seat while we played "Not It," "Freeze Tag" and "Tickle David until he cries." The backseat was our country and we had free rein over it as long as no one awakened Mom's attention. Eventually someone would start crying (usually Celeste or David) because someone had been too mean (usually me). Then Mom's yell would invade our territory and we'd have to sit up straight and face frontward, seat belts slung over our waists. We could not fasten them; the seat belt claps had broken years before. Safety wasn't the concern, seat belts were merely indications that we had heard and would behave.

In the summertime we never knew where the station wagon would go. A trip to town might become a glorious two-week journey to northern Manitoba or just a no-thrills ten minute trip back home. We'd never know for sure until we saw which direction the hood ornament pointed. If turning left led back to the reserve, then we would whisper, "right, right, right." Up front, Mom's hands would drum on the steering wheel until her internal compass pointed her in the right direction.

During the school months, road trips weren't eliminated but they were shorter and tended to be inspired more by necessity than lark. Most of these trips were of the midnight run variety and as I got older they became more complicated. It's tough to explain to your teacher why your homework isn't done, tougher still to explain why you left all your books at home and that you don't know when you'll be going home to get them. Extra points if you can explain all this without referencing your dad's alcoholism.

One night our trusty station wagon stalled on us. We were at the t-stop where the reserve ended and the highway began.

It was November in Saskatchewan, which is a recipe for frostbite. Mom reluctantly opened the door to investigate under the hood. Tabitha slid over into the driver's seat and all of us in the backseat envied her.

We watched Mom by the light of the car's beams, jiggling the battery cables with a pair of pliers she kept stashed in the glove compartment for such emergencies. Then she asked Tabitha to start the car.

Tabitha turned the ignition. No comforting roar, no encouraging grunts. Even the inhabitants of the backseat knew that was bad.

Mom moved the cables around some more. "Try again," she yelled, her voice sounding lonesome in the cold wind.

Nothing.

Her knowledge of cars fully spent, Mom slid into the passenger's seat and blew into her hands. "It's cold out there," she shivered. "Colder than the tits on a witch."

We giggled in the back seat.

As she formulated a plan, Mom lit a smoke. "Well, no big deal. We'll just wait for someone to give us a boost." Once again, nicotine had failed to quicken her synapses.

Tabitha looked out the driver side window at a light far into the distance. "Is that a train coming?"

Five heads turned in unison. David, Celeste and I got on our knees and looked out the windows. The light was huge and coming closer. It shone like a flashlight, except several hundred times brighter and scarier.

I looked at Mom. "We crossed over the tracks, right?"

Mom nodded her head. "Of course." Then she got out of the car and checked. She jumped back in. "Lots of room." Nobody sighed in relief. We were all too busy reviewing everything we knew about trains in our heads.

For years Mom had been telling us that trains could suck you under. According to her, it wasn't even safe to stand ten feet away and throw rocks at the train. To back up her point, she would tell the grisly story of her uncle who had graduated from the seminary and was travelling home in his long priest robes. A breeze had blown his dress too close to the wheels and the train had sucked him under. "They had to close the coffin for his funeral," she'd finish. Everyone would shudder at this part, silently imagining what the closed coffin held.

The moral of the story was that trains were dangerous, even to the very good and holy. For years I thought it was a warning not to become a priest or a nun — those long dresses were a menace.

The train roared again. I could almost feel the engineer's annoyance at our car. I'm sure he was thinking, "What kind of idiot parks that close to the tracks?" But he did not stop and soon the train was practically on top of us.

Trains sound loud from miles away and when they are fifty metres away, you have to cover your ears. David lunged over the front seat and perched himself on Mom's lap.

Ignoring our mom's admonitions to stay still and put on our seat belts, Celeste and I jumped over the back seat and got into the back-back. (Well, Celeste did it first and being the older sister, I felt obligated to do the same. At times like these it really sucks to have a brave younger sister.)

There we lay on our tummies, our faces in our hands watching the train lumber past us. Unlike celebrities, sports heroes and priests who shrink with proximity, trains get a lot bigger up close.

Celeste counted every car. I silently observed our position on the road and watched to see if the train was pulling us closer. When the car remained stationary, I was pleased to conclude that trains had no magnetic or gravitational pull, at least not where station wagons were concerned.

"How long is this damn train?" Mom wondered from the front seat.

When the caboose finally sailed past, David cheered happily from the safety of our mom's chest.

Mom celebrated with a deep drag on her smoke.

It was hard to decide which was more exciting, almost getting run over by a train or getting to see a train up close. Probably the latter because we all hoped that another train would come by soon.

"Our cousins are going to be so jealous."

"I know, we are the luckiest!"

"Are we going to sleep here, Mom?"

This road was busy as it was only one of four main roads leading into the reserve. In no time at all someone, probably a relative, would pull up beside us and offer their aid. This time, however, help came from an unexpected quarter.

On the edge of the reserve lived a family of Mormons. The land they squatted on belonged to the local town and was dirt-cheap for the simple reason that it was near the Indian reserve. However that suited the purposes of the Mormons for they saw the reserve as an infinite wellspring of converts.

They were often seen driving from house to house, fighting off rez dogs and having tea with the house's inhabitants. The Native population tolerated them well. It was nice to be visited by a white person who smiled a lot and treated you as their equal. Their church also had the best picnics — or so I heard. We could never go because Mom was fiercely loyal to the Catholic Church that her parents had raised her in. Her brother, our Uncle Larry, felt no such loyalty and belonged to the Mormon, Catholic and United Churches. His kids loved picnics.

Mom recognized their truck as it stopped beside us. "Oh shit, it's the Mormons."

Two neatly dressed men stood outside Mom's door. They were tall and slim with cashew-coloured hair. Standing next to one another beside our car, they looked like that photo you get with your picture frames before you pull it out and insert the one of your sloppy relatives.

The man addressed her: "Ma'am, do you need some assistance?"

In the backseat, Celeste and I whispered to each other.

"How come he called Mom, Man?"

"Are Mormons the same thing as cops?"

"Why are their pants so neat?"

Up front, Mom considered her options: wait for help in the cold car or take help from strangers? She looked in her rear view mirror. There were no car lights coming up the reserve road so she reluctantly admitted that our car would not start. We were transferred to their truck in a few minutes.

The Mormons lived nearby in three large trailers. Even though we were poor, we associated trailers with poorer people. For instance, Uncle Larry lived in a trailer.

The Mormons were well off. They lived in trailers because the conversion business sometimes had them moving from place to place in search of a better source of souls. They had not yet established a permanent church on the reserve (and never would) but when they did, the trailers would be sold and they would set down roots and basements.

Their trailer was welcoming. We were astounded by the size of their living space. Not for the last time I realized that trailers were like icebergs; you will always underestimate their true size by forty per cent. Even more shocking was the realization that they had no TV. My siblings and I noticed this immediately, but we were too polite to mention it.

Two lady Mormons greeted us at the front door. They took our jackets and hung them up in the closet. My mom, suspicious, kept her jacket by her side.

One of the women offered us some cold juice. With the minus twenty-degree weather outside it was an odd choice. Perhaps the Latter Day saints do not feel the cold.

My mom thanked the woman. I could tell she was troubled because Mom drank only coffee from morning until night. However, she was respectful of other people's beliefs and instead of complaining, said, "Orange juice, what a treat. Yum, that hits the spot."

After the sharing of juice, the Mormons stared at us and we stared back at them. With no TV, we were at a loss. They had children but they were in bed as it was way past six PM. One of the Morman ladies brought my brother a blanket as he fell asleep on the floor. First, of course, he bounced his head rhythmically for about two minutes before finally dropping off into unconsciousness. With nothing else to do, everyone in the room watched him. The Mormons looked from David to Mom, back to David again.

Celeste kicked David. He grunted and continued knocking his head on the floor.

"It's how he gets to sleep," Mom explained.

The women continued to stare at him. None of us thought they were being rude. It was a strange thing to witness; even we thought so.

After David fell asleep, the silence in the room threatened to crush our skulls.

"Do you have any books?" I asked the Mormon lady nearest to me.

Mom glared at me. We were under standing orders not to make a fuss in someone else's house.

I couldn't help myself. Unlike Anne of Green Gables, I had no imagination. I had to be constantly entertained with cartoons, a book or a wrestling match with one of my siblings.

Already I could feel my shaking hands creeping towards my sister's long hair.

One of the women smiled broadly and left the room. She returned with a large book, the Mormon bible. Eagerly, I grabbed it from her hands. I loved its heft. Inside there were no pictures but there were words, oh so many words. I began to read immediately. The woman was overjoyed, Mom decidedly less so.

"We're Catholic," Mom said suddenly with no small amount of defiance.

The woman nodded. "We respect all religions."

"She's . . . made her first communion, y'know, the ceremony where children commune with God." Mom was reaching and she knew it.

"That's wonderful. However, it is important to allow children to explore."

Mom gave up. She was no match for someone who had been trained in evangelical tactics since she was ten years old.

I read until my eyes began to glaze over, the whole time aware of my mom's glares boring into the back of my head.

Finally the men came in from outside. They had recharged our battery, fixed a tire that was going flat and done a quick oil change. They were truly miraculous, these Mormons.

Mom offered them some money. Of course they would not take it. For them the giving was the reward. And the chance that it would lead to new converts was a possible secondary reward. Mom picked up my sleeping brother, pushed my sisters towards the door and dragged me away from my bible. The woman pressed some pamphlets into my hand as we left. "Come back anytime," she said joyously.

Outside Mom smacked the back of my head. "What were you thinking?" she asked, "You have a church."

I shrugged. If the Mormon lady had handed me a copy of Satan's Bible I would have read it. If she had pressed a copy of *Mein Kampf* in my hands, I would have given it a go. For me, the real reward was a book to distract myself from our ever-changing landscape. No matter where we went or how we got there, I wanted to know that I could depend on a book to centre myself. Books were my cigarettes.

We drove out of the Mormon's yard back onto the main road. Mom turned the wheel north towards our cousins who lived in the valley. We would either go visit my auntie Squaw and her kids or my auntie Bunny and her kids where we would stay for a night or a week or a month. Those decisions would be made in the front seat, and the inhabitants of the back seat would accept them, knowing that it did not matter where you rested your head as long as you woke up with family.

A Spooky Halloween

I n Saskatchewan, Halloween occurs shortly after the first snowfall and right before snow makes itself a permanent nuisance. Sometimes, however, the weather turned bad even before Halloween, which meant our costumes had to fit over our puffy winter jackets. The number of princess costumes ruined by Saskatchewan winters must number in the millions.

Halloween was the night when we would stand beside our mom and hand out candy to the local kids and young adults. I remember the cold wind flowing into the kitchen as my mom drew the trick or treater inward. We'd see plenty of princesses and cowboys and Star Trek uniforms. The real highlight of Halloween was a teenage boy dressed in his mother's dress, his chest padded with his own sweat socks, his deep voice mocking a lipstick-smeared mouth. My mother would grab onto the boy's arm and yell for the rest of the family to come enjoy the show. A boy dressed as a woman! Was there nothing funnier in this world? Not in Saskatchewan, apparently.

Finally, it was our turn. We'd run to our bedrooms and pull our pillowcases off our pillows. Although we would often beg for the fancy store bought candy bags, our homemade versions were even better. They never ripped and leaked out precious candy, and they could fit thirty pounds of candy with ease.

Costumes were the next concern. They were never more complicated than whatever mask our mom found in the drug store the night before.

"Celeste, didn't you say you wanted to be a princess?" she would say handing the mask with blonde hair and blue eye shadow to Celeste.

"That was me!" I always wanted to be the Princess. I felt it was my right as the girl with the longest hair in the family.

"Oh Dawn, don't be such a grouch. Take the ogre mask."

Sometimes we would attempt to create our own costumes. Since all of us lacked even a shred of artistic talent, this always ended in failure. One year Tabitha tried to make Celeste into a bum. She layered Celeste in oversized clothes and socks, put marker on her face to imitate whiskers and as a finishing touch, exhaled her cigarette smoke over Celeste. Celeste still looked like Celeste at the end of the day, albeit a dirty-faced, smelly version.

Celeste stamped her feet. "I look stupid!"

"Well, I don't know what else to do," Tabitha said abandoning her project like it was fifth period Chemistry. She returned to her teenage interests (stealing smokes from Mom and pouting.) Celeste cursed her trust in her big sister's ability and went to scrub her face in the bathroom mirror.

Jolene and Adelle, our cousins down the road, lacked even our limited funds, yet they outshone us. They never had store-bought costumes, make-up or masks. Still each Halloween they wandered into our house convincingly clad as witches, grannies and yes, even bums.

"Your whiskers look cool," I said enviously.

"Wet coffee grounds."

"Where'd you get your pants and shirt?"

"We tore apart Dad's suit and sewed a patch on the ass."

"How did you make the smoke stains on your teeth?"

"Oh, those are real." Adelle and Jolene had been stealing smokes for years.

Every year we watched the Halloween warning films in school: do not walk alone, do not walk down unlit streets, do not wear masks with narrow eyeholes, and do not eat candy before it goes through an x-ray machine. None of these warnings made much sense to me.

I lived on the reserve where there were no sidewalks and the closest house to us belonged to our Great Uncle Ed who handed out candy, money and kittens if you knocked on his door and yelled "trick or treat" — he didn't really get Halloween. Also, he would hand out those things any old night of the year, so where was the novelty?

Even if you had the energy to walk from house to house, you'd only make it to one or two before it got dark and the coyotes started howling. As for the poisoned candy fears, there was no x-ray machine within forty miles so you had to take your chances. Besides it wasn't like we got candy every day. This could be it until Christmas time. Let the city kids throw out their unsafe candy. If there were razor blades in our caramel apples, then damn it, we would chew around them.

One year Geraldine came around to pick us up for Halloween. Geraldine or Gerry was a friend of our mom's. She had two foster children, Dylan and Shane, two boys a little older than me.

Gerry was the same age as our mom but seemed years younger. She wore tight jeans, had short hair, and rode horses. She was energetic and daring; these two qualities were apparent when she volunteered to take us trick or treating with her kids. Mom was shocked. "You want to take ALL the kids? By yourself? Have you been drinking?"

"Sure, what the hell. What's three more? Just adds to the fun, right?!" Gerry looked at us and we cheered. We weren't the cheering types but her enthusiasm was contagious.

Hoping to impress Gerry and her kids, I made an effort for Halloween night. I took two hours to get ready. I put on dark eye makeup intending to make myself into Cleopatra. After lining one eye, the eyeliner crumbled in my hands so I abandoned that plan. I used the left over pieces to draw cat whiskers by my nose. Half way through I realized that without cat ears, I'd look like an ugly man wearing eyeliner. I scrapped that plan. Time was ticking and I had no idea what to do.

Celeste entered the bathroom. "What are you?" she asked.

I shrugged. "What are you?" Her hair was pulled back and there were freckles drawn all over her face and coffee grounds on her chin. She shrugged. "Dunno."

We stared into the big mirror and knew we had failed again. I had an idea. "Punk Rockers?" We did not know that punk rock was a movement about rebelling against authority; all we knew was that punk rockers dressed weird.

We applied the remainder of Tabitha's make up to our faces. David joined us in the bedroom; he had struggled all afternoon to build his costume. He held a round piece of yellow paper between his teeth and wore an orange hat. "I'm a duck," he said and the yellow paper fell out of his mouth.

Our costumes impressed him. "Cool, zombies. Wish I'd thought of that!"

Quickly Celeste dissuaded him. "You can't copy us or I'll hit you!"

We walked into the living room to wait for Gerry.

Mom looked up from her book. "What are you? Clowns?"

"No we're punk rockers. And he's a duck that can't quack."

"If you say so, Sid Vicious," she smirked.

"I don't know who that is." I slumped on the couch. "All I know is we wouldn't look stupid if you bought us good costumes."

Mom denied her part in the Halloween disaster. "Hey, I bought you three perfectly good masks that are just lying on the table. I did my part."

"Other kids' moms sew their outfits."

"They're idiots. Why put all that work into a costume that you're gonna wear for one friggin' day and prolly get chocolate all over it? They may have that kind of time to waste but I don't," she said and returned to her book.

Mom had a point. Still it would have been nice for at least one year to have an outfit that went over your whole body and completely changed your identity — like a fishbowl or a table with cutlery and dishes. I'd seen costumes like that in movies and even on some kids at school. Their costumes said, "We're totally thriving. This child will be a complete success because we know how to plan, sacrifice and sew. This child can do anything, be anything, even a Martian." Next to those masterpieces, a plastic mask with a piece of string hooked over your ears, looked pathetic. The mask said, "We're getting by, thank you very much. Now, put the candy in the bag and look away."

Gerry squeezed the three of us into her black Bronco with her three kids. Then she hit the gas like she had a vendetta against staying still and drove us farther and faster than my mom ever had. "We gotta move kids, if we want to hit all four reserves!"

We lived on Okanese, which was located in a block of four reserves, collectively known as File Hills. The others were Peepeekisis, Starblanket and Little Black Bear. Peepeekisis was the biggest, Starblanket was the smallest and Little Black Bear was the rankest (according to my mom and the local police.) Altogether, about 2000 native people lived on File Hills; if you were willing to put in the work, you could amass a tidy sum of candy.

The idea of hitting all four had never occurred to us before. Mom had a tendency to pack it in as soon as the bottoms of our pillowcases were full. Even when Mom got ambitious, she'd only hit houses on Okanese and her relatives who lived on Peepeekisis.

With Gerry, we went to every single house that we saw. And if there was no one home then we would pile up garbage in front of the front door. Before Gerry came along, I didn't even know what the "trick" part of Halloween meant.

"I thought trick meant that people could give you candy or do magic tricks for you," I said to Gerry as we dragged an old car hood onto someone's porch.

"You poor kids. Didn't anyone teach you the true meaning of Halloween? It's all about getting up in people's asses and showing them how to have a good time."

"What if they get mad?"

"Then screw 'em for not being good sports!"

Gerry really got into those tricks. They took more time than the treating. After we had dragged a lawn mower, a doghouse and a bag of soil onto an unfortunate family's doorsteps, it was already late.

My siblings and I stole a glance at our driver; surely by now her mouth would be forming a frown that would only become deeper as the sun went down. Her voice would become sharper each time one of us didn't shut the door hard enough. And like our mom, Gerry would start muttering under her breath about how no one understood how tired her legs were.

Gerry showed no signs of slowing down. Her eyes were fiery as she steered the Bronco over ruts. As our heads bounced against the Bronco's ceiling, we admired Gerry's energy. What would it be like to have a mom who could go and go and go?

After we had reaped our destruction on a few homes, she sped away from our reserve onto the next one. We were eager to see what candy the other reserves had to offer.

"Stop at the Youngs! They're rich, they have two trucks!" Instinctively we knew which families would hand out quality snacks. "Mrs. Klein will have caramel apples. Look how fat her grandchildren are! She might even have brownies; I always smell chocolate and nuts on their breath!"

Everywhere we wanted to go Geraldine was prepared to go. Never before had our pillowcases seen so much candy. Celeste and I weren't even tempted to steal from our brother's. We had eaten so much that our mouths were dry and we had to reach for our caramel apples to wet our pallets.

"Where do you want to go next?" Geraldine asked us. I looked over at our other passengers. Her three kids were unspoiled cowboys in the making with their lean legs and hyperactive personalities. I could tell that sweets did not enthrall them as it did my siblings and me. They didn't have what it took to be greedy; that was evident from the way they dug into their bags and chewed their gum first. Gum! Such amateurs. Even now they had lost interest in our quest and were trying out wrestling moves on one another in the back seat. They didn't know lucky they were to have a tireless mom. It was true what the Bible said, "To whom much chocolate was offered, much was neglected." Or something like that.

It would be up to me to keep this dream going. "Um . . . how about into . . . town?" I pretended to speak hesitantly as if it had just occurred to me. It had always been a fantasy of mine to go trick or treating in town: all those houses, so close together and even, the dream of going door to door inside an apartment building. Imagine it: less effort for a higher volume of candy! Mom never appreciated my elegant breakdown of candy economics, preferring her own logic. "The more crap you eat, the more likely you are to shit your pants."

I held my breath as I waited for Gerry's answer. I prepared myself for a "no." "No" was what I was used to. I understood "no," I told myself.

Gerry was prepared to take us on a new adventure into the land of "yes."

"All right then, let's go into town!" she said and swung the jeep in the direction away from the reserve, away from mediocrity and acceptance of less towards a future of unlimited mini chocolate bars and cavities. I released my breath and sat back revelling in our good fortune.

Celeste elbowed me. "Look it's almost dark. Mom will wonder where we are."

"Shhh . . . " I told her. "There's street lights in town." They would light the way to our chocolate dreams.

Celeste looked afraid. This is what our mom had done to us, made us afraid to reach out for the unknown, for the big kahuna, for the giant stash of candy in the sky. I patted her on the leg as it if to say, "Hang with me, kid, and I'll take you all the way to the top."

We were nearly off the reserve when Gerry spotted a side road. "Who lives down here?" she wondered aloud, then shrugged and went down the road anyway. As was the fashion all over the reserves, the road twisted around and around with no rhyme or reason until it came onto a clearing. There was a small house with no car in front of it.

"Aww, nobody's home," I whined, which was difficult since my mouth was stuffed with fudge.

Then there was a movement behind one of the curtains. It was furtive but this was enough welcome for us.

"Yay!" Another home to plunder!

All six of us paraded up the steps and pounded on the door. David laboured behind on his short legs, his pillowcase nearly as big as him. We pushed him to the front, as his cute face was always a favourite with old ladies and this had to be an old lady house with its squeaky porch and fussy plants.

The rest of us stood behind him, our chocolate smiles fastened in place. They faded a bit when a young woman opened the door. Oh no, not a babysitter!

A babysitter meant that the parents had forgotten about Halloween, gone to bingo and left a young person to dole out the disappointment. Behind her, a baby boy and girl were sucking on their thumbs. They had no costumes, just big smiles at seeing a group of children in their kitchen. They hung onto the young woman's jeans shyly.

She invited us inside where we screamed our greeting. "TRICK OR TREAT!" It came out as a rowdy soccer hooligan yell.

The little boy held up his hands and begged her to pick him up and protect him from us. He called her Mommy as she slung him onto her hip.

"Mommy?" I mouthed to Celeste. The girl couldn't have been much older than Tabitha who was sixteen.

The young woman feigned fear at our costumes. "Oh you little monsters! What am I going to do!" She asked our names. We gave them loudly.

I looked around the kitchen, a little confused. Where was the bowl of candy? Had she given all of it away? I searched the kitchen and noticed how bare it looked. There was no loaf of bread on the counter, half open, half closed with peanut butter and jelly confetti strewn in front of it. There was no bag of cookies with the cookie tray half in and half out where the last person had violently searched through it looking for the chocolate chippiest cookie. There was nothing on those counters that would tempt the skinniest mouse. The little girl smiled up at me. She didn't have a big belly or chubby cheeks like the babies in my family. Realization hit my brain like an ice cream freeze on a warm day: we had gone one house too many. This was one of the houses that Mom was talking about when she told us not to waste food. Mom wasn't full of shit.

I stepped away from the front wanting to slink out the door and slide back into the Bronco. It wasn't right to be here, taking from this house. Surely the young woman's fresh smile would transform into a pursed mouth as she shook her head side to side. "No candy here, sorry."

She didn't do that. With more grace than hostesses twice her age, she complimented our costumes and gently pinched David's full cheeks (everyone had to do this, they were that plush and tempting.) Then she opened her fridge, which I knew even before she opened it would be as barren as a wintry grainfield. Somehow she produced two oranges. She sliced each orange into three pieces and wrapped each piece in plastic wrap. Then she dropped the small packages into our bags. We said 'thank you' reverently — even my little brother whose lisp made it come out, "fank you."

Into the Bronco we went, one little monster at a time. Gerry could tell something was wrong. She'd sent a bunch of marauders into the house and five sad zombies had emerged.

Dylan, Gerry's eldest, showed her his orange pieces. Gerry examined them. We sat silently in the driveway as she decided what to do.

Finally, she put the jeep in gear and we sped down the windy road away from the young girl and the two small children. I knew that the Bronco would not be turning towards town — I was disappointed — but less than I normally would have been.

By the time we made it home, it was already dark. My mom stood on the front steps puffing on a smoke and watched us drive up the approach. Her face had a worried frown. Even though Mom knew Gerry was energetic, I don't think she ever expected to see anyone keep her kids out later than sundown.

Though Mom smiled as she thanked Gerry, her eyes were on our baby brother sleeping in the back seat with his head at an odd angle. "Wow, looks like you really wore them out."

"Lots of kids come by?" Gerry asked.

Mom shook her head. "Not for the last hour. Most people pack it in pretty early."

"Lazy. Never understand that myself." Geraldine helped Mom slide the Bronco seat open.

Mom pursed her lips. She gathered Dave into her arms and waved goodbye to Gerry with her free hand. My sister and I carried his bag of candy in for him as the little Bronco roared out of the yard. Most of his candy made it into the house.

Mom immediately sent Celeste and I to bed. We sat on our beds and ate our candy in the dark, quickly and methodically. When I reached the slice of orange the young woman had given us, I unwrapped it gently and popped it into my mouth. I imagined that it would taste sweeter than all the chocolate in the world. It was quite dry. I ate it anyway.

NOBODY CRIES AT BINGO

BINGO TIME WAS AN UNDERSTOOD RULE IN our family. Just as we knew that if there was a band meeting held on a Friday then Dad wasn't getting home until Sunday, or that my brother David would bounce his head rhythmically until he fell sleep each night, or that if my sister Celeste and I did not get *exactly* the same doll, toy or T-shirt then we would fight until we did, so too we understood that bingo was something that Mom had to do — every night. (Mom vehemently denies that she played every night. My siblings' eyewitness accounts contradict her statements.)

Bingo was held everywhere. In the city, in small towns, on the reserve — as long as you had four walls and some balls then you had a bingo, my friend. There was a bingo every night of the week if you looked for it. And many did.

Around six PM, Mom, Grandma and assorted aunts and uncles would feel compelled to crowd into a car together. No matter that they spent the day fighting over who stole whose hoe or who hocked whose television, at the end of the day they were all willing warriors in the same noble fight. They would hurry one another into the car with their little margarine containers filled to the brim with red, blue, and green button markers and head to the nearest bingo.

Us kids would see the bingo players off as we sat on the front steps, a dog or cat tucked between our legs as we inspected them for wood ticks. We'd interrupt our picking to wave at the grown-ups. Then, as soon as the car was out of sight, we'd squash the fat bloated ticks into bloody mush under our sneakers and head to the backyard to do stuff we weren't supposed to. Having a bonfire and chasing each other around with fire-tipped sticks was always a relaxing way to spend the evening.

If we complained to Mom about how much she went to bingo, she would remind us that our dad was off somewhere drinking to his heart's content. Others of his ilk surrounded him, and at the moment they were draining our bank account dry. "Would you like me to be like that, a drunk who never comes home and never helps out with his kids?"

Presented with the other choice, bingo seemed to be the correct one. Besides, a mom only got in the way during our busy schedule of dangerous evening activities.

The first bingos our family attended were held in band halls, scheduled between the chief's meeting and the first aid training. Our bingo players dutifully travelled from one reserve to another in their crowded car.

Their need for different games and bigger jackpots drove them to try different bingos. First they branched out to Catholic Church bingos, then, disappointed by the lack of high jackpots and the prowling nuns in the aisles, they added Protestant bingos to their schedule. When they ran out of those, they expanded their area to include bingos held in small towns. At first it was awkward sitting next to the same white people who glared at Native people when they walked into their stores, but after sharing a few fingernail-biting jackpots, racism faded into the background as they concentrated on the true enemy:

"Goddamn fuckin' bingo caller!"

"I only needed one number for a fucking hour."

"Last fucking time I play at this hall!"

Finally when their appetite was whetted and they felt ready, like truly ready, they went to a bingo in the big city. You had to be prepared for that bingo though; you had to feel it in your heart that you could make it among the big boys. (You also had to have enough gas in your tank.)

City bingos were held in huge monoliths built to honour the bingo gods. Dedicated players could attend bingo from morning until night until morning again. Once you entered such a bingo palace, there would be no reason to ever leave again, if you played your cards right, that is.

My mom took me to my first bingo game as a reward for being a good girl which in my case meant not hitting my sister or brother for sixty minutes in a row (or more likely that Mom hadn't *witnessed* me bullying them in said time frame.) I was suitably excited. It was one-on-one Mom time, which was rare in a house where four kids and an infinite number of cousins were all clamoring for her attention.

Lots of people brought their kids to bingo. The hall was located next to a playground for this very reason. I knew that my friends Layla and Trina would be perched on that playground equipment. When I arrived, I waved at them and headed in their direction only to be pulled short by my mom.

"Where you going?"

"To play with my friends."

"You're here to play bingo, not to have fun."

I mouthed the words, "I have to play" to my friends as she escorted me inside the hall.

Instead of being disappointed, my heart surged. I was gonna play bingo! I had played in school before but that wasn't real bingo because in school, everyone won. Even Boris who spilt his milk all over his cards won, for god's sake. This would be real. There would be a bingo caller who had dedicated his or her life to pronouncing numbers in a numb monotone. There would be runners who would hurry to the side of a person who yelled bingo, grab their card and then race the card to the front where it would be verified by the caller and the manager. The runners were like fleet deer and someday I wanted to be one of them.

The games outside the bingo hall were just as exciting as the ones inside the hall. The kids would play hide and go seek among the cars, or rummage through the ashtrays looking for butts to smoke. The games always left the kids red-faced and sweaty as they headed back into the hall to visit their mothers.

"I changed my mind, I want to play outside," I told my mom as an overheated kid walked by me.

"No, you play your card. Look, you're missing numbers."

"Mommmmmmmmmm . . . "

"Maybe I should have brought Celeste."

My mouth slammed shut as I placed my red markers on the card. I was playing a three-up, the easiest card you could play, whereas Mom played twenty-four cards at once. That was bush league compared to Auntie Squaw who played thirty-six without breaking a sweat. What's more, if someone had to go to the bathroom, Auntie would dab his or her cards as well.

The game required your full concentration because not all the games were the same. The standard was the standard; it was one line across the card, anyway you could make it. There were also four corners, two lines anyway, crisscross — the games designers had worked overtime to make bingo even more engrossing. It made no difference to the true bingo players. As long as the balls kept bubbling up, they kept dabbing.

The games that paid the most were the blackouts; these were also known as the jackpots. This was the game that made you tighten your butt cheeks as you waited for the next number to come out.

"Look Mom, I only need two on this card. And two on that one and three on that one."

Mom shushed me with a shush that communicated how truly pathetic my card was. "Oh hush, I've needed only one number for the last ten numbers."

Now that was a true bingo player. They could handle the tension of needing one number for as long as it took without succumbing to even a hopeful smile.

That's because true bingo players had a jaded view of life and their cards:

"Where's that damn 75? Did it fall under his chair?"

"He's too busy playing with his balls to call any of our numbers."

"Watch, with my luck, I won't win anything!"

The goal was to bring yourself and those around you as low as possible so that if by some miracle the number was called, the rise to the top would be that much further and faster.

When a player from another table called "Bingo!" bingo players would make a face and say something, oddly conspiratorial. "Of course, she won. Look whose mother she is."

I stole a glance at the elderly woman who smiled warmly as the runner handed her card back in one hand and her forty dollars in the other. The winner didn't look like a person who would participate in a complex bingo scheme, but who knew what people were capable of when the stakes were so high?

My table mates were even angrier if a player won more than once in a night. They would shake their heads at the greed of the winner. "She just won three bingos ago, what is her problem?"

At every table, someone was munching on a bag of Cheezies. They popped one in their mouth, crunched it into Cheezie paste, wiped their hands and resumed dabbing their cards. I watched a woman at the next table go through this rhythm and my stomach began to growl.

"I need some Cheezies."

"You need Cheezies like I need a hole in the head," Mom replied.

"C'mon, Mom, one bag, please, please, please."

"Nope. Not until you win." Then she winked at Auntie Squaw who laughed.

I looked at her in disbelief. How could that be the rule? I was young but even I knew that winning was based on chance. You couldn't good-bingo-play your way into winning, if you could, Auntie Squaw would be the richest woman in the universe.

If I had to depend on my luck, then I was going home hungry. I knew from listening to the bingo players discuss their winnings that certain people in the family won more than others. I noticed that my chubby Uncle Larry, who was always grinning and playing tricks on people, won a great deal. Uncle Frank, stolid and grumpy, (hence the nickname, "cranky Frankie,") almost never won. In fact, his tantrums at bingo games were legendary. Before each bingo game, his sisters would argue, "The hell with you, I am not sitting next to him. So embarrassing!"

They took to telling him off before each game, warning him to rein in his temper or else he would get no more rides. He would forget. After the last bingo of the night, he would let out a tortured war cry that conveyed a lifetime's worth of disappointment: "HOLY FUUCCCCKKKK!"

I knew I wasn't one of the lucky ones. My wiry, curly hair, short stubby legs and potbelly had already demonstrated my lack of that quality. No, people like Celeste were lucky. Our cousins Malcolm and Jolene were lucky. They were the kind of people who were always finding quarters on the ground or five-dollar bills near their mother's purses. They could win a bingo game at the beginning of the night and then build up enough luck during the game to win another one at the end of the night.

Luckless, I had to whine my way through life.

"Mom, if I don't get Cheezies I'll die."

"Then you better not miss any more numbers," Mom said, as she sanctimoniously dabbed my card.

"Mom, my stomach hurts from hunger."

"You missed a number."

"This isn't fair."

"Life isn't fair."

My stomach growled in agreement.

I stared down at my card. The numbers began to mist in front of me as tears fell out of my eyes and dropped onto my card. My Aunt handed me a Kleenex. "Stop that! Everyone is looking at you," she whispered angrily. "You're not supposed to cry at bingo. That big man over there will come and steal you."

When required, any random, large and scary looking man served as a threat. It was an effective tool as it meant we always avoided that person in any public setting. My aching tummy made me fearless.

"Good, I hope he does. Maybe he'll have some chips and candy."

Auntie and Mom looked at one another and shook their heads. What had happened to kids these days? Back in their day, a kid was lucky to get to go anywhere. Growing up in a family of twelve, you were lucky if your mom remembered your face, never mind took you to bingo. And if you did want to go to bingo, it wasn't just a quick five-minute drive; it was a two-day journey involving a horse, a wagon and three portages. Now those were days when people appreciated bingo, when they understood that it was an important part of the community. Not only did you get to spend time with everyone you cared about but also you got to do it within the healthy confines of gambling. And all the money that was lost went to the money grubbing church. It was win-win. Of course kids couldn't understand that. They were only interested in feeding their guts.

My tummy growled. It was a surprised growl — my tummy was unfamiliar with denial. My tears increased in intensity. People were staring at our table now. The woman with Cheezies was shaking her head, mumbling something about "kids not being allowed to play," with her cheese stained lips.

I was a trooper and kept playing. The first number was called. I placed my marker on my card and went back to constructing my tower of markers. It was no higher than my thumb but I felt that if I shored up the side with another tower, I might be able to get it three inches off the table.

"You're missing numbers," Mom hissed next to me.

I could not figure out how she could watch her own cards and mine and her sister's and the stranger to the right of her and yet not notice how gaunt I was growing!

I carefully moved my tower out of her reach and pulled my card closer.

"What are we playing again?"

"Standard."

"Oh. I think I need two numbers."

My aunt laughed bitterly. 'You and the rest of the hall."

The next number was announced. Everyone tensed waiting for a bingo to be called.

I had heard about a kid, not much older than myself, who had once yelled bingo — when he didn't have one. Legend said that when the runners came along to confirm his bingo, he was forced to admit his lie. Nobody ever saw him again.

I could see the temptation. You could so easily pop the tension in the room with that one word. I wasn't daring enough to call a false bingo. The best I could do was to utter a series of words that began with B.

"B-B-Bananas are a tasty fruit."

"B-B-Birthdays are fun."

"B-B-Bastard, that's what they say my friend Jack is. B-B-But, I think that's unfair b-b-because he had no choice in his b-b-birth."

My b-b-brilliance was awarded with a slap to the back of the head.

The next number was called and it was mine. I was down to one. Bells started to go off in my head and my vision suddenly narrowed. I pulled my card closer. Mom noticed my sudden hoarding and looked over.

"She's down to one."

Thirteen pairs of eyes turned towards me. I was suddenly hot from the heat of twenty-six retinas.

Mom massaged my shoulder muscles like a coach in a boxer's corner. "Stay loose, be alert. You can do this."

She whispered to Auntie Squaw, "She needs B10. That's all."

Auntie pursed her lips together and nodded as if to say, "Okay, I'll get right on that. I will make this happen." She glared up at the bingo caller with renewed purpose.

My hands tapped a rat-a-tat on the tabletop. Would this idiot never call the next number? What the hell was he doing? Did he know he wasn't getting paid to sit there with his thumb up his ass?

"Don't swear."

"You and Auntie say that."

"That's different. We're adults, you're a child."

"Isn't it illegal for children to gamble?"

"Shut up and play your card."

I stared down at my numbers. Was it going to happen? Was I going to finally break my six-year unlucky streak? I was not a nice person — just that morning I'd put my sister's shoe in the toilet. I did not deserve to win.

The bingo caller cleared his throat and called his next number. B10. I looked up at my mom. She stared into my eyes and she knew. "Say it."

"I can't," I croaked.

"Say it!"

"Everyone will look at me."

"Say it!"

"Bingo!"

Heads swiveled around the table as everyone heard the word. The runner, a slim mother of six, ran over. I gave her my card and she brushed it clear of the numbers. I showed her where my line was and she called out the numbers to the bingo caller. This was scarier than the game itself. What if I made a mistake? What if everyone thought I called a false bingo? Would they turn on me like a pack of rez dogs? Or would my age make them think twice? Just in case, I kept one foot on the floor to run out the door. If I could make it out into the parking lot, I'd get lost among the other sixty brown kids out there. Blending in, that was my only chance.

"It's good!" The runner held up her hand and another runner ran up with a wad of cash. They counted out the money in front of me and pushed it towards me. Mom grabbed it before I understood what was happening.

Women around the table glared at me. No longer was I the cute kid in pigtails, I was real competition like the chicken who played tick- tack- toe at the Fair.

I had won forty-five dollars. Not a fortune even back then but it was more than enough to buy me chips, a drink and a chocolate bar, although my mom wouldn't let me have the latter two until the second bingo game.

As I sat there eating my Cheezies, I reflected on the bingo game. Was there anything to learn from this experience? I had wanted Cheezies. My mom made me wait until I won. I cried. And then I won. What was the moral? If I cried, then I would win? A dangerous conclusion as it would mean carrying tissue in my pocket for the rest of my life.

It would be worth it if I could continue this streak. I wouldn't have to get a job, just a lot of markers. No margarine tins for me, I'd have specialized pockets sewn on the inside of my jacket with a different pocket for each colour. I would learn how to play with both hands and I would be good — crazy good. I wouldn't play a pathetic 24 or even 36, I would play 56 cards, a feat that had been attempted only once — by a drunk guy who had wandered into the bingo hall, bought a bunch of cards and then passed out before the first game started.

I would be different. I would be a prodigy. People would speak of my quick hands, my perfect eyesight and my luck — oh yes, my luck would be legendary.

"You're missing numbers again!"

Mom's annoyed tone jerked me out of my reverie.

"Go on, you're fired." She jerked her head in direction of the door.

"Really?'

I tucked my Cheezies into my pocket and headed outside into the night deciding that winning was something that happened to everyone, even the unlucky and sometimes, when you needed it the most.

A Weighty Matter

EVERY NIGHT AT FIVE THIRTY, OUR FAMILY met around the dinner table. Dinnertime was orderly: we each owned a chair at the table and there could be no squatters. I sat to the right of Celeste, my younger sister, and to the left of Dad. Celeste refused to accept her seat in life. She and I had an ongoing rivalry about who was Dad's best girl so she frequently attempted to steal my chair. Every time Celeste tried, Mom firmly told her to sit in her own damn chair.

"Mom, the chairs don't have names on them!" Celeste argued. "Anybody should be able to sit anywhere. After all, isn't this a free country?"

An argument based on Canada's principles of peace, order and choice of chairs wouldn't work on Mom who had never voted in her life.

As Celeste grudgingly moved, I plopped down into my chair and delivered a pinch to her arm to acknowledge that I did not appreciate her attempted coup d'état. I found it annoying that she refused to give up because it meant that I couldn't give up. I could never miss a meal because then Celeste would take my chair and smile up adoringly at our dad. Fortunately my appetite, never, ever, waned. I could have the bubonic plague and I'd still drag my boil-ridden carcass to the table.

Mealtimes were about eating and Mom liked to keep it that way: "No laughing, no singing, no fighting while you're eating, or else you'll get an ulcer."

"What's an ulcer?"

"Shut up or you'll get one."

Her rules never stopped us from annoying one another from across the table. "Mom, David won't stop whistling."

"I'll stop whistling when she stops snapping her fingers," David said.

"Then I'm gonna click my tongue. How do you like that?"

"Then it's time for pig eating noises." David was really good at pig eating noises.

"I'm getting an ulcer just listening to you all! Art, do something," Mom said.

Dad had gone to his happy place: a place where there was no shortage of gravy, where the TV was on and tuned into a hockey game, where a man could eat his pork chops in peace.

Another one of Mom's rules was that we had to finish everything on our plate. If you took something, you had to eat it. In Africa, India and even in some other houses on the reserve, there was a food shortage and any decline in our appetites would make it worse.

"If we don't finish our food, doesn't that mean more food goes to other people?" I asked her once.

"No, because we're gonna just throw it out to the dogs."

This prompted a glance out the window at the dogs who sat on our verandah, their tongues hanging out of our mouths waiting for the scraps that were promised to them.

I had no issues with the plate-polishing rule. With fourteen hands reaching for food at the same time, I was lucky if I got seconds. In our house, leftovers were a quaint idea, something you might see on TV. The cherub-faced TV kids groaned when their mom put a casserole dish on the table, "Not leftovers, again!" At our meals, we always saw the bottom of the pan, cake dish, or pie tin. Sometimes Dad would even mop up remaining grease with a piece of bread.

David and I polished our plates until we could see our own reflections in them. Then seeing hunger in the eyes staring back at us, we moved onto other people's food if no one stopped us. Celeste was a picky eater and David and I had learned to hover over her.

We didn't understand why someone would turn down food so we teased Celeste for what we called "being snotty," like when she dropped food on the floor and didn't pick it up and eat it.

"Look at her, thinks she's too good to eat off the floor," I said rolling my eyes at David. My gloating was lost on him, as he'd already be under the table clambering for the food.

Wieners and beans. Pork chops and rice. Deer steaks and onions. Rabbit stew with dumplings. These were the dishes Mom knew best. With five kids, a full time job and an addiction to bingo, Mom didn't have time to research new dishes or experiment with fancy foods like vegetables. However, a foray into Asian cuisine introduced her to canned mushrooms. She mixed them in with some rice and soy sauce and David and I devoured our plates in mere seconds.

Celeste ate her way around the mushrooms and piled them high in the middle of her plate. Mom was feeling plucky that day and said something she had never said before: "If you don't eat that, Celeste, then you'll stay there until you do." Celeste made her face into the shape of a pout and folded her arms. The game was on.

Three hours later, Celeste still sat at the table. Every half hour Mom would walk in and glance at Celeste and then at the clock. Mom was more curious than angry. It rarely took this long to break a child.

David and I perched on the chairs beside Celeste. "Just eat them already and come play."

Celeste shook her head. "I can't. They're gross."

"They're just mushrooms," David said.

Celeste looked at him in confusion. "Is that what they are?"

"What did you think they were?"

"Poo."

David and I both laughed. "Mom would never feed us poo!" I said. "Mom is not a crazy poo-cooker!"

It turns out that I spoke too soon; two weeks later Mom brought home tripe. She spent all day boiling it and we spent all day making gagging noises whenever we walked into the kitchen.

"What smells so gross?" I asked.

"Get the hell out of here," Mom replied.

"Is that food?" I peeked a look at the grey thing bubbling on the stove.

"It's tripe and it's good for you," she said and took a deep satisfied whiff. I could not have been more shocked if she had turned her head in a complete circle like an owl.

"What's tripe?" I asked.

Mom ignored the question as she stirred the pot. I consulted Tabitha, my older sister and my expert on everything.

"Tripe is the guts of an animal," she explained.

"That doesn't sound too bad," I replied. Pretty much every meat we ate was the guts of something.

"It's where the shit comes from."

I left the room and went to relay the information to David and Celeste. When suppertime rolled around, we hid ourselves in the basement and snacked on a bag of chips we had stolen from the cupboard. Upstairs our parents ate the tripe with relish. Every once in a while my dad would call out, "If you guys don't hurry, there's not going to be any left!"

Downstairs we shuddered.

Later that evening, our uncles and aunts alerted to the tripe meal — probably by the smell — dropped in and filled their bowls with the crap. I guess tripe was their generation's pizza pops.

My favourite meal was something a lot less "fragrant"; meatloaf day was the best of times and the worst of times. I loved it and so did David, and because he was the only boy, Mom always gave him an extra-large serving. Then David would eat it while I glared at him from across the table, silently planning future "accidents" for my accident-prone little brother.

I started hanging out in the kitchen on meatloaf day. When Mom pulled it from the stove, I volunteered to set the table. Then I delivered it to the table with one serving already missing. My brother figured out my game and started hanging out in front of the stove with a fork in one hand and a bottle of ketchup in the other.

I had a healthy appetite for a ten-year-old girl, healthy even for a thirty-year-old construction worker. I used to polish off two, sometimes three pork chops at the dinner table. My dad and I once fork-wrestled over the last one.

"What's with this girl?" he blustered. "She eats like a horse."

"She's ten, she's growing," Mom explained.

"I'm growing," I reiterated through a mouthful of meat.

"Are you planning on being eight feet tall?"

"That would be awesome! Then I could play basketball!" I exclaimed. "These are good pork chops, Mom," I added with a winsome smile.

My mom never gave a moment's thought to her weight. Taller than average, her hips had always been narrow and her waist, if not small, was never thick. "I've got better things to worry about than a few pounds."

One of our aunties left a Nutri-System shake at our house and Mom drank it more out of curiosity than anything else. "Damn thing tasted so bad I had to have a whole bowl of ice cream to get the taste out of my mouth."

If she did gain weight, she'd start wearing my dad's jeans. "Women waste too much time worrying about what they look like," she'd say as we watched a daytime TV heroine add another layer of lipstick to her face as she tried to seduce her sister's husband.

"Tell me about it," I'd add as I polished off a bag of chips on the couch beside her.

※

Mom had twelve brothers and sisters. Most of them had families and most of these families averaged four children each. I tried counting them once and I always forgot someone. Nowadays trying to count the offspring of my cousins is beyond me. I hope one of us is up to the task before the next generation starts getting married.

We labeled our cousins according to geography. We belonged to the Saskatchewan cousins, which included two other families in the Qu'Appelle Valley along with another family in Prince Albert. Then there were two families of Manitoba cousins who had a lot of kids around our age.

The Manitoba cousins were frequent visitors. They were bigger, bolder and more numerous than us. Each summer their parents, Auntie Beth and Uncle Jack, opened the back of their camper truck and our cousins piled out in a clamber of legs, arms and insults. They descended upon us like passenger pigeons, blocking out the sun with their squawking.

My siblings and I observed them curiously from behind our blanket of shyness. Everything about us was weird to them as well. "Why do you talk softly?" "Why do you read books?" "Why don't you shoot more things?"

They thought up all the fun things to do. "Let's build a big fire. Then we'll throw some kerosene on it. Then we'll jump over it."

Their sense of fun permeated everything they did. They went from activity to activity, greedily sucking the enjoyment out of it. I envied their hedonism but I couldn't tell them that. Mostly because uttering a word like hedonism guaranteed a pile driver.

Thanks to the wonderful world of wrestling, my cousins learned a variety of wrestling moves like the pile driver, camel clutch and the suplex. My sister, girl cousins and I got to experience these moves firsthand. The pile driver is when someone much stronger than you — let's call them the attacker — picks you up, turns you upside down with your head between their knees. Then the attacker drops into a sitting or kneeling position. Your job is to scream for help that never comes.

Once the Manitoba cousins arrived, summer vacation began to move at a breakneck pace. There were three-hour long soccer games played against the fading sun, diving competitions off the dock at the beach, and games of Sasquatch in the woods late into the night.

Sasquatch: there have been few things I've done in my life that have inspired such a heady mix of excitement and intense fear. Every night as all the kids headed out the door to play the latest game, I could feel my legs shaking. "This is a bad idea," I would whisper to myself. But I would never turn back from those dark woods.

The game began after the sun went down. Sasquatch was best when the only light came from the Bics carried in our back pockets or the whites of our eyes. We'd tramp through the woods, crushing leaves beneath our feet, our joking voices and laughter scaring the rabbits and deer across the prairies. There would be anywhere from seven to twenty of us spread through the woods.

The game began when one of the older cousins, usually Malcolm, tied a scarf around his neck until he "passed out" and "became crazy." I don't understand why this step was necessary, as the mere act of putting a scarf around your neck on the reserve would at the very least qualify you as eccentric.

Malcolm was a showman. He would wrap the scarf around his neck multiple times and pull on the ends until his eyes began to bulge. He'd continue pulling even as he slowly sank to his knees. His head would fall forward and his dark hair obscured his face. The more naïve of us would approach him with concern. "Malcolm, are you okay?'

Malcolm would begin growling. Experienced players knew it was time to run. The younger ones wouldn't budge because they were worried about their older cousin. Malcolm would reward their concern with a painful beating.

After "becoming crazy," Malcolm hunted every one of us. If he found you he threw you down and delivered hard fast punches to your thigh (these were known as charley horses). Sometimes, he got out of control — usually with his younger brother Nathan — and the punches would be delivered to more sensitive areas and then a fight would start. While hiding, the little kids would hear the scuffling of the older kids and we knew that it was a matter of time before one of them, or both, would begin crying violently, as boys do.

When the game went well, the best you could hope for was getting to huddle in the dark, cold woods without getting a beating. Yet the whole game was worthwhile for that 30-second chase that happened when the Sasquatch spotted you. You'd run as fast your short legs could take you over the uneven terrain. The Sasquatch toyed with you, sometimes running past you and slapping the back of your head as he passed. You'd try to turn but he'd already be ahead of you again. You both knew there was no chance you could escape him at this point but you'd run anyway. And giggle nervously. This took away most of your breath so finally you'd fall onto the ground, paralyzed with laughter and fear. The game taught me a lot about night navigation and reconnaissance work. More importantly I realized I could run and pee myself at the same time.

Another reason we loved having our Manitoba cousins around was they always had at least one extra boy with them: a boy that we weren't related to! This was something new for Celeste and me. One summer they had a foster child named Adrian Fox staying with them. Fox: even his name suggested how cute he was. If you were wont to have daydreams about tall, dark and handsome princes, as I was, then Adrian fit the role perfectly. Even better, he came neatly packaged with a sad story of abandonment by his equally beautiful but depressed mother.

"She went crazy and tried to kill herself, right, Adrian?'
Malcolm said behind the barn as he teased a rooster with a
stick.

Adrian nodded with a soft smile on his face.

I was in awe of his reticence. Here Adrian had the saddest
story in the world and he wasn't taking advantage of it. I
talked about everything bad that happened to me. Once one
of my uncles said that my younger sister Celeste was prettier
than me and I didn't stop talking about that for two years.

I didn't even need to tell people in order to derive satisfaction from the story. On days when I was particularly bored,
I would sit on my bed and replay those fateful words, "You're
pretty Dawn but Celeste is like a wildflower . . . " until I could
make myself cry all over again.

Then after my supply of tears had run low, I rehearsed my
brave speech to the offender. "A wildflower! Then what am I?
A weed? A dirty stinkweed! What do people do with weeds?
They cut them down! I am not a weed you mean, old man — I
am a flower and there is no such thing as an ugly flower! You
cannot appreciate my beauty because you are a sad, old man
and you have no imagination."

Now if I'd had a crazy, yet beautiful, mother and
abandonment under my belt, I would have been set. Such
unfortunate circumstances would have supplied me with
enough self-pity for two lifetimes.

Adrian's story made him even more adorable to us. What
girl wouldn't want to heal Adrian's broken heart? Celeste, our
cousin Rachel, and I had crushes on him. Publicly we declared
that we loved Corey Haim but we all knew that a real Adrian
was a thousand times better than a distant Hollywood beau.

Each summer while the boys spent their time taunting
the farm animals until the animals chased them, the girls

decorated our playhouse in the woods. That summer, however, Adrian's presence lured us out of the bush more and more often.

At Malcolm's suggestion one night we were even cajoled into a game of strip poker. The game was a favourite of Malcolm's who thoroughly enjoyed mooning his younger cousins as they hid their eyes and screamed: "Gross!" He drank our disgust like ambrosia.

Strip poker was a new game for us. If one of the boys had suggested it before, all of us girls would have said, "No way, as if!" Adrian's presence made strip poker less repulsive, exciting even. We had no cards so we improvised with a bottle. Wearing three sets of clothes each, the game moved pretty slowly. Sadly the bottle never went near Adrian. Malcolm got impatient with the evening's pace and mooned everyone; unfortunately this was the moment that our parents walked in the door.

After our first foray into nude gambling, we girls began to play strip poker on our own. Strip poker gave us insight into one another's progress through the mysterious, and mostly gross, miracle of puberty. Some of us had breasts, some of us had hair in new places, some had neither. The dark light we chose to play in obscured anything else. Our cousin Dotty was the oldest of all of us and we were in awe of her breasts.

They were huge and Dotty was understandably very proud of them. Dotty had always been big. At least once a day someone called her names like huge cow, fat slob, and lazy pig. Adults can be very cruel. Unfortunately, having a life-long experience with obesity did not make the insults go down easier. But, the breasts took the sting out of the insults about her weight.

"I don't know why they tease me," Dotty said to me one day. "It just makes me eat more."

"Tell me about it," I said, as I tossed another handful of potato chips into my mouth.

At the end of July, Auntie Beth had enough of living out of a suitcase and decided it was time to return home. My brother, sister and I begged my mom to let us go visit our cousins in Manitoba. My mom wouldn't let my brother go — he was only nine, six in personality — but she agreed to send my sister and me.

As this was going to be the longest visit ever away from home, Mom figured I wouldn't be able to do it. I was notorious for trying to walk back to our house in the middle of the night or calling my mom and tearfully asking her to come get me. She tried to give me an out: "You don't have to go. You can stay home and play with your brother. I'll tell the kids you have to help me out."

I blanched at the thought of hanging out with my brother for the whole summer. His idea of fun was making car crash sounds while sitting on a pile of gravel. Not exactly an eleven-year-old girl's style. Besides, I knew it would kill me — literally — if my younger sister was off having fun and I was not. And then there was the Adrian factor. This morning, he had spoken to me. Sure he just said, "Can you pass the milk?" But it was the way he said it!

Even though we would be gone for four weeks, I didn't see the weeks so much as I saw it as twenty-eight days and twenty-eight chances to kiss Adrian. I replied that I would not need my brother's company for I was travelling north.

༂

My aunt and uncle loaded us kids into the back of their pickup truck. As I look back, I wonder at the generosity of this couple.

Who takes on another two kids when they already have seven? What drives people to want to be around children in such numbers? I suppose locking them in the back of a pickup makes the job easier.

The camper was its own country with its own customs and conventions. First of all, you weren't allowed to sleep. That was clear from the get-go. As soon as you lay down your head, the other kids descended upon you like a flock of hungry crows. You'd be teased, kicked, pinched and tickled. You would have no rest until the leader — Malcolm — was ready to rest. Unfortunately, Malcolm had the constitution of an ox and never slept. So neither did we.

Malcolm was one of those rare individuals who enjoy torturing others. Physical, emotional or verbal — it made no difference really, all forms of torture brought a gleeful smile to his face. I suppose child psychologists could have found the root of his anger and given it a diagnosis. I liked to think that he was mean simply because he was good at it.

The second rule of the camper was that you could not cry. Only pussies cried. If you couldn't hold it in, then you had to do it quickly and quietly before an adult noticed and started asking questions. Questions could lead to adult interference, which would inevitably lead to less fun. This rule was difficult for me because crying was a hobby of mine. I cried over pretty much everything including things that had not yet come to pass.

"Why are you crying now?" Mom had asked the week before, the "now" declaring her impatience with my favourite pastime. She didn't even stop sweeping the floor as she listened for my response.

"Someday Barkley is going to die," I hiccupped. Barkley was our giant brown German Shepherd whose hobby was hiding in the grass next to the main road and chasing after cars that drove past our house.

A car eventually killed Barkley. Considering his daily itinerary, I think that's the way he would have wanted to go. Ironically, I didn't cry when I heard the news, although I did cry when I imagined our new dog, Barkley II, getting hit by a car.

It was a six-hour drive to our cousin's reserve from ours, and in between we stopped off at a provincial park. Aunt Beth pulled a plastic tablecloth over a picnic table and unpacked a few KFC family meals as all the kids made a long line in front of the table. I put two pieces of chicken onto my plate, looking forward to the fun that we would be having this summer.

"Two pieces? I never saw a girl eat two pieces of chicken before." I looked up into my Aunt's surprised face.

"I always eat that much." And more, I thought to myself. This would definitely not be a four-piece day.

Her question was uttered in a soft tone, not judging, just surprised. That softness was enough to awaken the wolves. Malcolm, in particular, smelled blood in the air. His head cocked to the side as his cunning mind began to formulate the insults that were to come.

After lunch was over, my uncle locked us in the back of the truck. While I would have rather spent the time napping from the heat of the sun beating down on the camper, the others wanted to play a game of Truth or Dare.

Without consulting one another, all three of us girls had decided in advance that we were going to dare each other to kiss Adrian. We would all respond to the dare with exactly the same high-pitched giggle, a softly uttered, "Gross, I can't" and then a reluctant dive towards his handsome face.

As anyone who has played it knows, Truth or Dare is a dangerous and revealing game. Before the ride was over, we discovered that Nathan did not like to eat dirt off of Malcolm's sneaker, that Adrian had a crush on Rachel and that I had a chubby belly. I already knew this. I had stared at myself in my mom's bedroom mirror enough times with my shirt lifted. I had memorized each and every curve of my tummy. I also knew that if I stood on my toes and sucked in deeply, you could almost see the shadow of my ribs. "That's what I'll look like when I grow up," I whispered to the mirror nightly. The ritual was completed with a quick dance as I hummed Madonna's "Like a Virgin."

I acknowledged that my tummy was chubby, but that did not mean I was fat and I said as much to the camper crew. Malcolm begged to differ. "You are fatter than everyone else here. So that makes you: fat." Nobody dared disagree with his logic.

Malcolm also noted that my tummy had the consistency of bannock dough and so my new nickname was born: bannock belly. On their own, those two words weren't so awful except when you put them together, then they packed a nuclear punch. The repetitive "b's" gave the name additional power. Thank God my name didn't start with a "B" or the nickname would have stuck so firmly I would have been obligated to add it to my driver's license. As it was the nickname preceded my name awkwardly. "Bannock Belly Dawn." It didn't quite fit and I would have suggested something more alliterative like "Dumpy" but that was hardly in my best interest.

By the time we reached our destination and Uncle Jack opened the back of the truck, I was ready to pack it in. I mentally rehearsed my phone call. "Mom, I've decided to accept your offer. Now if you can just drive six hours north and pick me up, I will gladly spend the rest of the summer making car sounds with David."

When I saw the phone sitting on my aunt's living room table, I did not run to it. Six hours was not even close to one month and I couldn't give up so quickly.

Auntie Beth showed us around the house. There were three bedrooms, one for my aunt and uncle, one for the boys and one for Rachel and my sister and me. There was one door left in the hallway. "That's the bathroom," Auntie Beth indicated. "The toilet doesn't work." She pointed at the outhouse about twenty metres away from the house. "That's where everyone goes."

Celeste and I stared at the outhouse.

"I'm kind of sorry I came," I whispered to Celeste.

Celeste shuddered. "I'm sorry I drank two cokes."

That night as I fell asleep next to Rachel and Celeste, I resolved to be stronger. Everyone got teased, at one time or another. This could be character building, I told myself. Someday I would thank Malcolm for his teasing. For a few minutes, I imagined various scenarios in which I delivered my thanks to Malcolm. In each daydream I was thin, beautiful and rich as I delivered the words, while Malcolm did not fare so well as he fought off leprosy, morbid obesity and a severe goiter.

The next day the boys were gone before the girls woke up. They had woken at the break of dawn and run off to do boy stuff. Before they had left for our reserve, they had set a bunch of traps in the woods and needed to check them. They returned later that day with the desiccated remains of gophers and gopher-like creatures.

While they were tending to their rodent guillotines, I felt a sense of relief. My sister and Rachel were not interested in calling me names. Instead we went bike riding . . . sort of. Rachel rode her bike while Celeste and I walked beside her. We mostly talked about Rachel's relationship with Adrian, which had been upgraded, to "going out." Rachel was rather blasé about the relationship and refused to giggle or act excited. Her lack of giddiness grated on me.

"You said that you wanted to marry him when we were talking in our playhouse," I pointed out.

"I didn't say that. I said that he would make a nice friend."

"You said you wanted his babies. Now are you going to have his babies or what?" Everything else on the trip had turned out badly; I wasn't going to give up on Rachel and Adrian's happily ever after. No ambivalent eleven-year-old was going to ruin the dream.

"I don't know. Okay!" Rachel rode faster on her bike forcing Celeste and I into a light jog. As blood rushed from my head, I no longer had the energy to keep up my line of questioning.

Our cousins lived on the Big Eddy reserve. It was named after the river that cut through it. On one side of the river was the city of The Pas and on the other side was the reserve. Even though we also lived on a reserve, there was still a sense of culture shock. Big Eddy had over a 1000 band members while our reserve had fewer than 300. The reserve had its own shopping mall, rink, school and various band stores. It even had a paved road!

There were similarities too. As Celeste and I walked, the sight of the same cheap bungalows, yards filled with old cars and skinny yapping dogs, comforted us.

Big Eddy teemed with young people. At night, crowds of teenagers and pre-teens walked down its highway looking for something to do. Kids here had social lives. This was new to Celeste and me. At home, our social lives consisted of hanging out with our cousins who lived a mile away or, if we got ambitious, our cousin who lived two miles away. Once we'd walked one of those treks, there wasn't much energy to do anything other than walk back home.

Rachel's friend, Mandy, rode up on her pink bike. Mandy was the same age as us but looked younger because she was so small. She was curious and checked us out from afar before riding closer. I found that people from Big Eddy had a need for the upper hand . . . or maybe they just though they were better. That was a huge insult by the way. Telling someone that they "thought they were too good" was the worst thing you could say about them. With the exception of calling them fat.

Despite still smarting from the insults from the day before, I still had some confidence, inborn from being an older sister. I asked Mandy if I could ride her bike. She said no, explaining that I was too big for her bike. I knew this was unreasonable. I outweighed her by about twenty pounds not two hundred. I pointed this out to her. Mandy continued to demur so I snapped. "Is that a real bike or is it made out of papier mache?"

"You're fat!" Mandy said and then pedaled out of my reach. I thought about chasing after her but there were too many unknowns — like who were her cousins? And how mean were they?

"That Mandy is a jerk," I told Celeste and Rachel on our way home.

"Oh, yeah. Well, she's cheap, that's all," Rachel replied. "You can ride my bike."

I looked up excitedly.

"When we get home," she added.

Mandy's insult worried me more than I could admit to Celeste and Rachel. It showed me that it wasn't just my cousins; I was too fat for Big Eddy reserve. And if I wanted to make it through the next four weeks, I had to learn to deal with the insults.

Being the fat kid makes you a lot faster on your feet. You must anticipate the insults and be ready for them. I would leaf through the TV guide, making sure to avoid those shows that would call attention to weight. Anything starring Dom Deluise or Dolly Parton was to be avoided at all costs. I didn't anticipate all the jokes that could be made out of Orca or even Jaws. I silently cursed the producers. How could they not know that a movie about a creature composed of blubber or one with razor sharp jaws and huge appetite was an open invitation to fat jokes?

I was the fat kid and barring some inexplicable thirty-pound weight gain in one of the other kids, I'd better buckle down and accept it. I tried to find other labels for myself. I made sure to fix the beds every morning and asked my aunt if I could help her with the dishes. "Well, aren't you a hard worker," she said.

Yes I am, I smirked to myself. A hard working kid was a helluva lot better than the fat kid.

Malcolm saw through my act, "Hey, brown-noser, get your lardass out here to play some tag."

(Halfway through the visit, Malcolm decided that it took too much effort to say "Bannock Belly" and started calling me, "Lardass.")

At home when I felt stressed, I could retire to my bedroom with a book. Here I had no bedroom and they had no books. The only things to do were to play outside with the judgmental wolves or stay inside and watch TV with my uncle whose idea of good programming was back-to-back taped hockey games. I was caught between a rock, and a slightly bigger — way more boring — rock.

I stopped eating dinner with everyone else. There was no real dinner time anyway, not like at our house where we sat around the table and told our mom about our day. This was more like a scrimmage through the fridge and cupboards and then a free for all when one of the kids would decide to cook some Kraft Dinner. I stayed away from the kitchen and ate only when no one was looking.

"Isn't it strange how Dawn is fat but she never eats?" Nathan mused while wolfing down a half cooked cake.

I stared at his chubby cheeks and soft belly and knew that when I wasn't around he was the fat kid. In fact all of the kids, except Malcolm and Celeste, were within a few pounds of me. It was that I had been passed the torch and it wasn't possible to give it away.

I decided to fight back. I studied a picture of Malcolm in the living room. He had to have some weakness that I wasn't seeing. He had dark eyes, slightly slanted — I suppose I could get some mileage out of calling him "chinky eyes."

But I knew better. My mom had taught us that racial slurs were wrong. My aunt had different views and one of her nephews had the nickname, "Nigger," on account of his darker than average skin. Celeste and I cringed every time one of my cousins said the word. We asked Rachel what his real name was.

"Gaylord, but he likes Nigger better," she said without a trace of irony.

Celeste and I avoided directly addressing him for the rest of the visit.

Malcolm had a long hawk nose which some might say was too big for his face. My own chocolate bar nose was a constant source of disappointment to myself and I did not want to invite the comparison. Malcolm's only flaw — if it could be called that — was that he had a set of Mick Jagger-sized lips. My own lips were more big than small so I knew I was taking a chance with this one but it was all I had.

The next time Malcolm fired one of his zingers at me, "Hey, Lardass, I found some gum under the table, you want it?"

I was ready.

"Maybe you should use it to keep your big lips closed," I replied.

Silence filled the room. Malcolm looked shocked for a second, and then his pillowy lips broke into a wide grin.

"Oh so you noticed I have big lips? What else did you notice?" His eyes crackled with laughter as he welcomed the challenge.

I swallowed. "That's it. The lips. But they're really big!"

In my peripheral vision, I could see Celeste shaking her head ruefully. I had entered a gunfight with only one bullet.

Malcolm laughed. I admired his laugh; if only I could laugh then I could beat him. Malcolm wiped tears from his eyes and began his attack.

For the next few minutes, I listened as Malcolm discussed my weight problem and its possible implications: being harpooned after being mistaken for a land whale, falling into a well and being wedged in it, being shot by a moose hunter and ending up on someone's living room wall. He probably would have gone on but I escaped into the bathroom and locked the door.

"You can't take a joke!" Malcolm yelled from the other side.

Rachel and Celeste urged from nearby, "Ignore him!"

"Don't use the toilet!" my aunt yelled.

Celeste sidled up to the door a few minutes later and whispered. "Just come out. Or let me in."

It was too late by then. I'd already started crying and once I started it took weeks to finish. Even after I was done, my face turned red and swelled like a tomato. I had to put cold compresses on it to return it to normalcy, which was impossible in a bathroom with no running water.

I climbed on the dusty sink and stared out the window at the dark bushes behind the house. Even though there were bears in those woods, at that moment I felt like I could walk home if I wanted to. Sure it would be hard in the beginning but once I got used to sleeping outside, I'd be all right. I could eat blueberries ((which I loved) until I reached the border, and then once I got into Saskatchewan, I could switch to Saskatoon berries (which I also loved.) The best part was after I got home I would be thin. Way thinner than Rachel, maybe even as thin as Celeste.

I heard everyone settle down around ten PM and came out of the bathroom. The boys were in their bedroom planning the murder of Rachel's favourite cabbage patch kid. Rachel and Celeste were in her room discussing the injustice of Barbie doll clothing not fitting on all dolls. Celeste pointed out, "What if my cabbage patch doll wants to wear a mink coat? Now she'll feel too fat to wear nice clothes."

My heart jumped at the word fat. I didn't feel like facing them. I walked into the backyard and sat down on the picnic table. The woods looked a lot darker and scarier close up. There was no path through the woods, just brambles and sticks blocking you in every direction. No wonder bears always looked so rough and matted when we saw them down at the dump.

I looked down at my legs as I swung them. Were they fat? They looked the same as they had always looked. (Though a lot less skinned since no one would let me ride a bike since I'd been here.)

I heard a noise a few feet away and looked up. Adrian stood by the camper. He was leaning his beautiful head against it and his shoulders were curled inwards as he silently wept. While every hormone coursing through my body told me to go over to him, I held myself back.

The next morning, I decided to bring in the big guns. My heart told me it was time; I called home. I tearfully asked my mom to come pick me up. She was either having a crisis of money or perhaps she was enjoying her vacation. I turned the tears full blast, and claimed that I was having migraine headaches and that I might be going blind and deaf.

"Well, if you go deaf and blind, then I guess it wouldn't really matter where you are then," Mom reasoned.

I hung up.

A day later my mom called back. Her cousin Wha-hoo was travelling through Manitoba and said that he would stop by and pick up my sister and me. It was only 500 kilometres out of his way. He was a tall, friendly guy who had stopped by our house a few times and had coffee with my parents. I didn't like the idea of travelling with a relative stranger with a strange name but it was the best plan I had.

Wha-hoo pulled up at my aunt's house in a camper truck just like my aunt's. My aunt and uncle greeted him warmly as they set out the coffee cups on the table. Nobody asked him why he was there. I sat around the corner in the living room and nervously waited for him to tell them that he was taking us away. Mom had expected me to tell my aunt and uncle that we were catching a ride with Wha-hoo and I had not . . . mentioned it.

I didn't even know how to begin. "Um . . . I'm leaving because you think I'm fat." By saying the words, I would be making the fat real. Instead I chose the far more awkward route of walking out the door after Wha-hoo carrying my backpack and dragging my sister's hand.

"You're leaving?" My cousins were stunned. Why would anyone want to leave Big Eddy reserve? Sure people went away for jobs and school and jail. But kids? Kids LOVED Big Eddy. It was made for kids, it was run by kids! It was the last kid stronghold in the world.

I wanted to pretend that it was my sister who wanted to leave. Unfortunately, her sad face would never back up that lie.

"You can stay if you want," I had whispered to her the night before. She was loyal and didn't want to stay if I wasn't there. I felt there was some hope for her after all.

I knew I had to say something. I dropped my sister's hand and faced the confused people lining the verandah. The muddy yard was my pulpit and it was my obligation to deliver upon them the truth.

"I must leave you. Not because I want to . . . but because I must. You see, I have a brain tumor. And I'm dying. My mom told me I have to come back and spend my last few days with her."

I thought my speech might inspire a few shocked gasps, perhaps a few tears, maybe even some regret at the ways in which they had abused me. Instead they only stared.

Malcolm bravely broke the silence. "You got a tumor alright. A big fat stomach tumor."

Everyone snickered. Even my driver.

Aunt Beth told Malcolm to shut up. Then taking a look at Rachel and Celeste's sad faces, she suggested that Rachel go visit with us in Saskatchewan. The two girls ran inside to pack.

The three of us rode back to Saskatchewan in the back of Wha-hoo's camper. He offered to let us sit up front. We were smart enough to know that awkward conversation was a fate worse than death. We sat in the back of the truck and discussed the one-week visit. Celeste had had a pretty good time. There'd been cookouts and some rowdy games of tag. She'd even managed to weasel a cabbage patch doll out of Rachel's extensive collection.

Rachel confessed that she had broken up with Adrian before she left. "In the hallway as I was passing him," she explained.

My sister and I showed her shocked faces.

"He's cute but he always wants to be by himself," she said. "That's weird."

We nodded in acceptance of her decision while secretly shaking our heads. Then again, Rachel didn't know what it was like to be surrounded by nothing but trees and cousins. A few weeks at our house would teach her to appreciate a gorgeous — though somewhat emotionally scarred — young man. Hopefully someday, he would find a way to thank us.

The whole ride home, nobody brought up my weight or my impending death. As each mile took us closer to Saskatchewan, I left the labels further behind me. In Manitoba, I was fat; in Saskatchewan I was normal. Weight like real estate was just a matter of location.

THE BEAVER DAM

SHANE AND DYLAN WERE GERRY AND RICHARD's foster kids. Geraldine and Richard needed boys because they were ranchers. Nobody told me this; I figured it out for myself. Richard was a real live cowboy who looked after the reserve's cows.

We met the boys outside Geraldine's house. In a rare burst of extroversion, Mom had driven us over to Geraldine's house to visit. "I hear she has some foster kids about your own age," she said as she pulled into their yard.

"So? Who cares?" I said under my breath, annoyed that I'd been dragged away from my books.

"What are foster kids?" asked Celeste, who was forever curious.

Mom explained. "They can't live with their own mom and dad so Geraldine and Richard took them in. They even got separated from their brothers and sisters."

Celeste and I exchanged shocked looks.

Our own family had survived a rickety time a few years before when money problems had forced Mom to split us up. Celeste and Dave got sent to our Uncle Johnny's house on the reserve while Tabitha and I were sent to our Auntie Bunny's in the valley. Mom had stayed at the boarding school where she worked looking after other people's children. Our separation had lasted only a couple of weeks until she found a place for all of us to live. It was the worst thing that had ever happened to us and we were still wary.

"Where is their family?" I asked.

Mom shrugged. "Who knows?"

I made a face at her behind her head. She did not understand the importance of solving other people's problems, especially kids'. If a child needed something, it was an adult's responsibility to get it immediately. These boys needed their brothers and their sisters and their mom . . . probably not their dad . . . and they needed them now!

"I'm not discussing this with you," Mom said. "It's none of our business."

Geraldine and Richard lived about ten minutes away from us, high on a hill. Their house was perfectly situated with views of the country from every window. Their driveway went all around the house in a way that would have driven my mom crazy. She said it was a lazy way of avoiding backing up and proper parking; I could tell that it saved a lot of time.

Their house had a special surprise. Just behind it was a long road that led to stables and a few corrals. Down in the corral we could see horses pulling at bales. Right next to the house there were two towering stacks of bales. We could barely take our eyes off them as Mom ushered us into Geraldine's tiny kitchen.

Once inside, Geraldine just as quickly swept us out the door. "The boys are out there somewhere. Go meet them."

Obedient and silent, Celeste, David and I walked outside. We were bundled up in coats and scarves with socks on our hands because there was still snow on the ground. We had recently moved from town where we had spent a lot of time playing indoors. As a result we were unfamiliar with making fun by ourselves or using what Sesame Street called our imaginations.

"What should we do?" asked Celeste.

David plopped himself into the gravel and began making truck noises with a rock.

"I know I'm not doing that," I replied, impatient as usual with my brother's lack of creativity. "Maybe we could go down to where the horses are and ride them?"

Celeste looked doubtful. "They look pretty big. And we've never ridden horses before."

"You guys are such chickens," I declared. And then I sat down on the steps. (I immediately lost interest in my plans if they weren't enthusiastically supported or if I was nervous about carrying them out.)

Celeste and I stared up at the stacks of bales that loomed two storeys high beside us.

"How many bales you think is in there?" asked Celeste. "I think about four hundred."

"Pfft. Probably more like two thousand."

"Wanna climb them?"

I was raising the necessary courage to go nearer to the bales when a fair head poked its way out.

"Who are you?" the voice called. It was a squeaky voice, high pitched for a boy. He didn't look like anyone we'd ever seen on the reserve before. This boy was even whiter looking than Celeste.

We introduced ourselves. "We're Odie's kids." This was our Mom's nickname on the reserves and it was how people described us when we ran into them on the street. "Look here, it's Odie's kids. You can tell by the socks on their hands."

"What's your names?" he asked. We told him and then asked his.

"Shane." Even his name was different.

"Wanna see something cool?" Shane asked.

We nodded.

Shane ran the full length of the pile of bales and then jumped. He flew over the gap like a flying squirrel and landed in the other stack with a couple inches to spare.

Wow. Our mouths flew open. Celeste and I had never seen such daring.

"Holy cow, you could have died," I said.

"That looked like fun," Celeste added.

David only nodded sagely. He had always known that such daring was possible. He was so used to being thwarted by his sisters that he had retired most of his dangerous instincts.

Shane laughed at our amazement, then turned red from the excitement and jumped down the back of the bales. We heard a voice calling his name; it was Richard, his foster dad. Without saying good-bye, Shane leapt off the pile of bales and ran down to the stables, his body crackling with energy.

Another head popped up on the bales. The head was darker, the body longer and leaner. He smiled at us. "You're Odie's kids, right?"

"Yeah, that's us. What's your name?"

"Dylan." He chewed on a piece of straw and stared down at us.

"Are you gonna jump?" David asked.

Dylan looked at the other stack of bales. Then he walked to the edge of the bales, stared down at the drop to the ground. "It's too far," he said finally. "I could break an ankle or something."

"The other one did it," I said. "That other boy, he jumped."

Dylan smiled and chuckled. "Yeah, that's something Shane would do."

Dylan was two years older than Shane. I found it interesting that he knew his younger brother was more daring than him and that it didn't bother him. At home I had to endure the comparisons with my sister, "Celeste has such pep, and Dawn . . . she sure reads a lot." They pronounced the word "read" in the same pitying tone you might describe someone with a metal brace on her leg.

Dylan wore the mantle of "the less daring one," proudly and while it didn't make me feel better about being the "chicken shit one," I respected him for it.

"How many bales are in there?" Celeste asked Dylan.

"About four hundred," he replied.

Celeste smiled smugly at me.

We lived less than a kilometre away, which made us the luckiest kids in the world. At school, Dylan and Shane had already been declared to be the cutest brothers, with Shane having the overall title of "cutest boy in the school." And they were also the most fun.

When we were at their house, nothing was off limits. We could chase after the cows and swim in the dugout. We could run through the horse pen trying to escape Ruby, the white horse who used to bite everyone on the ass.

Shane glared at her every time we passed her pen. "Ass-biter," he would say under his breath.

Dylan would laugh. "Nobody told you to go in there."

"You did!"

"Nobody told you to listen."

Up on the hill next to the house, the hay bales were a constant source of amusement. Inside them we played hide and go seek which more often than not turned into huge wrestling matches, the soft bales giving us a reason to be violent and take more risks.

In the wintertime we went on skidoo rides. Dylan drove (Shane had been banned from driving after an ill-fated game of chicken with a stack of bales) and the rest of us kids piled onto the sled at the back. The heat of everyone's bodies and the struggle to stay on would keep us warm in the minus thirty-degree weather. Inevitably the jostling of the bodies turned into a struggle for survival as each of us tried to maintain a hold on the edge of the sled.

I lost the fight one night and ended up falling off into the snow. The sled and skidoo drove away even as I ran and yelled for them to stop. I kept expecting them to turn around but they didn't. As the light and the sound of the skidoo faded into the distance, I stood alone in the snow and the black night. I stopped yelling. Who knew what I would wake up — a wolf, a bear, a Sasquatch?! So I stood by the skidoo track and waited. Above me, a billion stars filled the sky. If I hadn't been so cold and frightened, I would have enjoyed it.

The skidoo came around again and Shane jumped off. "I was so scared for you," he said and pulled me back onto the sled.

Over at our house, we didn't have skidoos, horses or bales. We had something better: a beaver dam that stretched a football's field length behind our house. When spring came along we introduced Dylan and Shane to the mysteries of it.

The dam was a huge collection of dry sticks and logs along with a dozen mud huts half exposed by the water. We knew that the doorways to the huts were under the water and I was always curious to know what it looked like inside. How big would the beavers' rooms be? Did they make bedrooms as well? Did the beaver kids get their own bedrooms?

Since the beaver dam was surrounded by water it was difficult to play there. We weren't allowed to play in water — this was one of our mother's cardinal rules. We swiftly found a way around that rule. You see, falling into the water is something far different from wading in. It's an accident, an act of God, if you will, and certainly not something you can be punished for.

We took logs and created bridges from one beaver house to the next. Then we dared one another to walk across the bridges. Some of us needed to be challenged, like Dylan who always examined a problem from a few different angles. Others would not do it, even if dared. That was me. There were others though who didn't need to be dared, people who were always raring to put their lives and limbs in peril. That was Shane and Celeste.

Shane was the first one to run across the skinny log bridging two beaver homes. He laughed at how easy it was.

Celeste was the first one to stand on the bridge. She stood in the centre with a pole held horizontal in her hands. "I am the great Celest-tini!" she said as she tightrope-walked across it.

Shane, emboldened by her daring, joined her on the log bridge. Their combined weight had an immediate effect on the log. It broke in two and let out a loud bark; the daring duo toppled into the water. Celeste ended up standing waist high in the water. Shane, in a decidedly dramatic turn, fell in headfirst.

Dylan and I laughed from the sidelines, proud of our forethought and envious of their lack.

Being that Shane and the great Celest-tini had spankings waiting for them at home, we stayed out late that night. In keeping with his reckless nature, Shane swam under the murky water into one of the beaver houses, and re-emerged with a beaver skull, white and small, no bigger than my fist. "So they really are dead then?" I said, as I held it in my hands. For some reason, I thought we were sharing this dam with the beavers. It seemed impossible that anyone would build something so amazing and then leave it all behind.

I was into God during these years. Really into God. I prayed all the time and I felt that someone was communicating back to me. I had been reading about Catholic saints and how their devotion to God was rewarded with miracles. I wanted a miracle to happen to me — hopefully, the power of flight — so I told Him that I was ready to do His work. A pretty easy proposition considering that nobody had been into sacrificing Christians for at least a thousand years.

"Whatever you want from me, God, I will do. I will be your willing servant. I am ready to serve you. Just tell me what you want and I will do it."

I sat still on my bedroom floor and listened. Eventually, a voice popped into my head. It sounded like my own voice. I figured God was just using my voice because he didn't want to drive me insane. The voice told me that I was supposed to help Shane.

"Help Shane?" I asked.

"Yes, help Shane," the voice repeated impatiently.

I couldn't figure out what God meant by that. Shane wasn't in need of my help as far as I could see. He was the handsomest, cutest boy in the school. He could run the fastest and everyone loved him. He would run down the hallway at recess and make roadrunner sounds as he passed people, "Beep, beep." He would grab at girls' bums and sing, "feelings, feelings" and we would cover our bums with our hands because that's what we were supposed to do. He would stick his head into the girls' bathroom and scream, "Are you having a bloody good time?!" He was all kinds of charming.

At school Shane was king of the playground. A group of boys followed him and copied everything he did. The girls would whisper to one another about him. Once they found out that I was "his girl," they also whispered about me. There was no need to be jealous as Shane had plenty of love to share. He flirted with every girl in turn and then ran on to the next one.

Besides it wasn't so great being the "special girl." One winter Shane found some ice in a ditch by the edge of the playground. Soon he was sliding across it.

"Don't do that," I said.

"Why not? It won't break," he said.

I took a tentative step onto the ice. It creaked beneath me. "It's too thin," I said, as I backed up.

"It's thick!" Shane said, and then he jumped on it to prove it to me.

The ice cracked and his foot went through. The crack moved quickly towards me and my feet sank. The water was only up to our ankles but I still yelled, "You dumb idiot!"

I slogged out of the water only to see a large fire-engine red coat stalking towards us — it was Ms. Reynolds. She was eight feet tall and husky like a football player. I'd seen her ball out other students, particularly Shane, until they were blubbering messes. I'd never been on the receiving end of her wrath. She grabbed my hand in her huge paw and then Shane's and pulled us behind her.

I was too scared to ask where we were going. I looked at Shane; he winked at me.

She led us to the front doors of the school. There, in front of a hundred elementary school students, Ms. Reynold's spanked both of us with her racquet-sized hands. It didn't hurt since we were both wearing ski pants but emotionally it scarred me for life. To this day I get chills whenever I see ice, red coats, and Reynold's wrap.

After our beating we were placed in opposite corners and told to stand there for the rest of recess. Little girls wandered close to me and asked what happened. I told them about the ice and about how Shane had told me it would be okay. They nodded sagely; this was exactly why they did not play with boys.

"I am never playing with you again," I told him after our punishment was over. "Leave me alone."

Shane sat down next to me and then said. "Hey, did you know I had pizza last night? It had pineapples."

"It did not."

"It did. I promise you! It did!"

"You are a liar."

"No! I'm SD Best!" This was Shane's name for himself and also his catchphrase.

"Shane!"

"That's my name, don't wear it out!"

Shane and I built forts in our basement and planned our life together. I would draw a picture of our house and show him all the bedrooms and the multiple living rooms.

"This is your bedroom, this is mine, this is Celeste's, this is Dylan's, this is David's." The houses were always mansions because our future was bright and we planned on sharing it with everyone. We were going to need a very large house.

"I like you, Dawn."

"I know."

"I want us to be together forever."

Moments later the fort would be destroyed, usually by Shane, but the promises remained.

*

I could hear mumblings through the walls. That's how you found stuff out. Mom and Geraldine's voices were lowered to whispers. It didn't matter how low they spoke because tension flows right through drywall. It would take years to piece the story together but I knew something was wrong, that a door was closing.

In my bedroom, I sat on my bed and prayed. "What do I do God? How do I help my friend?" He was silent so I knelt on the floor, sure that the sacrifice of my knees would show the heavens that I was serious. "Please tell me what to do, God."

There was no voice in my head.

So I just went on as before. It was hard, though, because everything was changing at once. We hardly got to visit Shane and Dylan anymore because Mom never knew if they were going to be home or not.

"I don't know where Gerry is taking them," Mom said. "I don't know if she'll even be able to keep them now that her and Richard are breaking up."

My heart would leap into my throat. I knew a bit about foster children from my aunts who had kept children for years and years. Sometimes the children went away and you never got to see them again.

I carefully chose my next words. "If she's gonna lose them, could we adopt them?"

Mom pursed her lips together and turned away without speaking, which means *no* in every single language in the world. I went to my bedroom and stared up at the ceiling. Was that my moment? Was that my chance to help my friend? When the saints did God's work, it was usually something big like defying a king — of course, they did usually get eaten by lions afterwards.

Things had changed over at our friends' house. Shane wasn't as smiley and Dylan was even quieter.

One day Celeste and I gathered together all the change in our drawers. We even rifled through Mom's jeans and found a few bills. On our next visit, we gave the money to Dylan and Shane.

"What's this for?" asked Dylan.

"It's for you guys. So you can run away."

"All right!" said Shane, "we can buy some food with this money and go live in the woods."

Dylan frowned. "Where did you get this money?"

"We found it."

"We can't keep this, we'll get in trouble if someone finds it." He pushed it back towards us.

"It's yours!" I was getting angry. For God's sake, didn't they realize that I was trying to do God's work? Why did helping people have to be so damned hard!

In the end, we compromised. On our next trip to town we spent the money on snacks and comic books that we read sprawled out on the boys' bunk beds.

On one of the last days, Shane and I went down to the stable. There was a single horse standing there and Shane caught her. It wasn't Ruby the assbiter, but a calm sorrel horse that had never been ridden (I didn't know that at the time.) Shane grabbed her by the bridle and coaxed her next to the fence where I was perched. He brought her close enough for me to climb on, clambered up in front of me and we rode around the barn.

"I love this horse," I said. I loved all horses, except Ruby.

"Watch this!" Shane said, as he put his hands up in the air. I'm still not sure what he was trying to show me because at that moment one of his sleeves got caught on a nail on the roof of the barn. The sorrel kept going but Shane's progress was paused. Frantically he tried to pull himself free but we ran out of horse before it could be accomplished. I fell to the ground first. Shane lingered a moment longer in the air, then his shirt ripped and he came tumbling down.

"You idiot moron!" I jumped to my feet and dusted off my behind.

"That was great! Let's do it again!"

"Why do you have to ruin everything!" I said.

Shane laughed.

He ran off and found the sorrel that had wandered out of the barn. He pulled her back and we repeated the process. This time, Shane kept his hands down.

There was a trail that led away from Geraldine and Richard's house. We had never gone that way before. On this day Shane steered the pony in that direction. I clasped my hands around his narrow waist as we rode down the path.

BOYS CATCH THE GIRLS

FOR THE MAJORITY OF MY SCHOOL CAREER, I went to Balcarres School or BS as it was known on the side of our school jackets. Balcarres was a small school with less than five hundred students in total even though it included an elementary, junior high and high school. At some point in history the school had been huge. The classrooms had teemed with students and new additions had to be built to accommodate the overflow. Reminders of the school's glory days still lingered; it had a regulation sized football field and old football uniforms locked in the gym supply room. Its heyday had passed a long time before I walked through the door.

Unlike most of the schools in the area, this one was surviving. As other shut down, Balcarres greedily absorbed their students.

Part of Balcarres survival was due to its close proximity to File Hills. Each morning five busses carried the Native students in from the four reserves. Together the Native and white students could barely fill the classrooms, still we managed to create two separate worlds. The segregation began in elementary and grew more defined with each year. You might know Nina Buffaloskull's name in Kindergarten, that she could stuff three carrot sticks up her nose. By graduation you would not acknowledge her or her talents.

I had chosen my world on my first day at the school, as a new student, after February. My parents' — always thrilling — relationship had taken us from northern Manitoba, to Fort Qu'Appelle and back to the reserve in less than six months. My older sister and I had attended two different schools by the Christmas break. I was glad to be starting again; I hadn't liked my other two teachers. Both of them had been young and shrill and really adamant about singing every day.

When I saw Mrs. Green with her salt and pepper hair and her smile, just the right amount of friendly, and the right amount of firm, I knew I was in the right place. That's how everyone felt around teachers like that. You could trust your academic career in their weathered hands.

After the twenty-five year mark, such teachers no longer feared their students. They could size you up in thirty seconds and know exactly how much trouble you would give them. They knew which kids would make it and which kids would be shunted to the back of the classroom. Mrs. Green took one look at my messy hair that had fallen out of its braid, my clothes that were ill fitting but clean, and knew that someone was trying to steer me straight despite my natural proclivity towards sloppiness. It was my eager smile that gave away my defining quality — a desperate need to please. Mrs. Green placed me at the front of the classroom.

At my first recess break, she held me by the shoulders and pointed me at all the students. "Who do you want to play with?" she asked me.

My eyes searched the rows of expectant faces. I recognized one face from a few weeks I had spent at a nursery school on the reserve. "Trina," I said pointing at a tall girl with long braids. Trina came up to the front and took my hand. Everyone nodded as if this was what they had expected. The matter was decided; I was Native.

From then on there was no expectation that I would ever associate with the non-Native girls.

That didn't mean I wasn't curious about them. I would watch them walk together at recess. They would often surround the supervising teacher and hold her hand as she walked through the playground. Elsewhere, they played in clusters. I observed them from time to time but could not figure out their games. "Hmm . . . it appears that the blonde one is the leader. However, the brunette always gets her way if she pouts. The girl who always has new clothes never wants to do anything. It must be hard to get a good game of wrassling together with this bunch."

Inevitably my interest would fade and I'd run back to a group of Native (or Indian kids as we called ourselves at the time.)

In our group, I was a much-requested wrestling partner during recess time.

My girlfriends did not share my interest so they would cheer me on from the sidelines as they played "practice smoking."

"Go on Dawn, take him down," Trina, now my best friend, cheered. My face was red and sweaty, my hair stuck to my face, but that didn't matter. The only important thing was to wrestle your partner into submission. The boys were surprisingly weak. I threw one boy to the ground with one hand. My feat of strength made my jeans button snap off.

He laughed from the ground, 'Ha ha, look at her. Her pants snapped open. Ha ha!"

I refused to become embarrassed. What was the point when my face was already fire-engine red from exertion? I calmly buttoned my pants and lunged at him. It wasn't hard to grab his wrists and make him slap himself in the face as I asked, "Why are you hitting yourself? Why are you pinching yourself? Why are you unbuttoning your own pants?"

Though strong as a bull moose, Trina rarely joined in unless someone decided to cheat and attack from me behind. Then she would summon her incredible strength and without rancor grab the boy and deposit him a few metres away. "No ganging up," she would say and return to watching the match.

We played in shadows cast by the brick walls. That way we didn't overheat. Also, wrestling was against school policy, but as long as we didn't make it obvious and didn't bang into the law abiding students, the teachers were prepared to ignore us. They did not have the energy or the manpower to pull us off one another and send us packing. Once in a while the supervising teacher would walk to the edge of the circle and plaintively ask, "Don't you know any other games?"

We would stop immediately and stare at her. She would stare back. We would stare harder. She would look away and then move away with that slow, steady walk that every playground supervisor had mastered. Each step took at least a second. Watching the teacher stroll through the playground was almost meditative. I wonder if they taught it in teacher's college: Recess Walking 101 — How to Create a Sense of Authority with Your Gait.

⁐

The Native girls played on the tire fort, which we shared only with the Native boys. Nobody wanted it anyway because it was so dangerous. A girl had broken her arm the year before;

it was a bad break that necessitated surgery and pins and ugly stitches. We had all been dragged into the gymnasium for a school assembly on safe play. Afterwards, all the other kids abandoned the tire fort, so we took it over.

The tire fort had a staircase of tires that led to a wooden platform at the top. To get down you had four choices. You could take the slide, slide down a pole, go back down the tire stairs or take the broken arm route.

One day Celeste led a blonde, pretty white girl over to the tire fort. We welcomed her with curious stares.

"What's your name?"

"Sandy." She spoke softly.

"Sandy, so . . . " I wanted to ask her about being white and what it was like and how come she wanted to play with us but it seemed rude to put her on the spot. "Do you wanna play race to the top?" I asked.

She nodded.

It was kind of cool having a white girl hanging out with us. She brightened up the fort. She was also well off which made her and Celeste even more unusual friends.

There was a caste system that everyone on the playground unquestioningly followed. The white girls played with the white girls. The Native girls played with the Native girls. The only exception was the poor white girls who played with us from time to time. Like us, their clothes had seen the inside of a second hand store.

There was an Asian girl and a South Asian girl who went to the school — they played with the white girls. I figured that was because they lived in town. There was one Native girl who went back and forth from the white girls to the Native girls. She was very rich because her dad had won the lottery.

Sandy played with us for a few days. We accepted her as our own, even going so far as to give her a nickname, "the white girl." Then one day she didn't come over when the recess bell rang. We saw her across the playground, standing in line for hopscotch. I asked Celeste why she went away. Celeste shrugged. My sister had a lot of friends, what was one less?

Walking through the playground one day, I observed the other clusters of students and noticed the hierarchy. I relayed the theory to Trina who listened to my theories with unquestioning patience. This was an important quality in a best friend.

"I notice that there is prejudice here."

Trina's eyes widened. Everyone knew that prejudice was bad. To call someone prejudiced was to say that they hated Indians.

"The rich white kids are at the top. Then next is the poor kids and then at the bottom are the Indian kids."

"What about the Chinese girl and the East Indian girl?"

They were always screwing up my theories. "Well they're sort of like white girls aren't they? They live in town; they go to the same birthday parties. It's like they are white."

Trina nodded in agreement. It all made perfect sense to her. Also, she didn't really care.

Elementary school taught us that we lived in two different worlds. In a classroom setting, the worlds would sometimes bump up against one another. You could not always choose where you sat in a classroom and even if you could choose, inevitably a Native would have to sit next to a white or vice versa. It was simple geometry. Out on the playground where the teachers could not interfere, the separation was complete. They played their games; we played ours.

In the Native student world, people were always coming and going. A girl might show up at the school for a month and then leave, only to be replaced by another girl with new knowledge of the city or a different reserve. I was always curious to hear their stories. They were worldlier than us having lived in the country and in the city.

One year a girl named Cassandra showed up right after Christmas break. She was ten going on thirty. She had both ears pierced, more than once. She wore nail polish and frosted lipstick that she applied every chance she had. She had a boyfriend too, in the city. The city was one of her favourite subjects.

"In the city, there's like thousands of kids in elementary school. And recess isn't fifteen minutes, it's like half an hour."

"Half an hour? What do you play?"

"We don't play." She laughed at my conventionality. "In the city, we just . . . y'know . . . hang out."

"Hang out? What's that?"

Cassandra laughed and other girls joined in with her laughter. "It's . . . y'know . . . hanging out."

In practice, hanging out turned out to be sitting around on the tire fort talking about boys. In my opinion, hanging out was a giant waste of time. My sister and I were country girls — used to walking wherever we went — and our legs begged to be stretched each recess. Standing next to Cassandra and the girls gathered around her was torture. While they leaned languorously, my legs jiggled nervously.

"Hey, everybody, how about we have a race?"

"Why would we do that?" Cassandra had no interest in being a good runner. Instead she would light a smoke and pass it around the circle of girls who were eager to cast off their country values in favour of city vices.

A few days later, a teacher caught Cassandra smoking in the bathroom and confiscated her smokes. After a few detentions, she sauntered back onto the playground with a new plan for our recess time. She suggested a game of Girls Catch the Boys.

"How do you play that?"

"We run after the boys and then we catch them."

"And then what?"

"Then you do what you want to them."

"Like . . . ?" Beat them up? Make them eat dirt? Spit on their faces? There were a lot of possibilities out there, each with a different level of difficulty. I needed to know how to play this game if I was going to win it.

Instead of answering my question, Cassandra raised a plucked eyebrow like a ten-year-old Mae West and smiled. The other girls twittered. I rolled my eyes. They didn't know either but they didn't want to look stupid in front of Cassandra.

"Sure sounds like fun." My voice dripped with fake enthusiasm. How could chasing down smelly boys be any fun? Wouldn't pushing one another on the swings or having races to the top of the monkey bars be a better use of our time?

Even hopscotch was preferable — and hopscotch was the dumbest thing anyone could do. Hamsters would find hopscotch boring. (A giant wheel, on the other hand, would have kept me busy for months at a time.)

At least you knew when you lost hopscotch — it was when your kneecap fell off. I couldn't see how a winner could be proclaimed from the game, Girls Catch the Boys. Would it be the girl who caught the most boys? Or the girl who caught the fastest boy?

We did not notify the boys about the game, we just ruthlessly ran them down. One second they were standing in the ball field waiting for a fly ball, the next a group of giggling girls had descended upon them. Once the first boy was captured, the other boys knew to run. And soon they were half way across the sports field.

The captured boy looked from one female to the next as they discussed his future.

"Let me go!" He struggled. We ignored him.

"What do we do?"

"Tickle him?"

"Please God No!!!" He got an arm free and tried to make a break for it. He had no chance against our snake-like arms and vise-like grips.

Cassandra pushed her way through the crowd of girls and looked at our wriggling boy.

"You are our prisoner," she proclaimed.

He laughed nervously. "You can't do this."

She pointed at the tire fort. "Take him there and make sure he does not escape."

She looked at the rest of her girl soldiers. "Catch me another one. An older one this time." Then she retired back to the tire fort. Cassandra wasn't one for running.

I ran down the next boy, Jackson. I grabbed him by his arms and pulled him backwards. Jackson was small but he had a bad temper. "What the fuck are you doing?"

"Cassandra wants us to catch boys."

"What the fuck for?"

"I don't know," I handed him to the waiting arms of two bigger girls. "I'm going to grab another one," I yelled back and left.

I noticed quickly that the less-cute guys were easier to catch as I dragged them back to the tire fort. It helped that at our age a girl was at least a head taller than a boy. It also helped that the boys were more curious than afraid.

"What are you going to do with me?" asked Michael, a skinny eleven-year-old from Little Black Bear.

"I don't know. Maybe beat you up."

"I thought you were gonna . . . y'know do girl stuff." He puckered up his lips. I gagged and pushed him away.

He gave me a strange look and ran away from me. He ran slowly though and looked back frequently. "Aren't you going to catch me?" Michael said, circling back.

"No." I walked over to an empty hopscotch square that the white girls painstakingly drawn on the sideway, and began practicing my footwork.

Trina wandered over. "Cassandra wants to know why you aren't playing."

"It's a stupid game."

Trina agreed but she couldn't say so as she was Cassandra's cousin. "It's too hard to catch the cute boys."

"I don't see the point. What do we get if we catch them?"

Trina gave me a look as if she wanted to tell me something and decided against it.

My mom had a word for the girls like Cassandra — boy crazy. "Those girls only think of boys, that's all they can think of it. It's sick."

I didn't understand why the girls got so giggly and silly about it. Don't get me wrong; I liked boys. I even had a boyfriend, Shane. This meant that when he wrote his name it was always SD plus DD. And when I signed my name, I did the same. When he looked in my direction and winked, I smiled back and gave him the thumbs up sign. (The thumbs up sign was cool because of Fonzie.) Even though Shane had moved away two years before, I assumed I was still his girlfriend.

The next recess, Cassandra gathered the girls together again. She agreed that the game wasn't as fun as it was in the city. In the city, the boys didn't run so fast and there were more girls there so it was easier. Also the city playground was fenced in so the boys couldn't run a kilometre to get away from us.

Taking these factors into account, Cassandra devised a twist on the game: girls catch the boys would now become boys catch the girls.

The girls twittered with excitement. I was nervous. I knew that Jackson wanted his revenge for his captivity. Jackson wasn't exactly what you would call stable. He smiled when he doled out beatings to his friends. And he was fast.

"That's a bad idea," I said.

Cassandra glared at me. "How come you always make trouble? Are you jealous of me?"

"Ohhhhh." A murmur went through the girls. Everyone knew that being jealous of someone was a horrible thing to be accused of.

I forced myself to laugh. "Ha. As if."

Another ohhh followed. Cassandra was now within her rights to call me out. But, she didn't because like most true leaders, she knew when to be tough and when to be magnanimous.

Cassandra smiled and patted me on the shoulder. "You know what Dawn? It's okay if you don't play with us. We'll have a good time without you."

She stressed the words "us" and "we" and I silently cursed my lack of leadership skills. If I didn't play by her rules, I'd be thrown out of the tribe, forced to eke out a playground existence with another group.

I looked around the playground. There white girls and their token South Asian and Chinese members played politely with one another on the sidewalk. I wasn't looking forward to introducing myself into the non-Native group. Like an anthropologist being introduced to an isolated South American tribe, I'd probably spend a few weeks observing the tribe and learning their customs before they would allow me into their circle. Even after that it would still take me years to learn the intricacies of their language and why they ate so many egg salad sandwiches.

Trina tugged on my arm, "C'mon I need you to help me. I don't want to get caught."

I capitulated for her. Trina was a slow runner and therefore a sitting duck.

Led by Jackson, the boys hit us hard and fast. They were everywhere at once. Unlike the boys who split up and ran in different directions, the girls stayed together and huddled against the fort. The plan was to thwart the boys by pushing them off the fort every time they tried to jump onto it. It was a good plan except that few of the girls had ever engaged in hand-to-hand combat. Instead, they kept climbing higher and higher up the fort until we were all squeezed onto the top of the fort, huddled together like refugees on a raft. We dared not let a hand or foot slip over the side.

I fought hard next to my sister and Trina. My sister and I were quick but Trina was strong. One heave from her and a boy was going all the way to the bottom in a hurry.

Cassandra stood in the middle of the girls and called out orders. "To your left. To your right. Behind you. Kick them with your feet." We knew without asking that the goal was to protect her. If she was captured the game was over. It was also important to avoid Jackson and his hard little fists.

I climbed up on the monkey bars to survey the scene. Native boys chased down Native girls with ease. I'm not sure if I was imagining it but it seemed like the girls . . . wanted to get caught. I was pondering this when Michael from Little Black Bear, grabbed my arm. "I got you now." He grinned up at me from below me.

"No you don't," I said and tried to shake off his hand.

"Yes I do."

"If you don't let go, I'm going to kick you in the face."

Michael let go of my leg. "This game is just for fun, you know."

"So what? You're not catching me." I climbed higher, out of his reach. As I watched him chase after another girl, the feeling of victory was swiftly replaced with disappointment: shouldn't he be trying harder?

I was distracted by Trina's yell. Jackson had his arm around her neck and was dragging her backwards off the fort. I hurried to my friend's defense. I grabbed one arm and Jackson hung onto her other one. We wrestled back and forth with our Trina wishbone. I was on the verge of losing when Celeste peeled Jackson's arm off Trina. Frustrated, he let go altogether, then jumped back up on the platform and raised his fist at Celeste.

Tweet! Tweet! Tweet!

A whistle shrieked through the air hysterically. Boys and girls froze in their positions, confused at the sound.

I looked down and saw the young teacher in her long coat, flanked by little white girls on each side. She shook her hands loose and put them on her waist in proper pissed off form.

"What is going on here?" She asked, surveying the carnage scattered all over the tire fort. "Jackson, were you going to hit Celeste?"

Jackson shook his head.

"Don't lie to me." She drew herself to her full height of five feet four.

"I wasn't!" His anger hit out at her like a fist. She flinched, not knowing where to go next.

"Boys don't hit girls. You know that. That's not acceptable." She looked at the girls for verification. We stared back blankly.

Jackson shrugged as if to say, you have your rules, I have mine.

The young teacher held her whistle and its lanyard in front of her like a sword. There was something else she had to do here, but where to begin? Her eyes moved up and down the fort studying us — "The Native kids."

"I don't want to see anymore fighting or hear any more yelling from here. You understand?"

She made eye contact with a few of the students. When her eyes touched mine, I felt a frisson of fear run down my back. She may have been a thin twenty-two-year-old teacher a few months out of Teacher's College but authority of any kind scared me. Especially since my mom always found out what we did on the school grounds.

My fear was not shared. Cassandra didn't acknowledge the teacher; she looked down at her fingernails and flicked off the nail polish. Jackson stared straight ahead at a point on the horizon.

Finally, feeling that she had won for at least a few seconds, the teacher decided to leave with her meager victory. She re-clasped hands with her chain gang and made a wide turn as they headed in another direction.

Back on the tire fort, the Native kids started to laugh.

"Did you see the look on her face? Looked like she ate a rotten orange."

" *'Jackson were you gonna hit Celeste.'* Well, duh."

"As if she could even do anything!"

We laughed until our guts were sore. We laughed because we almost got caught, because we got off scott free, because we were still separate and wild. We laughed because they could not touch us with their rules, not out here on the playground. We laughed because they had everything else, but we had the best games. Scary, dangerous and violent games — but ours.

FAMILY WEDDINGS

Mom's Wedding

Mom and I went through the family pictures about twice a year. It was never a deliberate thing. I would be climbing on the cupboards, searching for a hidden stash of candy and I would come upon the photo albums stacked in the cupboard over the fridge. Somehow the stack of photo albums would make its way down to the kitchen table. Then Mom would sit next to me, light a smoke and begin turning pages. The albums filled the centre of the table and cascaded down towards each of us. Loose pictures fill in the gaps, eagerly seeking a new home. I opened the oldest photo album, which was also the thinnest, and dedicated to my parent's wedding.

"How come you chose green for your bridesmaids? It's so ugly." The pale green colour flattered her brown-skinned bridesmaids, but I had a natural aversion to anything green. It reminded me of the algae that choked out all of our swimming holes.

"I liked that colour," Mom said.

"How did Dad ask you to marry him?" I already knew the answer to these questions. It was a ritual we went through whenever we looked through her wedding album.

"He asked me."

"What did he say?"

"Well, it was after you were born and I found out that I was pregnant with Celeste and your dad says, 'I guess we should get married then, eh?'"

"That's not romantic." I turned the page. In the next picture, Dad's face was front and centre and Mom appeared behind him in silhouette as though he was dreaming of her. His expression was a mix of confusion and annoyance.

"So we set a date and we booked the hall and the church."

"Why's Dad's hair so long? Was he a hippie?"

"He went to get it cut the day before—"

"Why did he wait so long?"

"—the wedding, but the barbershop was closed so he didn't."

I turned to a photo of a tiny church where the wedding party stood outside, neatly arrayed in a v-line.

"Where was this taken?" I asked.

"We had the wedding out at the old church that burned down. And then we had the reception out on Starblanket at the old hall that burned down."

"Was it nice?"

"It was. Except your dad passed out at the reception."

"What a classy guy." We knew that Dad was an alcoholic although it always surprised me to find out that Mom had known this from day one.

"And so Alvin Rat and his girlfriend helped me get your dad into the car and then we hit the ditch. Went right off the road at the T-stop and flew into the ditch."

"You were pregnant!"

"We landed in five feet of snow. I got out of the car and I was up to my chest in it. And that stupid wedding dress just billowed out around me on top of the snow as I walked. Froze my legs off." Mom held out her coffee cup and I went to the counter to refill it along with spoonful of sugar and a pour of carnation cream — the good stuff.

"What about Dad? How'd he get out of the car?"

"I can't remember," she said.

"Did you leave him there?"

"I should've."

"Where was I?" I asked. Celeste walked past the table and I glared at her not to join us. She ignored me and took a seat on the other side of Mom. Mom-one-on-one time was always scarce and none of us let any of the others hog her.

"At home with Grandma and Tabitha," Mom replied.

"Where was I?" Celeste chimed in.

"In Mom's gut like a giant tapeworm!" I replied, and then, "Did you have a honeymoon?"

"No."

"Wow. Did you even get an engagement ring?" I had heard about them from watching a soap opera. A guy would fall in love with a woman and then he would ask her to marry him and she would say yes and take the ring even though she really loved his brother or his dad.

"I had a wedding ring," Mom said.

"Where is it?" Celeste and I asked together.

"I hocked it last year. Remember? For your brother's hockey camp."

"You lost it in a pawn shop?" Celeste asked before I could.

"It was the bingo caller's fault. He should've called my numbers."

"You think you'll ever go on honeymoon?" I asked.

"Ha."

Tabitha's Wedding

As she pinned a flower to my dress, Tabitha's hand shook. I wanted to grab her hand and hold it in mine. She was too proud for that. Tabitha was the oldest and she took care of us, not the other way around. Her dress curved around her, the scallops defining her slender frame. "She is too good for that dress," I thought to myself. I wanted her to look like the glamorous model she was in my eyes. Her actual dress was conservative in order to hide her pregnant tummy.

I wore a soft pink dress with a crinoline underneath. It felt like I was constantly walking through a bush of brambles. My parents went all out for the wedding and paid for the brides-maids to get our hair and makeup done. Unfortunately all our esthetic services were performed by the town's Greek hairdresser who believed in a more is more approach. I was sixteen- years-old and wearing so much make up I could have passed for a fifty year old who lived a hard life. My hair was teased into a lovely helmet-like shape and for the entire day I received no compliments except when a drunk relative bumped into me and called me Snow White.

"Can I wash my hair?" I said as I scratched it and hardened hair spray fell onto my shoulders.

"For the last time, no!" Tabitha's normally soft voice was starting to sound strained. "Now put your shoes on, we have to go."

My shoes were pink to match my dress and they were two inches high. This pleased me.

One of the other bridesmaids glared at me for being a pain in the butt. She was from the groom's side of the family and pretty in a buxom, sulky way. The maid of honour — and let's face it, the only bridesmaid that really matters — winked at me before taking her position to watch over my sister's train. I liked the back of Tabitha's dress. A train meant that you were taking this wedding business seriously. Also, when else would you ever get to wear a train? People should always take full advantage of their train wearing opportunities.

Tabitha walked down the aisle with my dad who looked as shaky as her hands, though his shaking came from a three-day drinking binge. He wandered into the house the morning of the wedding, looking dark and handsome as usual. His face was sweaty and he wore a Mona Lisa smile on his lips.

My cousin Nathan, who dotes on him, polished Dad's shoes as the rest of us ran around the house frantically searching for the secret to a perfect wedding. Dad and Nathan sat in the dining room and laughed as he teased Nathan. Nathan was drunk.

Tabitha cried during the wedding. One of the other brides-maids murmured under her breath. "Tabitha's crying." And everyone teared up because she was one of the family pets.

We drove to the valley for pictures. Then the rest of the wedding party went to the bar for a drink. I went directly to the reception, being the only one in the wedding party under age.

The dinner and dance was held in town — this was unusual among Natives. Most receptions were held at the band hall or the reserve school. We chose to stick ourselves right in the middle of town. It was a risky move considering the local RCMP's aggressive policing of Native males like my dad. But Mom wouldn't do it any other way — no child of hers would be stuck on the reserve like some backwards hick. Besides, unlike many Native people, Mom did not fear or resent the police as she had briefly dated an RCMP officer in her youth. Much to the annoyance of my dad, this fact came up quite a lot during my childhood.

The town hall was done up in pink and white, my sister's favourite colours. It was packed with family, friends and the uninvited. It wasn't a great wedding unless it was crashed. Tabitha had been popular in high school, a fact that haunted me, and all of her old high school friends showed up in their dark jackets and jeans. They looked sexy and dangerous to me. I lingered behind them, hoping someone would mistake me for an eighteen-year-old. A girl whispered to another girl, "Why's Tabby getting married? Just cuz you're knocked up doesn't mean you have to settle down." The other girl nodded in agreement. Tabitha's six-hours-old husband, Mike, glared at them from the head table, as if he could read their thoughts.

When I found out that Tabitha was pregnant, I wanted her to move back home. I would have gladly shared my bedroom with her and the new baby. She didn't need to go off and get married and be all grown up. But this was hardly something you could say when everyone was swept up in the excitement of wedding planning. My sister was married. I had lost the battle and now I had the crinoline scarred legs to prove it.

I sighed deeply and reminded myself that what was done was done. At least her wedding afforded me the chance to attend a party. There were a lot of people at the wedding and I wanted to meet everyone. First I had to get drunk.

My sister Celeste, my cousin Jolene and I had found a stash of beer the night before. Found, stole, it's hard to remember which now. We hid the beer in the back of the hall while everyone else was decorating. When Jolene went to look for the secret stash, it was gone. Of course now when I look back, beer had a way of disappearing when Jolene was around.

It was no matter. Everyone got their hands on drinks. All the adults were drinking and the liquor was spilling over into the mouths of the teenagers. My fourteen-year-old cousin Cindy passed out on the table at ten PM, her head in her hands.

I was the youngest bridesmaid and was paired up with my brother-in-law's nineteen-year-old brother Charles. I hoped that he would have been a tall, lean Corey Haim look- alike.

Not quite. Charles was a shorter, heavier version of my brother-in-law with a buffalo-sized head. Charles and I danced together for a waltz.

"Your parents let you date?" Charles asked.

"Not until I'm in grade eleven and I'm only in grade nine." (This was a lie — the topic had never come up — but there was no way I was gonna let Buffalo Head know that.)

"You're in grade nine? What a coincidence, so am I."

"Quit lying!" I said giving him a playful swat.

"I'm not." His voice was hard.

I looked at him in disbelief then wiped the look off my face when I saw him redden.

"Oh right, I think I remember my sister mentioning that." I nodded my head as if that was a normal thing. "How are you finding chemistry?"

He'd seen the shocked look in my eyes and the waltz was awkward after that, as has been every other encounter since.

The dance with the groomsman ended my bridesmaid responsibilities. Sitting alone at the head table, I sipped cranberry juice from a plastic cup and cursed my heavy dress. It was long and scratchy. There were grandmothers dressed cooler than I was. Everywhere I turned everyone seemed to be tipsy, half cut and fully wasted and I wanted to catch up! I went in search of my extra clothes that I had given Celeste the night before and told her: "Bring this to the wedding, Celeste, so that I won't have to walk around looking like the tooth fairy all night." I found Celeste at a table in the corner, building a pyramid of plastic beer cups with Jolene.

"Where are my clothes?"

"Hey, it's the pink lady!" Celeste elbowed Jolene and they laughed in that happy, euphoric way that only stolen beer causes.

"Where are my clothes?"

"What clothes?" she asked.

"The ones I asked you to bring for me."

"Oh, I knew I forgot something. You look nice," Celeste said. A lie. My skin was red from the scratchy pink dress and I was limping in my one-inch heels. Celeste, on the other hand, was comfortably dressed in a pair of tight jeans with cool Reebok sneakers on her feet.

Nothing, absolutely nothing was falling to place. No cute escort! No cute jeans! It was gonna be the worst night of my life.

My sister finished another beer and piled it onto the top of her beer pyramid.

"Hey, you know what?" she breathed Budweiser into my face.

"What?"

"I think I left a skirt in the change room from the rehearsal dinner last night," she said.

"Are you sure?"

She nodded as she took a sip from another beer that Jolene had placed into her hand.

"What about a shirt?"

"Here you go."

Jolene drunkenly pulled her T-shirt off to reveal a white tank top underneath. And a black bra underneath that. A pretty risqué look even for the eighties. But like I said, Jolene has always been ahead of her time.

I ran to the back of the hall to the change room. I found my sister's wrinkled black miniskirt. I held it up next to Jolene's beer-stained T-shirt. Wrinkled and dirty, or prissy and pink?

I had nowhere to put my dress so I bundled it up in a ball and stuffed it into a black garbage bag. Days later my older sister would find it and confront me for being an ungrateful brat but that was in the future and I was living in the NOW. I wanted to meet someone, a cute guy, with black hair who played hockey and who looked cool drinking a beer. "He" would be here. I had no doubt.

I looked around the wedding. I couldn't see any cute guys or at least not any that I wasn't related to. I saw a lot of women. Most of them performing the same desperate scan I was making. My eyes locked with an older girl cousin who had been single longer than I had been alive. I quickly looked away.

My brother walked up to me. David's face was red and his hair was stuck to his head.

"Where's Mom?" His voice had a thick milky quality.

"I don't know, why are you talking like that?"

"I'm sick."

I sniffed him. "You're drunk. Hey, where did you get those?" I asked pointing at his neck.

David's neck was ringed with giant hickeys. You could have matched the mouth to those hickeys, they were so dark and distinct. Wow, even my twelve-year-old brother was getting lucky.

"What are you talking about? Where's Mom?" he asked. Then he stumbled and grabbed onto me. I tried to pry his hands off me. "Go play with our cousins or something," I told him.

"I want to go home." His big eyes were watery. I rolled my eyes, now here was someone who could not hold his liquor. Although in retrospect, I'd be frightened to meet a preteen who could.

I went to find Tabitha. She would know what to do with David.

David followed along behind me. "Quit walking so fast," he complained.

"I'm not walking fast, you're really slow," I replied. I headed out of the hall over to the bar/motel. To escape her family and friends, Tabitha had booked a room in the motel next to the hall with her husband. I knocked on the door of her room. Tabitha opened it looking like she was tired of being asked for things.

"Where's Mom?" I asked.

"I don't know. You better get him home," she said, looking at David who staggered under the weight of her gaze.

I had no intention of doing that — I was pawning him off on Mom as soon as I found her. "Where are the keys to the truck?"

"Dad must have them," she replied and shut the door.

I ran next door to the bar. I heard my dad's giant laugh from outside. "You stay here," I told David.

"I'll do whatever you want, I just want to go home," he said. (Whenever David drinks, he becomes oddly obedient.)

I pushed my way into the bar, sure that my heavily made up face would get me past the bouncer. I was right. I stood in the bar and enjoyed the ambiance for a moment. The ceiling was low, clearly no one anticipated any NBA players popping by. People were crowded around the bar, talking loudly. A man sat by himself at a table with his head in his hands as he sobbed. The air was stale, like it had died and lingered. (There was also a smell of burnt cabbage but the bar served no food. Odd.) My heart beat excitedly to be in such a glamorous environment.

My dad was holding court among old friends and new. He had married off his oldest daughter; not many men at the table could say that. He knew he had done something right. If you asked him to tell you what that was exactly, he would have been at a loss to explain.

I asked him the question that I've surely asked him a thousand times since I've learned to drive. "Do you have the keys, Dad?"

"How's your dad gonna get home?" one of my uncles asked.

"I'm gonna ride Nathan home," Dad said, and the whole table broke into laughter.

By this time Nathan was passed out in a chair beside my dad, his face looking young in an old, grey suit.

Dad handed me the keys and I hurried out of the bar. With the keys to the family vehicle in my hand, I still believed that something amazing could happen. In order of most exciting: 1. A cute guy would kiss me. 2. I'd get invited to a really fun party. That's it. At fifteen, there was not much else on my mind.

I went back into the hall and was disappointed to find that it, and the opportunity for the best night of my life, had emptied out. The tables were bare now and one of my more formidable aunties was cleaning up. I edged into the shadows so that I couldn't be enlisted to join the cleaning patrol. This is where my mom found me. She walked out of the bathroom and ran straight into me. My mother rarely drank. When she did, she made it seem like a tedious job. She was only tipsy and already seemed hung over.

"Find your sister and brother," she demanded. "We're going home."

I was caught.

A few minutes later, five people had piled into our pickup truck. It was a single cab, meant for three at the most. I drove; Celeste, Jolene, my mom, and my brother sat next to me. It was too cold for someone to sit in the back, although if someone could have, my vote would have been for Celeste who spent the whole trip dry heaving beside me.

Celeste was in good spirits, however, and laughed at everything she saw. David complained that Celeste's laugh was hurting his ears. Mom kept telling everyone to shut up and Jolene sat quietly, calculating the quantities of beer in each of her secret stashes located throughout the province of Saskatchewan.

I was happy to be the driver, as I didn't even have my license yet. My happiness would have been complete if: 1. A cute boy had kissed me, or 2. I had been invited to a cool party, and 3.

My mom had passed out instead of giving me frequent orders to slow down.

We got to the house and I thought, there's still a chance. I enlisted Jolene as my wing woman because she was one of those rare creatures who was always up for fun and because Celeste was already snoring on her bed. I couldn't use the truck because Mom wisely tore the keys out of my hand before heading to her bed to pass out. So Jolene and I snuck out of the house. At the very least, I knew my family members would be partying next door at Uncle Frank's house. It was less than five minutes way at a brisk jog. The path was dark but we had walked it a million times.

The path was wet with dew. The sky looked half awake and I ran faster because I knew my chances for a fun night were running out

We got into my uncle's yard just as three cars pulled into the driveway. I didn't recognize any of them and I was glad because I knew it was my older sister's friends, the leather and jeans clad teenagers. I ran up to one of the cars and the driver rolled down the window.

"Hi!" I said brightly (I had been aiming for cool). "Do you know where a party is?"

Before the driver could reply, the voice of God rang out from my grandpa's porch. And he sounded exactly like my Aunt Beth. Normally, she was my sweetest and gentlest aunt, except it seemed, when her sixteen-year-old niece was leaning into a car full of strange boys.

"Dawn, get your ass over here!" she yelled. I was still young enough that an adult's voice had power over me. I immediately backed away from the car. My uncle stepped out onto the porch next to my aunt. For the past four days they had hosted a bachelor party. (Yes, a four-day bachelor party.) They had bought beer and hard stuff and even a Texas mickey. They had driven to town to pick up more booze and snacks. They had helped write naughty words on the faces of my cousins when they passed out and had taken pictures of the bachelor party guests in embarrassing positions with goats and other livestock. All of that was over. Now their faces wore the looks of people who had never partied and never would again.

The driver rolled up his window and turned his car around. The other cars followed him out of the yard. I still remember the look of their lights as they all turned in the same direction, away from me.

"Good night Dawn!" my aunt called gleefully from the front steps as she walked back inside the house. Her cockblocking efforts had put an extra bounce in her step.

Minutes later Jolene and I trudged back to my house down the same path, the smell of spring rising up into the air as we crunched the grass and gravel under our feet. I silently cursed my bad luck. Jolene sipped a beer she had procured from one of her stashes.

The next day Tabitha and her new husband came by the house for brunch. My brother-in-law teased my siblings and me with newfound confidence; God had officially sanctioned his obnoxiousness. Tabitha sat beside me on the couch as she drank her coffee and I worked my way through a stack of pancakes. "Did you have a good time at the wedding?" she asked.

"Yeah, it was fun. I didn't meet any cute guys though."

She smiled with the confidence that comes from wearing a gold ring. "Don't be in such a hurry. Everything comes in time."

Mom's Wedding

In the picture, Mom's wedding gown ballooned around her as she clasped her bouquet to her waist.

"Wow, you look so chubby," I said.

"Cuz I'm inside her belly, right Mom?" Celeste asked.

"Yup. Five months, pregnant." Mom added, "I had the worst case of hemorrhoids."

Behind Mom stood three bridesmaids. All of them wore excited smiles as if to say, "I can't believe we're getting away with this." Mom touched her own photo, smoothing out the corners. "I can't believe I ever looked that young."

A new question occurred to me. "Hey, when did you and Dad meet anyway?"

"I knew him from school and we had dated this one time when we were teenagers. I broke up with him because I thought he drank too much. I was much smarter back then." She got up to refill her coffee cup.

"Then what happened?" Celeste asked. "Did he stop drinking for you?"

"I moved to the city and then after a couple of years, I came back and started working at the band office."

"And Dad was chief!" Celeste and I said in unison.

"He was the band administrator then."

"Was he like really cute and you were like all weird around him, like you couldn't even breathe right when he walked into the room?" I asked.

"He was okay," Mom answered as she stirred sugar and cream into her coffee. "I was too busy looking after your older sister. I wasn't thinking about dating anyone."

"He asked you out on a date?"

"I was living with grandpa and grandma so he came over and asked grandpa if he could go out with me."

"See, now that's romantic!" I crowed.

"I guess so."

"Where'd you go on the first date?" Celeste asked. "Somewhere fancy in the city like Red Lobster?"

We had never been to Red Lobster because Mom always said it was too expensive.

"As if. There wasn't even Red Lobsters back then," I told Celeste.

"I'm not a dinosaur," Mom said dryly.

"So there *were* Red Lobsters?"

"Well, no there weren't. That's not important cuz we didn't go to the city, we went down to the valley. To the old pizza place. I wasn't used to going out so I got really drunk and your dad had to take me home early. I'm surprised he even asked me out again."

"But he did."

"He did."

"Then you had me. In a blizzard," I added, turning the page in the photo album to a baby picture of me.

"And then you got pregnant with me!" Celeste said and pointed to a baby picture of her.

"God, you were an ugly baby," I said.

"Dawn!" Mom said in her warning voice.

"Then Dad said, 'we should get married, eh?' That's the worst proposal I've ever heard," I said even though it was the only one I had ever heard of.

"Life isn't like the movies," Mom replied as she brushed Celeste's bangs out of her eyes.

"Did you love Dad?" Celeste asked.

"Well, yeah, why else would I marry him?"

"Cuz you had me and you were pregnant with that one," I said.

"That didn't matter. Grandpa told me, 'you don't have to do this if you don't want to. We'll help you look after the little ones.'"

"Do you ever wish you didn't marry Dad?" I asked. It was a fair question because Mom complained about Dad's drinking to us all the time.

"Every day," she said.

"Really?" Celeste asked, her eyes big with worry.

We could never tell when Mom was being serious. Neither Mom nor Dad were romantic and they mocked their relationship every chance they got, like a Catskills comedy team. "You're a nag." "You're a cheap bastard." "Your face makes me want to puke." "People say I look like you!" Despite their protesting, we suspected that love was keeping them together, or a shared part in a homicide.

A.J.'s Wedding

My cousin A.J. married a white girl nearly a decade after Tabitha's wedding. It was the first mixed wedding in our family. "So what if she's a white girl? It's not a big deal," everyone kept saying. A.J. had known the girl for years; the family all knew her. "It's not a big deal! So what if she's white?!"

A.J., like my older sister, was a family pet so everyone went to his wedding. The wedding itself, I missed. Having been a bridesmaid, I knew from experience that Catholic Church weddings were deadly boring. I knew that the real action was at the reception and this one promised to be the best reception yet — especially since I was legally allowed to join in the drinking fun.

The reception was in full tilt when we arrived. Everyone was drinking. The whites, the Natives, the grandmas, the grandpas, the teenagers, even toddlers were having a good time. The bride and groom were older and more laid back than any I'd ever seen. They seemed to be enjoying the party as much as everyone else.

Nathan walked past with a piece of wedding cake wrapped in blue tinfoil. He waved it in my face. "See this? Girls are supposed to put it under their pillow and then you'll dream of the man you'll marry."

"Why do you have it — you want a husband?"

Nathan showed his dimples. "Why not?"

I bought a beer. I sipped it because I never could drink beer fast. I had to work hard to get the beer down and by the time I'd finished it everyone else would be on his or her second. I'd try to force down another but my stomach would rebel against me.

Around midnight, a fight broke out between Elliot, the family troublemaker, and, well, everyone. Elliot had a troubled youth and a few years back a well-meaning uncle had thought it a good idea to give him boxing lessons. Now Elliot was well equipped to annoy everyone. He fought Nathan, then he fought the guys that held his arms back, then he fought the guys who held back the guys trying to fight him. He bounced off a bystander — who happened to be the bride's father — and took a swing at him. Then he fought Nathan again until finally he was surrounded on all sides. The men surged forward in a large group and dragged him to the nearest cop station, which happened to be across the street.

The white people left after that.

The wedding reception continued unabated until the hall closed. We lingered a few minutes in the foyer wondering what to do next before someone yelled, "Party on Big Eddy!"

I pulled up to the party address with Celeste and Nathan. A long line of people snaked up the stairs to the house, others stood around a bonfire behind the house. I went inside and went out again, too shy to make myself at home. I was surprised to see my mom in the living room surrounded by people, both young and old, as she sat on another woman's knee and laughed raucously.

Eventually Mom and her caretakers left but not before she assigned me an important task. "Look after your sister," Mom slurred as she fell into the car. "She's the only sister you've got."

Since I had two other sisters, I didn't take her words very seriously. Besides how could I be babysitting my sister, when I was looking for *him*?! "He" was the elusive cute guy who would kiss me and fall passionately in love with me. Then, everyone would be coming to my wedding! First, I had to find him.

I found him, or at least a reasonable facsimile, near the bonfire. He stood across from me, bathed in the warm light of the fire. Nathan called him Garfield. Garfield — it was a name befitting an angel. In my head I heard the Priest announcing, "I now pronounce Dawn and Garfield . . . "

Garfield's eyes flirted with me and with my sister. I pretended not to see him; I pretended not to care. He stared at me across the fire. I smiled and sipped my beer. I spilt my beer down the front of my shirt. I laughed it off coolly. "Uh oh, alcohol abuse."

He laughed, more at my stupidity than the joke. That was okay. Guys didn't mind if you were stupid; I knew at least that much about the opposite sex.

Garfield was older than me, a hockey player. He talked earnestly to Nathan about the team they were putting together. Nathan was having trouble concentrating because he had taken a handful of mushrooms earlier.

"I'm not playing hockey this season. My knee has a pin in it. A huge pin." Nathan held his arms about a metre apart.

Garfield laughed.

Celeste wandered over, hand in hand with a dude.

"Who's this?" I asked.

Celeste smiled, "This is my boyfriend, Chris."

"Albert," the boy said. Then he and Celeste began making out by the fire; the slurping noises made it impossible to ignore them.

I checked in with Garfield; this didn't seem to be throwing him off. Across the bonfire my eyes met his. He smiled. I half-smiled. What now? Was he supposed to walk over here and take my hand? Or was I supposed to say something witty and smart-assed, perhaps make fun of The Pas and its various idiosyncrasies such as the way that parents attended the same parties as their kids?

No wait, smart-assed had never ever worked for me. So I stayed silent.

"What's wrong with you, Puddinghead? Why you so quiet?" Nathan turned to Garfield. "You should hear this girl, she's got a real mouth on her. Say something mean! Go on."

"Oh Nathan," I laughed gently, and smacked him on the arm. Nathan reacted like I had beaten him with a coat wire. He reared backwards and fell into the grass.

"She hit me!" he cried.

Celeste stopped kissing Albert-Chris and looked down at Nathan and then at me. "Why are you so mean?" she demanded.

"I didn't do anything!" I looked at the faces around the fire; everyone was staring back at me suspiciously.

Celeste knelt on the ground and petted Nathan's head. "There, there. She won't touch you anymore."

Nathan nodded. "I was so scared. She was hitting me and hitting me."

A group of pretty girls walked past us, up the hill to the party. Garfield's eyes followed the pretty girls.

"So how do you like The Pas?" I asked loudly.

"What?"

"The Pas? You like it?" Someone turned up the AC/DC and it surged through the party. The raspy drawl of Brian Johnson fought the mosquitoes for sovereignty of the air.

"What?" Garfield asked, again.

"DO YOU LIKE THE PAS?"

"Sure. I'm gonna go get another beer." Garfield slipped away.

I looked down at Celeste, Albert-Chris and Nathan. Nathan had recovered from his "beating" and was now studying the stars. "I never noticed this before, but the big dipper looks sad," Nathan observed.

The other two agreed.

I sat on the hood of the car and pondered my beer: how was it that I was still in the same position? Wandering around at a family wedding looking for a cute guy? Evolution took millions of years. I wanted to jump ahead to a moment when I could stop thinking and relax and have things come to me. I looked up at a bright star and made a wish on it, "Dear North Star, or Venus, or Chinese spy-satellite, please hear my wish that I get a boyfriend someday." The star blinked twice.

I stared down at my beer. If only I could drink then my hormones could punch out my brain and I could have as much fun as everyone else. As if to mock my desire, Celeste began gagging.

"Oh crap, she's gonna blow." Nathan rolled away from her.

Celeste puked all over the grass and in her own hair. Dutifully I went to help her up.

"Why did you make me throw up? Why are you so mean to me?" she sobbed.

"That's it, I'm taking you home," I replied, grabbing her by the elbow, which was mercifully vomit-free.

"Take me home now!" Celeste commanded.

On the car ride home, Nathan played with the car stereo, convinced that he could find a station that only played Creedence Clearwater songs. In the backseat Celeste held her head and groaned. Albert-Chris sat next to her staring out the window trying to remember where he lived.

I dropped Nathan at his front door as the sun came up. "See you at the next wedding," I called to him.

Nathan laughed, "It'll probably be mine."

"Or mine," I said.

"Or mine," said Albert-Chris.

As I helped Celeste into the house, Tabitha walked from the kitchen with a coffee cup in her hand, a sly smile on her face. "How drunk is she?"

Celeste's head popped up. "I'm so drunk."

"And sick, don't forget that," I added.

Tabitha smiled and helped Celeste take off her jacket. "I met a guy," Celeste said. "He's beautiful. His name is Gary."

Tabitha looked at me. I shrugged.

We helped Celeste into bed. "My wedding cake!" Celeste said. "I need to put it under my pillow."

Tabitha reached into Celeste's pocket and pulled out a handful of wrapped pieces. She held them up to Celeste. "How many husbands are you planning on having? Seven?"

Tabitha looked over at me. "Did you meet anyone?"

I shook my head.

Tabitha handed me a piece of wedding cake. "For your dreams." My stomach grumbled.

"I don't think it's gonna make it to the pillow," I said, unwrapping it and taking a bite.

"Well, don't worry about it," Tabitha said pulling her expensive duvet away from Celeste's open mouth. "There's no rush," she added with the clarity of someone who has worn a gold ring for ten years.

❧

Mom's Wedding

I glanced at the wall and saw that it was almost our bedtime. I was in no hurry so I asked Mom another question. "How did you know that Dad was the one?"

"The one what?"

"The love of your life," I said sighing with the heavy effort of a lifelong coalminer. I hated the way she always made us spell things out for her.

Mom scoffed. Then she took a drag of her smoke. Then she scoffed again. "Why would it be him? I think my true love is Robert Redford. Or Paul Newman. Or Brad Pitt. Would you like Brad Pitt to be your stepfather?"

"First of all, gross," I said.

"How is Brad and me gross?" Mom asked.

"You're our mom, you can't have . . . " Celeste's voice dropped to a whisper, " . . . sex with Brad Pitt."

"I would make him the happiest man alive; you don't know your old mom."

"Again, gross. Seriously though, how did you know that Dad was the one you were supposed to marry?" I asked.

"Your dad told me something once . . . " Mom dropped into her story telling voice. Celeste and I leaned back in our chairs in preparation for a long Mom-tale.

Mom exhaled her smoke. "When I was about thirteen I went over to your dad's house with my friend Chris Starr. Chris and your dad had the same grandfather. Your great grandfather had three wives. That was the custom back then. "

"Cool," Celeste said.

"Not in my family," Mom was quick to add. "In traditional Indian families like your dad's."

I knew all about the polygamy thing because Mom had explained this after an ill-fated family tree assignment for Health Class. My teacher had asked us to go home and enquire about our ancestors.

The morning the family tree was due, I had sat across from Dad at the table and questioned him about his forebears. He told me the name of his mom and his grandfather and then stopped talking. I shot a questioning look at Mom who surreptitiously shook her head as she blew on her coffee. Later she took me aside and explained that Dad didn't like talking about his family.

"Why?" I asked.

"It makes him sad," Mom replied.

"Then what am I supposed to tell my teacher? 'Family makes my dad weepy?'"

I did my best with the tree. After an hour interviewing Mom, her side of the tree was filled out in detail. Each of her Métis relatives was noted and smugly occupying their lines.

In contrast Dad's side of the tree was barren and thin like a strong storm had stolen all the branches. (If I had put in all the wives, their predecessors and children, Dad's side would have dragged the tree to the ground. There was no room on the paper for multiple wives.)

The multiple wives thing would have probably impressed my teacher. I imagined standing in front of the class and explaining that Native custom to my classmates and loving their shocked silence. But Mom didn't know the names of those other women and she most definitely did not know the names of their parents as well.

There was no way I was going to turn in a blank family tree and risk getting a low grade. So, I compromised. When Monday rolled around I ended up scribbling fake names into the blanks. This is how I became a direct descendent of Pocahontas, Big Bear and Charlie Chaplin.

Mom continued her story, "And we went over to Dad's house because Chris wanted to see his grandpa about something. Chris wasn't my boyfriend, just a friend. Nobody could ever understand that. How I could be friends with men? Especially since my friends were always sleeping around and—"

"Yes, and you went to visit Dad's family. What happened there?" I asked. Sometimes we had to steer her back in the right direction.

"We got there and your dad's Auntie Emma was there. She was an old woman by then and blind. She used to lie on a bed in the living room. The whole time Chris and I were there she never said a word. I think she only spoke Cree anyway. Later that night, your dad got home and his Auntie Emma says to him, 'Your wife was here today.' And your dad says, 'I don't have a wife Auntie.' Cuz he was only fifteen at the time, y'know? Emma said it again. 'Your wife was here. Y'know that Dumont girl.'"

"How did she know Dad was gonna marry you?" Celeste asked.

"She just knew. She could see things." Mom waved her hands in the air to symbolize the kinds of things Emma could see.

"So it was kind of like fate then?" I asked.

Mom shrugged.

"Well, that's romantic," Celeste said.

"I guess." Mom let the smoke ease out of her mouth.

"I wish Auntie Emma was still alive," I said.

"Yah, so we could meet her!" interrupted Celeste.

"No, so she could tell me who I'm gonna marry," I said, and then remembering that relatives did not exist to satisfy my every whim, I added, "and uh . . . also the meeting her thing." Trust Celeste to make me look like an asshole every time.

"It's best to find things out as you go. That way you're always surprised," Mom said as she closed the wedding album.

"You should have a second wedding someday," Celeste said.

"One wedding was enough, thank you very much," Mom replied. Then she stepped on her tiptoes to tuck the wedding album back into its cupboard above the fridge.

Miss Gramiak

AFTER A TUMULTUOUS GRADE ONE IN WHICH I switched schools three times, our parents — meaning Mom — decided that for the rest of our school careers, we would stay in one place, Balcarres. It was hard at first because the teachers were not aware of my brown-nosing powers. Over time, my earnest smile, arrow quick arm, and need to do extra homework proved that I was a teacher-pleaser. By grade four, I had established myself as one of Balcarres first Native teacher's pets; it was quite an achievement.

On the first day of school, all the elementary school students were ushered into the hallway for an assembly. There was excitement in the air as the students whispered about the unfamiliar adults faces they had seen. It could mean only one thing: new teachers! They were as rare as rainstorms. Years had gone by without seeing a new face and then bam! Suddenly two new teachers appeared out of nowhere.

The new teachers were Miss Noble and Miss Gramiak. All the students declared them both beautiful, which was no stretch. They were both young and blonde; Miss Noble came to this colour via genetics and the latter found it through other means.

While I acknowledged that they were prettier than the rest of the elementary teachers who tended to be around the 100 year mark, I also thought they had big bums. At the time I was obsessed with the size of teachers' rear ends. It made sense: what else was there to look at when the teacher was at the board? My eyes were always drawn to their bottoms, snug in their tailored slacks or skirts. Compared to my butt, theirs seemed enormous. Which was hardly fair considering that that I was only nine-years-old and Native to boot.

"I never want a bum like that," I whispered to Trina who nodded in agreement.

"You're dumb," said Tyler Clark who overheard everything.

Trina and I ignored him. That was the best way to handle Tyler, a skinny kid with a huge voice. That voice! He was even louder than my mom and she spoke at twice the volume of a normal human being; if you had the misfortune of speaking to her on the phone, your ears would ring for weeks.

A big mouth is sometimes confused with charisma. This was true in Tyler's case. He used that preternaturally loud voice to control his followers. He wasn't witty but everyone heard whatever he said. One by one all the boys in class fell under the spell of his loud mouth. He was a natural leader; he knew that the only way to stay in control was to keep your men busy. Tyler decided that bullying quiet, shy boys was the best use of his and his acolytes' energies.

In grade one, I watched him psychologically destroy Mike Johnson, Craig Martin and Eric Lahaney. Every guy wanted to be his friend if only to stand behind him and laugh as he convinced his soldiers to shove other kids' faces in the mud.

Both of the new teachers gave short speeches about how they were happy to be in our community. Miss Noble smiled throughout her speech and when a child raised her hand and asked if she was a princess, Miss Noble giggled. Miss Gramiak smiled less and tapped her fingers against her leg. I recognized the movement; my mom did the same thing when her desire to smoke came up was in conflict with her setting. In church, Mom's hand became a blur.

Both of the women had moved from the big city of Regina to join our small town yet I don't think they were friends. I couldn't put my finger on what made them different, exactly. They both wore pastels and had their long hair pulled back neatly but with Miss Noble you had a sense of softness and with Miss Gramiak, thumbtacks.

Both women said they were excited about the prospect of teaching in a small town. I figured they were either crazy or lying. Why would anyone leave the city to move to the country? I knew that characters in movies thought the country had "charm." By the end of the movie, after being chased through a forest by a guy wearing a goalie mask, they would realize that the country was far more terrifying than any city ever could be.

Miss Noble said that she would focus on singing in her class. "Singing is fun and it makes other people happy." She beamed at the grade threes in front of her. They beamed back at her. My sister Celeste was going to be in her class.

Then it was Miss Gramiak's turn to speak. Her voice gave away her long and friendly relationship with nicotine. Her eyes were dark and deep-set. In an effort to make them visible, she had given them a generous coating of blue mascara. It looked like blue spiders were perched on top of her lids staring down at the students in front of her. She'd be teaching the grade three and four split and she said that she'd be concentrating on reading. "I want my class to have strong reading skills because I'm entering us in a year-long reading competition with schools all over the province."

I sat up straighter. Reading? Competition? Those were my two favourite words. So when my friend Trina and I were assigned to her class, I couldn't have been happier. Then I found out that Tyler was in the same class and my euphoria was downgraded to light happiness.

When we got home that day, Celeste and I fought over the rights to the story. We danced around our mom.

"There were new teachers!"

"I got one!"

"And I got the other one!"

"Mine is really pretty!"

"Mine smokes!"

Mom already knew because she was on the School Board. She went to a meeting once a month and from that meeting gleaned enough gossip to carry her through to the next month. At the band office she was the queen of the school news and would hold court at one of the big round tables the day after every meeting. She had learned about the new hirings a few months before and had even seen the women's resumes. Mom implied that she had used her connections to ensure that we would be in their classes.

"They're both smart young women and you're lucky to have them," she said as she set the table. "You can thank me by doing the dishes without complaining for once."

My sister and I felt that we were on the cutting edge of education. Most of the elementary school teachers had been around for more than thirty years and people complained that the staff room smelled like an old folk's home.

It was my first year in a split class. The grade fours would be sharing the same room as the grade threes. I wasn't happy about this. Younger kids were always a drag, as I knew from having three younger siblings.

The grade fours — my year — sat on the right side of the room and the grade threes sat on the other side. Trina sat in front of me, Tyler to my left.

"Here we go again, Dumont," Tyler drawled. "You must love me or something?" For the past four years, we had always been in the same classroom.

"As if."

Trina added for good measure. "You're gross, Tyler."

⁊

To improve our reading skills, Miss Gramiak invented the dictionary game. I loved it. She gave us a list of words in the morning and we had a race to see who could find the word the quickest. I sped through the dictionary and found the words and wrote down the corresponding page number. I knew the competition was an important one, as I quickly needed to establish myself as the smartest student in the class.

Tyler came in second but he was good-natured about it. "Hey, Dumont, what the hell do you do with your weekends, sleep on a dictionary?"

"Yup. That's what I do." With another victory in my pocket, Tyler's words could not touch me.

Just in case, Trina drew herself up to her full height; she was at least two heads taller than Tyler and looked down on him. "You have a problem with my friend?"

Tyler quickly backed away. "Hey, no need to get the whole tribe after me."

Trina and I laughed at his ignorance. "We're from different reserves, idiot."

I fully expected that my wins at the Dictionary Game would win my place at the top of Miss Gramiak's heart. I was used to being the teacher's pet. I had been one in grade one, two and three. I knew that teachers appreciated my ability to clean erasers, monitor the other students and smile on command. I liked rules and I often took on extra work to get extra attention. I was born to be a teacher's pet.

Miss Gramiak was different. Being a good student wasn't enough to guarantee her love. She appreciated different qualities . . . she liked a student to take initiative, to speak up and be cunning. She loved Tyler.

Trina and I watched open mouthed, as Tyler became the most powerful student in the class. Even Tyler was surprised. "Wow, she really likes me. And she hates everyone else."

Hate. That's a strong word. I wouldn't say that she hated the other students; rather she was . . . annoyed by their existence.

It wasn't her fault. She had specifically stated that she wanted to have the best readers in the province. So why were students resisting her? The slower ones were clearly not trying to be the best; they were still sounding out words with their mouths and reaching for their phonics guides. We started to fall behind in the provincial standings. By the second month, we were in fourth place out of five schools.

Like all good competitors, Miss Gramiak saw this as a challenge, not a failure. She had declared her intentions and now she would employ her big city methods. These consisted primarily of yelling and pounding on desks. Sometimes she was forced to shake a student until the knowledge worked its way into their medulla oblongata. Other times she relied on vocal motivation such as by shouting in the face of the student: "Stop being so stupid!"

Some might say that her methods were harsh; I felt they were effective. For instance, I never, not even once, failed to do my homework. Many nights I even lay awake, my mind frantically searching for a lesson that might have been overlooked. Who needed sleep when I had stress to keep my young body going?

Everyone reacted differently to Miss Gramiak. Trina and I kept our heads down and pretended not to hear. Other students checked their dignity and self-respect at the door. Not a single class went by without someone collapsing into tears. I don't know why: Miss Gramiak did not show pity. She would mock the crybabies by placing her head next to theirs and pretending to weep. "Oh boo hoo, I can't do it. I'm just a little kid. Oh boo hoo."

I felt the crybabies had chosen their reaction badly. "If they hadn't cried on the first day, if they had just held it in . . . they wouldn't keep crying," I whispered to Trina. She agreed with me and we promised that no matter what happened we would not cry.

The grade threes coped by developing a group mind. They became a single entity that worked with only one goal in mind: driving Miss Gramiak insane. They were like feral beasts. They dropped their books on the floor and took two minutes to pick them up. They refused to do their homework. They kept asking to go to the bathroom at different times and, when she refused them, they would urinate at their desks.

Miss Gramiak responded by screaming louder. Pencils flew across the room. She grabbed arms and roughly pulled students out of the classroom. We would hear her spanking them — which we knew wasn't allowed — then the kid, red-eyed and angry would appear in the doorway in front of Miss Gramiak, a tight angry smile on her face. Within minutes the pattern would begin again, this time with a different student. It was a furious little battle that continued through the day. We grade fours kept our eyes on our books and sent silent messages of thanks to the grade three Borg Collective for absorbing the weight of her anger.

Tyler, as Miss Gramiak's pet, could not avert his eyes because her eyes often went to his for support. "Tyler, can you believe these students?" she would say and Tyler would shake his head, a huge fake smile plastered to his face.

When a boy would burst into tears, she would make a face at Tyler and Tyler would replicate it back at her. Our classmates hated him and wished all kinds of cooties upon his head. I could sense his fear. Uneasy is the head that wears the crown, and Tyler's neck looked like it was ready to snap.

I began to pee my bed. Not every night, but even once is a problem. It meant getting up in the middle of the night, changing my clothes, and then pushing my sister over onto the wet spot before falling back asleep.

"I don't understand it," Mom said at the breakfast table. "Celeste's never wet the bed before."

Celeste crossed her arms. "I didn't do it!"

I smiled benevolently down at her. 'Hey, it's okay, you're still little."

At supper each night, our family sat around the table and discussed our days. Celeste bubbled forth about Miss Noble's class. "Today Miss Noble took us on a field trip to pick flowers and then she made us blow on the dandelions and make wishes. I wished that Miss Noble would be my teacher forever."

I silently reminded myself to find a dandelion after supper and make a wish of my own.

Celeste talked about chocolate prizes, and stickers that smelled like strawberries and sunshine.

Although I had nothing good to say about my teacher, I could not let my sister take all the attention. So I made up stories about how Miss Gramiak was teaching us to be good readers. "Every day one of us sits on her knee and she reads to us while she . . . brushes our hair."

Mom raised her eyebrows. "She has time to do that? With all of you?"

"Yes, because in Miss Gramiak's class, time seems to last forever."

My mom frequently told us that we got on her "nerves." In Miss Gramiak's class I knew what that truly meant. My nerves were shattered. I jumped every time someone slammed a door or dropped a book. When she lost patience with a student in the front row and her heels drummed from the back of the room to the front, my gut muscles would tighten until her footsteps passed my desk.

Every day I would stare at the door to the classroom willing myself to run. "Now," I would whisper, "now." My feet would not move. I was afraid of what would happen once I reached the other side of the door. Yes, there would be the momentary satisfaction of having escaped, but how long would that last? It would only be a minute before Miss Gramiak made it to the hallway and then escorted me back to the classroom. Even if I encountered another teacher, even if I could get my story out, what would they do? If they had ears, then they already knew what was going on in that classroom. Unless of course they thought that Miss Gramiak had discovered a new way to teach phonics — by screaming it down her students' throats.

Worst of all, if I ran for it — Miss Gramiak would know what I really thought about her class. She would know that she was getting to me. As long as my eyes were down, we could all pretend that everything was okay.

I had made the mistake of opening my mouth, only once. I was standing beside her desk as she corrected my work with her red pen. With each stroke of her red pen, I uttered the word, "oops." I'd said it three times when she put down her pen and stood up to address the class. "Instead of standing beside me and saying OOPS, do your work right the first time."

My face turned red and I pretended that I was someone else, like my brother David who screwed up all the time and was loved even more for it. I tried to make my mouth into the shape of a smile; my trembling lips would allow only a grimace.

At least I had Trina. Tyler was all by himself. She would turn on him eventually and he grew nervous waiting for it to happen. He started getting sloppy. We noticed that he took longer and longer to clean the erasers and when he got back to the classroom, there was plenty of chalkboard dust on them.

Miss Gramiak noticed. "Hey, Tyler, what's wrong? You don't like your job?"

"No Miss Gramiak . . . it's great!" His fake enthusiasm was becoming weaker by the second.

"Because you can always be replaced. You know that, right?"

Tyler nodded and sat down.

"It's only a matter of time." Trina would whisper to me, and offered to set up a pool for the date of Tyler's upcoming downfall. I couldn't join in the fun because I felt sorry for him.

"You feel sorry for that jerk? Even after he made Stacy Smithson cry by breaking her Strawberry Shortcake lunch kit? Even after he said that Jerrod was fat because he ate his own dog? Even after he called our breasts nibblets?"

On the playground Tyler was losing his confidence. His minions crowded around him panting for his leadership but he didn't know what to do with them. A chubby kid would fall during a baseball game and instead of yelling, "Hey, look, Blubber hit the dust!" Tyler would walk out to the field and help him up.

One day Tyler turned towards us and blurted out, "I have to talk to you!"

Half the schoolyard turned around, and then turned back around as Tyler walked directly up to Trina and me. Trina beckoned him closer.

"Keep it down, Tyler. Everyone doesn't have to know our classroom business."

He lowered his voice to a quiet yell, "One of you take it. You be the pet, Dawn. You love being the pet."

I snorted, like I hadn't thought of that a thousand times already! "It's not my choice, you know that."

Trina decided to goad him, "See, this is what you get for being a suck up. Now you're gonna suffer like the rest of us."

Tyler turned his scared eyes to her. "Don't you think I know it?"

⁂

It happened on a Wednesday. The day had been rough. The grade threes had been particularly rebellious. One of them had gas and was letting farts go at random. Miss Gramiak identified the student and berated him only to have another student let one go. It was only ten AM and she was already hoarse.

A few of the grade threes were in tears but two of them — Hope and Cindy — had crossed over into crazy territory. They had gone where they could not be broken. She would scream at them and they would only smile. It was a demented smile and you had to turn away when you saw it.

You also had to admire them. Where they lived now, yelling, spankings and banishments to the hallway had no more effect. In fact, I envied their trips. Once you were outside the classroom, you could run to the bathroom, the water fountain or anywhere you pleased. Inside, you were trapped.

On Wednesdays it was Tyler's job to water the plants. Miss Gramiak had a lot of them. "Plants create a joyous environment," she said at the beginning of the year. "They are for everyone to enjoy." As our year progressed, the plants grew listless.

Precisely at 1:20 that day, Tyler got up from his seat and went to the back of the room to do his job. The rest of us sat still in our seats as Miss Gramiak taught us about the solar system.

"The earth is the only planet in our solar system that can support life," she intoned. "Some of the planets are composed entirely of gas."

The grade threes snickered. Miss Gramiak glared at them.

Behind us, we could hear the water running and hitting the bottom of the plastic watering bucket. Then the water stopped running. Miss Gramiak looked back. Tyler was hunched over the sink with a plant in his hand. He smiled back at her. She returned her gaze to the board.

Then Tyler's tight control slipped and a word escaped him. "Shit." A normal person might have been able to murmur a profanity with no chance of detection. Not Tyler. His loud voice propelled the word across the classroom, past the front row, right into Miss Gramiak's breathing space.

Miss Gramiak called out to him. "Everything okay, Tyler?"

Tyler did not answer. He was too busy trying to balance the heavy plant against the sink. He had over filled the plant and was trying to pour the water out.

Miss Gramiak's eyes grew large as she saw what he was doing. She ran to the back of the room.

"Not my geranium!" She touched the fronds of the drowned plant. "Get away from it!" she hissed at Tyler.

Tyler backed away and dropped the plant on the floor. The ceramic pot broke and wet dirt sprayed across the floor over his jeans and onto her corduroy skirt. A swarm of profanities flew from her mouth into my belly making it lurch. I wanted to clap my hands over my ears but I worried that it would draw her attention to me.

Tyler held on. He nodded in agreement with her abuse. Tears were threatening but he held them in.

One of the criers sitting to my left whispered, "Just let it out, Tyler."

I understood what Tyler was doing. Holding in our tears was all we had. It was our only flag — she had not broken us — that we could wave proudly after this was over.

Miss Gramiak wasn't going to settle for agreement. Not today. She picked up the green plant and waved it in his face. "Look! You killed it. Are you happy Tyler? Are you happy!"

She stared at him waiting for a response. Tyler's loud voice failed him. His shoulders began to shake, his mouth trembled and then finally the tears came rolling down his cheeks, like big fat traitors.

Even kids he'd tortured since kindergarten felt for him. Trina mumbled beside me, "He's a jerk but he doesn't deserve that." I nodded. I dared a look across at the grade threes. They were smiling.

I told my mom about Miss Gramiak. It was hard to explain exactly what was the matter with her. I was only nine and lacked the proper similes, "She is like a powder keg waiting to go off." "She has a temper like a rabid wolverine." "She screams like a banshee." Instead I was left with meager statements like, "She's really mean and I don't like her."

My mom dismissed my worries and said that I was being too sensitive. Besides, Mom was too busy dragging Celeste off to specialists in Regina trying to figure out why she kept wetting the bed to concern herself with my classroom problems.

Each month meant a month closer to being rid of Miss Gramiak. The year had not made her any nicer but we had learned to cope better. For instance, twice a week a teacher's aide was in the classroom. We would cling to her like kittens and climb onto her lap. "I've never seen kids be so affectionate. Especially children who are so . . . old." We needed all the love we could get to balance out Miss Gramiak.

When there were visitors, Miss Gramiak never ever lost her temper. Her voice never went above the danger range. She kept her comments short and mostly positive. The grade threes shamelessly took advantage of her tied hands. They turned their backs to her and sat on their desks and ate their lunches. They ripped pages out of the books and wiped their faces with them.

Miss Gramiak would keep the same dead smile on her face. "Oh my grade threes, what am I going to do with you?"

We knew.

The principal, Mr. Macdonald, visited the class on a regular basis. When he first started coming around, I had hoped to slip him a note asking for his help. I lost faith in him when I saw how his cheeks turned red whenever Miss Gramiak smiled at him. Instead, we learned to keep him in the classroom by asking him questions about his job: Do you ever have to spank kids? Do you enjoy it? What if a teacher is bad? Do you have to spank her?

When we ran out of questions, Tyler would beg Mr. Macdonald over and over again to tell us his lame knock-knock jokes. We would laugh uproariously at each joke.

"Tell us the one about the banana and the orange again."

"Oh no, you've heard it."

"It gets funnier every time you tell it."

"I tell you, Miss Gramiak, your class is a bunch of jokers."

"Oh, don't I know it."

In a surprisingly strategic move that one might expect of a chess master, Miss Gramiak organized a visit to the beach. She had to, she had nothing left to use against the grade threes. In the war of wills, they were now about even. The grade threes had the look of weathered Vietnam vets. They would sharpen their pencils and stare at her desk. She would sense their eyes on her and shiver as she corrected spelling tests.

"If you behave, then you can go to the beach," became her new mantra. And it worked. It held the classroom together for the remaining month.

However, a day at the beach only increased my fear. Miss Gramiak would be even more dangerous away from the school. The beach was dotted with small thick bushes every twenty feet, perfect for stepping behind to dole out spankings. I decided I wouldn't go.

"We can't go," I told Trina at lunch break. "I told Miss Gramiak that swimming in water is against my tribal beliefs. And since we're both Cree, you can't go either."

Trina refused to go along with my plan and placed her permission slip on Miss Gramiak's desk along with all the others.

It was annoying to see Miss Gramiak happy that her plan was working: "We're going to have a great time at the beach — except for Dawn, of course. She has tribal beliefs. Dawn, would you like to come up here and explain them to the class? No? Oh, is speaking about your tribal beliefs against your tribal beliefs?"

On a piece of paper, I calculated how many seconds I had left in grade four: 166 billion left to go.

My mom decided to be one of the parent chaperones. She felt that a day at the beach was exactly what she needed after all the stress of the year. Mom had failed to discover the reason behind Celeste's bed-wettings. The doctor assured her that a few sessions of electric shock would solve the problem.

I tried to talk her out of it but she was determined to go. I consoled myself with the fact that Mom would finally get to see Miss Gramiak in all her tense glory. She would understand and I would be vindicated.

My plan quickly went awry. Mom and my nemesis immediately hit it off when Miss Gramiak bummed a smoke off of Mom. Then my plan went further south when they sat on the same beach blanket and introduced themselves.

"I'm Theresa, Dawn's mom," Mom said lighting Miss Gramiak's smoke.

"Theresa, I didn't think you'd come — isn't swimming against your tribal beliefs?" Miss Gramiak asked with a sly glance in my direction.

Mom replied, "The only tribal belief I follow is cheap smokes."

I lost all hope for retribution when Mom laughed uproariously at Miss Gramiak's impression of the ever-perky Miss Noble. "'*Okay my songbirds, all on three!*' Songbirds, my butt! It sounds like she's squeezing kittens. Twenty-four students and not one can carry a single note in key."

"What about the sounds coming from your classroom?" I wanted to yell. "What about the crying students in the hallway, what about my nervous eye twitch and my sharp pain in my gut that is probably an ulcer?! Grade fours shouldn't even know what ulcers are!"

Miss Gramiak surprised everyone with homemade chocolate chip cookies. I could see Trina and Tyler come around as they ate her cookies. I held out, whispering to Trina that they were probably poisoned.

"C'mon Dawn, they're cookies."

"Don't you remember the time she held us in all recess? She's crazy."

"So what? Recess is over-rated. You've said it yourself a thousand times. Who the hell wants to go play outside in a blizzard?"

I tried to get Tyler on my side. "What about the time she screamed at you until you cried?"

Tyler stopped chewing and stared at me. "You're thinking of someone else."

I glared at them and grabbed a cookie.

The grade threes ate the food greedily, not bothering to wipe their faces afterwards. They ran into the water in unison and splashed each other until their clothes were soaked. They and Miss Gramiak had an unspoken truce: you keep your mouths shut and I'll let you do whatever the hell you want.

I was silent on the ride home. I felt my mother's betrayal keenly. How dare she make friends with my mortal enemy? A person for whom capital punishment should be reinstated?

"She's not that bad."

"You don't know the real her. You just got to see the smoking her. And the telling amusing stories in the sun her. You don't know how she treats us when other people aren't around."

Mom was silent for a few minutes. Then as if to explain Miss Gramiak's behaviour, she said carefully: "Not everyone likes kids you know."

"Then why is she a teacher?" I demanded.

"She's quitting."

"She is?" I sat back in my seat, stunned.

"Yup, said she already resigned. The principal tried to talk her out of it but her mind was made up."

After the picnic, Miss Gramiak was a different teacher. She no longer yelled and her sarcastic comments were kept to a minimum. When students misbehaved, she rarely bothered to notice, preferring instead to look out the window at the flat Saskatchewan landscape or tend to her plants, which in the spring sun were perking up quite nicely.

On the last day, she brought more of her delicious cookies. We sat in a circle and each of us told her our summer plans.

Trina said her family would be camping on the pow-wow trail.

Tyler said he'd be helping his dad with the young steers, learning to bake with his mom and killing as many gophers as he could get his hands on.

I saw my turn coming and thought about telling her that I was planning on going to the police to report a bad person. When her eyes turned to me, I lost my nerve and said that I would probably just read some books.

Miss Gramiak smiled at me, "I can see that Dawn. You are a good reader." Her words hit me like warm sunshine on a cold day. Stunned, I began to cry. I hung my head and sobbed as the class watched.

Miss Gramiak went onto the next student, commenting dryly, "Let's keep it together, kids."

When the last bell rang, I collected my books and headed for the door, eager to be gone from the class forever. Tyler bounced against my shoulder in the hallway.

"Hey, Dumont, we survived another one."

"Yup. Hope the next one is better."

He shrugged his shoulders as if to say the Miss Gramiak's classroom was already forgotten, carefully stored away in a nine-year-old's memory attic along with being picked last for a sports team and accidentally seeing your parents have sex.

Down the hall, Miss Noble said her good byes. She was surrounded by her students, doling out loving hugs to each one and taking their gifts and placing them in a huge box at her feet. My sister was close to the front, on her sixth or seventh hug.

In our classroom, Miss Gramiak stood alone at the board, erasing the day's lesson, one last time.

PREP WORK

THE JET BOOMED PAST US. IT SWEPT across the flat ground and then suddenly, without hunching like a rabbit might, it leapt from the ground. One second it was right in front of us and the next it was in the air tucking its wheels into its tummy.

"How does it do that?" I stared into the sky.

"Jet engine fuel. Strongest thing in the world," Dad said.

"No, Dad, that's nuclear energy," I replied. I was keen to show off my learning to him.

"As if you could run a plane with fission," laughed Celeste, who was also keen.

"Brown-nosers," David said. He was not keen.

We stood on the second floor of the Regina airport watching planes take off. David had his body pressed against the window, his hands, nose and chubby cheeks leaving prints. Mom kept her hand on his waistband no matter how many times David tried to shake it off.

From a few feet away, a security guard watched us with a smile on her face. This was before 9-11 and the atmosphere at airports was different. You could wander in and take an impromptu tour of the area, including the part where the planes were serviced. If you were having trouble seeing the planes, you could walk into the traveller's lounge where the windows were much bigger and closer to the action.

Pamela, the baby of the family — born seven years after David — toddled through our legs. My uncles called her the "Hail Mary Pass baby." I don't know what they meant by that but my mom glared at them when they said it and Dad would throw back his head and laugh.

As a toddler, Pammy had no interest in airports, just in candy machines and animals. Dad caught her around the waist before she wandered into the lounge where people waited for their planes. "Where are you going?" he asked, "to Las Vegas?"

That was the only place my parents had ever flown together. The tribal council had chartered a plane for executives and their significant others (not their children). My parents had spent five whole days wandering the Las Vegas strip together. I had heard about the trip frequently. It was part of the family lore: "We barely slept at all. I hear they inject pure oxygen into the air conditioning system so that you never want to sleep. I believe it because we gambled for 48 hours straight."

After the trip, Mom could not stop comparing Las Vegas to Saskatchewan. As you would expect, the province did not fare well in such a comparison. "They have better roads in Las Vegas. Way better." "In Las Vegas, a girl your age would already be a cocktail waitress," or "Kids don't sit around watching TV, they're out there learning to count cards."

She made plans to go back every year. They had done it once, why not again? And why just Vegas, why not Atlantic City or Reno? The world was theirs to explore, why limit themselves? But other than leafing through some travel brochures, her plan never went further. "The tribal council needs to get off their butts and plan another trip, that's what they need to do," she complained.

My dad had other trips to compare to the gambling Mecca though they surely weren't as great as Vegas, either. He had spent a month in New Mexico attending the huge Albuquerque pow wow and a conference for native leaders. My parents had been separated a few months previous so it was confusing when he showed up with a bag full of New Mexican souvenirs including a giant velvet sombrero. We took turns wearing it around the house, and affecting Mexican accents: "Would you like some nachos, senor cat?" The sombrero was over-large and garishly decorated with rhinestones, but we thought it was authentic. Any Mexican who attempted to wear this on his head would die in a matter of minutes under the hot Mexican sun.

I thought Dad had left us to go live in New Mexico. For the first time ever, I wished that he had taken me with him. "I would like to live in a hot place where people wear velvet hats and eat nachos all day long."

My older sister Tabitha tried to explain that the trip had nothing to do with anything. It was just a work trip like many Dad took from time to time. But no matter what she said, my memory had made the connection between the trip and my parent's frequent separations. In my mind, Dad wanted us to move to New Mexico. Mom didn't want to. They fought. He moved to New Mexico but once he was down there he realized that the hot beautiful weather could never replace his family so he hired a donkey to take him to the airport where he said goodbye to the happiest place on earth . . .

"Holy crap you're dumb! People don't ride donkeys down there." Tabitha could get impatient with me sometimes.

"What do they ride then? . . . Camels?"

"They drive cars! They're exactly like us."

"Except that Dad likes us better cuz he came back to us," I said.

Tabitha rolled her eyes.

❧

During our early teens, our dad's job took him all over Canada. He flew to Edmonton, Ottawa and Vancouver with increasing regularity. We would proudly watch him carry his suitcase to the car. I bragged to my friends about my dad's globetrotting. "My dad is in Victoria, BC attending a conference on natives and casinos — he's doing a speech on gambling — he knows a lot about blackjack . . . "

It sounded so much better than when I had to tell them, "My dad didn't come home after New Year's Eve; my mom drives by the bar and his truck is always parked there." And yes, I did HAVE to tell them. I spent most recesses telling my friends all our family secrets because it made me feel important.

Our mother preferred driving rather than flying in planes. She was convinced that planes were inherently dangerous even though we pointed out that more people died in car accidents than in plane crashes.

"Well, how many of those accidents are caused by planes crashing into cars?" she argued back.

On our sight-seeing trips to the airport, Mom could barely stand to watch the airplanes take off, convinced that they were going to veer towards her at any moment like kamikaze pilots searching for a suitable target. "Aim for that window with that woman in the red coat surrounded by all those kids."

Mom didn't trust technology more complex than slot machines. She felt that planes were unnatural tools of evil. "What if someone steals one of those planes and drives it into a building, what are you gonna do then? And what if it's something really important like the Empire State building?"

We would shake our heads. Where did she come up with these crazy ideas?

She was so afraid of planes, I wondered aloud how she even made it to Las Vegas to gamble for a week straight.

"Listen carefully to what you just said, and the answer will be clear," Tabitha answered dryly.

⁂

Dad was eager to show us his old haunts on our visits to Regina. He had attended a year of business college right after graduating from the residential school. During that time he partied hard with his childhood friends. As we drove through the city he pointed out the places where they had hung out. "My friends were wild and crazy guys," he said. We already knew that, as he had spent our childhood hanging out with the same wild and crazy guys.

He took us to the secondhand bookstore where he used to buy his textbooks. We spent at least one afternoon there a month, picking through the stacks. We would only leave when each of us had a plastic bag full of comic books. A Ukrainian man ran the store and he remembered Dad from his college days: "See what happens when you party too much, you get a houseful of kids, yes?"

My dad would laugh and say something off-colour back, like, "and these are just the ones I know about!" Mom would make an annoyed sound and Dad would ignore her while he segued into a series of dirty jokes. We would wait, wanting the conversation to be over so that we could head to the back of the station wagon and start reading our comics.

Our next stop was on a street filled with second hand clothing stores. "When you're a college student, you have to watch every dime," Dad explained.

"Especially when you drink like your throat is on fire," said Mom, under her breath.

Dad's favourite second hand store was a mysterious place. It was dark and crammed to the rafters with historical treasures.

"It stinks in here," David said.

"That's the smell of a discount," said the woman behind the counter. She looked like she had been bought and sold in a second hand store, herself. She wore a pillbox hat on her head and a furry scarf around her neck. Her thick accent and indomitable manner told us she came from a tougher place. When she wasn't glaring at us as we picked through her wares, she stared out the window or *at* the window because the window was so dirty it would take x-ray vision to see through it.

Her bitter smile suggested she was wondering what she could have done differently with her life, particularly how could she have stopped herself from settling in Regina. "When the plane landed, why did I get off? Why didn't I keep going to Paris?"

While she daydreamed, we perused the racks of clothing. We usually shopped at places like the Saan store, Zellers and Superstore. The difference was staggering. At the second hand store, we had enough money to buy what we wanted. "How much for the fur jacket?"

"Fifty cents."

"The high heeled boots?'

"Fifty cents."

"This couch?"

"Fifty cents."

My first second hand store purchase was a black sweater with a lace collar. When I wore it to school, it drew comments from teachers. "Did that belong to your grandma, dear?"

"Maybe."

The sweater looked incongruous when I stood next to my friends who had taken to wearing heavy metal t-shirts everywhere they went. We were still in elementary school but they were preparing for high school where we heard that everyone was either a headbanger or a prep. As Natives, we would be automatically drafted onto the former team. My shirt confused my friends as the lace said *old lady,* but the black said *badass.*

While playing baseball one recess, the sweater gave off a special smell. It was as if the sweater had a memory that was awoken in the hot sun. Standing in the outfield, I relived its memories.

"Baby powder? Vicks? Cabbage?" I concluded that the former owner was a Ukrainian mother who was susceptible to colds.

One afternoon our dad took us to the south side of the city to see the university campus. Upon hearing our destination, a cold sweat broke out on my body. "Not yet, not now," I wanted to yell, "The smart, beautiful people will judge me." University was my Mecca, my heaven, my Hollywood and I always imagined that when I went I would be thin, well dressed, with super long thick hair and escorted by my football player boyfriend.

Instead, my first time on a university campus was in braces, with an unruly mullet, pimply skin, and my escort was my shy and awkward (yet abnormally loud) family. I told myself that nobody on the campus would remember when I returned in six years, or if they did, then they would say that this was my ugly duckling stage.

We parked in the lot and Mom marvelled at the price of parking. "Five bucks for the day? That's freakin' crazy! Do these idiots think we're made of money?"

"Everyone takes the bus. You have to watch every dime when you're in university," Dad replied. "To save money for your booze," he added with a wink.

Mom glared at him as she always did when he was trying to be cute.

"Hey!" Celeste pointed to the car where Tabitha was still sitting inside with her earphones on.

Dad knocked on the window of the car. "Hey, get out of the car."

Tabitha ignored him. She was good at ignoring people.

Dad looked at Mom for help. Mom shrugged her shoulders. "She doesn't want to go."

"But we made this trip for her."

"She doesn't want to go."

I cupped my hands on the car window and stared in at Tabitha. She was sixteen and university was only a year away. Was she too embarrassed to be seen with us? We were a motley crew, especially David who always had food on his shirt. I considered getting into the car too. But when I weighed the danger of humiliation against unfulfilled curiosity, my nosiness won out. I had been seeing university on TV and in movies for years. I had to see it in real life.

"Well, let's go then," Dad said. "Let her overheat in there if she wants." He marched ahead of us.

Under her breath, Mom murmured, "She can always roll the damn window down, she's not a puppy."

Dad walked confidently through the campus. The rest of us followed in a clump with the weak ones in the middle, the stronger ones on the outside . . . in case the university students were prone to attacking families.

I kept separating myself from the pack. My look said, "I am not with them, I am just a particularly short university student. I find them quite odd myself. Why is there a family of Native people walking through these hallways? Who brings a baby to a university?"

My cover was blown when Mom yelled at me to keep up. New situations brought out her bossy nervous self.

I expected the university to be filled with Hollywood stereotypes. The movies I had watched would have prepared me for the characters we would encounter. There would be the well-dressed blondes and their jock boyfriends. The girls would wear their cheerleading outfits to class and we would know the jocks by their huge muscles and their bullying of nerdy guys. The nerds would be wearing thick glasses, pocket protectors and shy smiles. They wouldn't be much to look at but they would be the best, most loyal friends you could ever have, and, if needed, they could make jet fuel.

But there were no jocks or cheerleaders or even nerds on the campus that day. The only people we saw were Asian students who sat on benches and talked quietly amongst themselves.

There were other things to look at that excited me. There was the huge library that was more difficult to get into than the airport.

My dad had to use all of his charm to get us past a middle-aged librarian lady. "I used to be a student here, a few hundred years ago," he said smiling roguishly. "And now I've brought my future students for a look around. Dawn! Celeste!"

I stepped forward and the librarian's beady eyes passed over my uncomfortable grimace and settled on Celeste's confident golden glow. She nodded and allowed all of us to pass through.

The family wandered around the stacks of books and I nearly fainted when my dad said there were three floors. I wanted to see each and every floor, and stick my nose into each book, smelling the knowledge inside.

"That would take a long time. And your brother and sisters have to eat."

"I'm prepared to sacrifice their health to stay here longer."

My brother's whines dragged us in the direction of the food court. Mom wouldn't let us get more than a cup of free water. The prices were at least twenty per cent more than they would be anywhere else in the city. Apparently, poor university students had to pay for convenience. "Lots of people stay on campus; it's easier to get to class," Dad explained. "Plus it's cheaper and -"

"Every dime counts." Celeste and I said in unison, Celeste slightly faster than me. She could be very annoying sometimes.

We walked past a concrete student residence as two girls exited. They looked no different from us except that their clothes fit them and their sweaters did not smell like someone else's cabbage. Still they weren't spectacular. I could not sense that they were inherently better than me so I decided that living with them in residence would not do. When I went to university, I would get my own apartment and I would decorate it how I wanted it. It would be a cool hang out for both the jocks and the cheerleaders. And I'd even invite the nerds over once in a while to play dungeons and dragons.

As we backtracked through the halls, I noticed that university was a place of opportunity. You could see that from the bulletin boards, which I studied in detail. Take Korean lessons, take karate lessons, buy a late model Hyundai — which would I do first? I had to do them all!

Eventually, my parents dragged me off the campus even as I argued with them. "I don't understand why I can't stay at least one night. Here's someone who's looking for a roommate."

The tour ended the way all our tours ended — with a visit to a Chinese buffet. We had a few favourites and we were known at each of them. My dad liked to be known, particularly from his university days. "Hello Mr. Lee," he would say as he slapped the tiny man on the back.

Mr. Lee fake-smiled and acknowledged their former relationship. "You can sit anywhere with your tribe."

"How about I pull up a chair at the buffet?"

And he and the Asian man would laugh and laugh. The rest of us would walk away and sit down at a table. Being friendly was important, but ordering your pop and getting to the buffet was more important.

Dad always encouraged us to try new things. "Don't just eat chicken balls."

"I like chicken balls," I said.

"Try the fried fish. C'mon try it."

"It looks gross," I observed.

"You don't know until you try it."

Celeste would then pipe up, "I love it, Dad!" which forced me to eat it.

"It IS gross," I whined through a mouthful of mushy fish.

Dad turned away from me and shook his head sadly in the direction of the velvet dragons hanging on the wall. 'You're not daring," his head shaking said, "you won't have what it takes to make it the city." I choked down the fish as if to say, you're wrong about me. I will do whatever it takes.

The drive home was always a quiet one and gave us a chance to absorb everything we had seen and heard. Next weekend we would spend on the reserve playing in the woods, riding horses at Uncle Frank's or sitting on the back steps drinking lemonade. That wasn't real life. That was the waiting time for what was to come.

The Indian Summer Games

MY ATHLETIC CAREER STARTED WITH A FIT of crying in the backseat of our car. Mr. Broderick, the most athletic teacher ever, had devised a system for improving athletics for all the elementary school students. He was an energetic and tireless person; this was evident in the book-length newsletter he released at the end of my grade six school year. In the newsletter he had assessed the grade point averages and athletic prowess of every single student from grades one through to six. Beside my name were my student average, my team name, "The Trojans", our intramural scores for the year, and then a short comment that summed up my worth as a person: "Not very athletic."

After I read the words, there was a stunned silence as my brain temporarily shut itself off. They say shock is a protective mechanism. Sadly it only lasts for a few minutes. The pain slowly dribbled through my mind's security doors. I expressed a rain cloud of tears and heaved myself around the back seat of the car. "Why oh why would he write that — for everyone to see!"

My mom had pulled up in front of the reserve's band hall where all the parents had been invited for an assembly about summer activities for the kids. As I cried in the backseat, she urged my sister and brother out of the car. "Get out. She's not going to calm down anytime soon."

David and Celeste stood next to my window and watched the tears stream down my red face as I pounded my head against the back of the seat. It kept their interest for a few minutes before they decided to wander inside.

I continued my crying war against injustice. Because of Mr. Broderick's cruel comments, I would now bear the dark brand of "not very athletic" . . . for the rest of my life. Everyone in the province was probably sitting around their kitchen table laughing as they read those words; "Look at this Dawn, not very athletic. Funny, I never noticed that before. Now that I think of it, Mr. Broderick is right. She isn't. In fact she probably never will be! *Ha ha ha!*"

My eye caught my sister Celeste's review. "Strong runner. Talented athlete." Oh great, more proof that my sister was better than me. Like that point hadn't been hammered home at every family get together. "Oh look how tall Celeste is! That Dawn sure is short!" "Celeste is growing like a weed! Is Dawn getting shorter?" "That Celeste could be a model and, Dawn . . . well, she could be her sister's agent!"

In order to torture myself further, I read through everyone else's ratings and no one, not a single student had received a comment as unflattering as mine. Apparently no one was less athletic than me. On our intramural team we had Karen who could not run more than a few steps before bursting into tears. "You can do it!" I'd yell encouragingly as she ran after the soccer ball. She'd only stop, bend at the waist and rub her lower back. Mr. Broderick wrote, "Tries very hard" next to her name.

Next to my brother David's name he had written. "One awesome guy." Mr. Broderick had been David's teacher and, for the first time, a teacher had found a way to engage David in learning; mostly by pretending to turn a machine gun on every student who wasn't listening. My brother adored Mr. Broderick.

I hated him. It wasn't fair. I was the captain of my intramural team. True, it wasn't because of my athletic ability; I had been chosen as captain because I was the oldest person on the team and because I was naturally bossy. I took my duties seriously. I made sure all my athletes attended as many games as possible. It sounds simple but have you ever tried to round up a group of students from ages six to eleven? I found that all grade one students look the same and had more than once dragged the wrong one to our field. My team was also disabled by the fact that we had more asthmatic players than every other team. They tried hard but it was difficult to chase after a ball when you had to take out your puffer every five minutes. How was I supposed to motivate asthmatics? "Run harder Ethan! Okay, stop and get some air. Ready, now? Okay, lie down. Um . . . teacher? Ethan seems to have passed out again."

We lost every game. My team found this amusing, particularly Roy Nokusis who was the school's best athlete. He was eleven years old, six feet tall and had muscles that would make a CFL quarterback jealous. For Roy, athletics were as natural as breathing.

Before each game, he laced up his sneakers and smiled knowingly. "Another game, another chance to lose."

I pointed at him. "This is why we lose: Roy has a bad attitude!" I said to the others.

"Whatever you say, coach," he'd say, laughing as he jogged onto the field, his long easy steps mocking the staccato bursts of my short legs.

Still my team had heart. They played hard and sucked even harder on their inhalers; there was no reasonable explanation for our losses until Mr. Broderick found one: "Dawn: not very athletic."

Now everyone knew. Now everyone would laugh at me. And I couldn't even shake off their laughter because secretly I believed it too. I had a younger phenom sister. She had been winning athletic awards since grade one. There weren't even athletic awards in grade one — they made one up just for her! Now her Top Grade One Athlete trophy sat on top of our TV and mocked me whenever I watched cartoons. My mom had thoughtfully hung my pink participation ribbons on it. They failed to console me.

Then too, every day my younger brother lost more of his baby fat and it looked like he would soon be as athletic as Celeste. Damn the genetic lottery.

I researched athletes every chance I got. Biographies about the athletically gifted were my favourites: Nadia Comaneci, Olga Korbut, and Pele. Their biographers wrote that everyone knew that these athletes were born to win; their excellence apparently showed a few minutes after birth as they held their bottle with fully developed bicep muscles or began crawling *en pointe*.

I dreamt of the day when my excellence would show up. It would be a special day, probably a Sunday, when I would put my running shoes on and suddenly I would be able to outrun everyone.

From my past performance up until now, it seemed that I was born to be mediocre and nobody ever wrote books about my tribe, the average people. "For her whole life, she struggled to be an athlete. She never succeeded but she was happy anyway and everyone loved her and everyone wanted to be her." Where was that book?

I cried for at least an hour. Finally, though, I was too tired even to sob and I slumped onto the seat.

I don't know how long it took me to find the silver lining but I did. Mr. Broderick's comment meant that expectations of me were as low as they could be. This meant when I showed them how athletic I really was, everyone would be surprised, oh yes, they would be very surprised. I would show that Mr. Broderick and his tight, spandex running shorts. Someday he'd be placing a gold medal around my neck as he remarked, "I can't believe I ever wrote that about you . . . "

No, strike that. Mr. Broderick wouldn't even remember writing the horrible comment. I would remind him innocently, and he would react with surprise. "No way, I didn't write that. I could never be so stupid." And then he would flagellate himself with my gold medal; twenty lashes ought to do it.

I drew up a plan for my future athletic success in the back seat of the car. I would run every day from now until school started again. No, strike that. I would run every day until I went to the Olympics and the biographers would comment that people had thought — mistakenly — of course — that I wasn't very athletic. They had no idea that my bones were still growing and my potential had not yet been seen. In fact, only a clever coach would see it in me and would . . .

"Hey, Dawn, guess what? The Indian summer games are in Gordon's this year." Celeste spoke through the car window as I had all the doors locked. She was licking a Popsicle.

"Where did you get that?" I asked as I rolled down the window. "And, what are the summer games?"

She handed me a melting Popsicle with her other hand. I hurriedly unwrapped it.

"It's a track and field meet for all the Indian kids in Saskatchewan with other sports and a pow-wow." She grinned. "I hope we make it on the team."

As Celeste was already known as a great athlete throughout the four reserves, I had no doubt that she would make it. Such an outcome was less likely for myself, no thanks to Mr. Broderick.

No, I couldn't let him hold me back. "This is good, this will give me more motivation to get into great shape," I said as I took a chomp out of my Popsicle.

The try-outs for the summer games were held on the Gordon's First Nation. Gordon's was less than an hour from our reserve. We knew it well; we'd driven through it many times while taking the back roads to the Candiac horse sales with our uncles who had been proudly refusing to get driving licenses for the past twenty years.

Gordon's was located on flat brown land with plenty of meager trees and modest bungalows like our own. In fact you could find the same type of bungalow all over Saskatchewan. No matter which reserve you went to, or whose home, you always knew where to find the bathroom.

All the File Hills athletes were travelling to Gordon's in a big yellow school bus, except us. Mom had signed up to be a chaperone for the games and decided she would drive us up herself.

"Not in the school bus!" I pleaded. Mom drove the school bus for our reserve. And when our other vehicle wasn't working or if she felt she needed additional seating, or if she felt like making us into social lepers, Mom would use the bus as our primary means of transportation.

"I didn't think of that. That's a good idea. Some of you can sleep in the bus if you want," Mom replied.

In the end, she decided against taking the bus. We were the only kids coming from Okanese so the band had refused to pay her gas costs.

I sighed with relief. For once, we would look like normal kids travelling in a normal.

🜚

It was great being part of a reserve and having lots of kids to play with. But meetings with other kids from other reserves were always uneasy. Trust is not big in our communities, particularly among the pre-teens. Wherever we went in Native country, no one ever greeted us with a smile and a "hi, how are ya?" No, we were the enemy until proven otherwise.

As we pulled up to the red-brick school on the Gordon's Reserve, a group of brown-skinned kids lounged on its steps. They surveyed our vehicle with little interest. The girls looked at us sideways from beneath their feathered bangs and the boys pretended not to notice us at all.

From inside our minivan, we pretended not to notice them back. "These kids sure look dangerous. Maybe we should go home," I said.

"Oh go on," said Mom. "You're such a chickenshit, I don't know where you get that from. Must be from your dad."

Dad was currently living across the reserve from us at his friend's house where his life had become one long party. We heard rumors of fistfights, police visits and drunk dogs passing out in the front yard. I sensed that Dad was slightly more daring than Mom.

The tryouts were simple. There were lists of teams and events and it was as easy as putting your name on the list for the File Hills team. Even though our team was made up of four reserves — Okanese, Little Black Bear, Starblanket and Peepeekisis — Charlene Bear, one of the organizers explained, "Everyone has to compete as much as they can because we have a shortage of athletes."

Charlene came from an athletic family. Her brother, Ricky Junior, was considered one of the best pitchers on File Hills; their dad, Ricky Senior, a tall, thick man coached his son's team as if it was a contender for the World Series. Charlene shared her family's love of sports but she took a gentler approach. She never yelled at anyone and preached respect for other players.

She gathered all the girls from ten to fifteen into a group. "I'll be looking after you gals. I'm proud to see so many athletes made it out!"

I was stunned. It was the first time I heard the word athlete in reference to myself. Sure the word was directed at an amorphous group of over fifty girls, but I was one of them. I was now an athlete and all I'd done was climb into the front seat of our family's minivan. In Charlene's opinion, a person was an athlete just because they showed up and put on a cute warm up jacket with the name File Hills on the back. It was like being innocent until proven guilty. I liked Charlene immediately.

I signed up for all the long distance running events. I knew I didn't have speed; it had been proven many times that anyone could beat me within sixty metres: chubby kids, kids with limps, once a dog with three legs. Long distance running was also perfect for me because there were so few athletes entered in the races. On any list, there were usually only three names. I liked those odds.

The campgrounds were next to the Gordon's Residential School. The priests and nuns had departed decades before and had left behind the giant red-brick school and some awesome ball diamonds.

We set up camp near the other File Hills students. Ricky Senior greeted us warmly. He and my mom were distant cousins and they had a playful relationship.

"Holee shit, you're late. We got on the road at five AM," Ricky Senior teased.

"Five AM? You ought to have your head examined."

His wife popped her head out of the tent and said hi to my mom as she began her warm up stretches. She wore a tracksuit that matched her husband's.

Mom often bragged about her lack of athleticism. "I played on a ball team once. I was in the outfield and was throwing a ball to the pitcher and the darn thing went backwards. I'm not even sure how I did that." Her story sent chills down my spine. What if I had inherited her lack of ability?

The day started with picking positions for the softball team. Charlene asked everyone what position they could play. I proudly raised my hand. "Pitcher." Charlene smiled, "Great! We always need more pitchers. What about catchers?"

Celeste raised her hand. Charlene was ecstatic. "Perfect! A sister-sister combo."

I had never pitched in my life, nor had I ever seen my sister catch a ball, but I was optimistic. Perhaps this would be one of those miracle moments when my athletic talent would reveal itself.

I grabbed a ball and headed out to the pitcher's mound. The ball felt heavy and big in my hand. "Err . . . do you have a smaller ball?" I asked Charlene.

"That's regulation size. C'mon on now, show everyone what you can do."

I pulled my arm back and threw the ball. It moved through the air, in a high arc, stopping about five feet in front of home plate. Celeste was still looking up in the air when the ball rolled across the plate and stopped against her foot. She hurriedly gathered it up and threw it back to me. Flawlessly.

"Good throw Celeste!" Charlene said. "Hey, Dawn, maybe you should let your sister try a hand at pitching?"

I pretended not to hear. I threw another pitch and achieved the same results. This time, however, the team laughed.

Wonderful. I'd been on the field for two minutes and proven that a) I could not throw a ball and that b) my sister was better than me.

Charlene came to the mound and put her hand on my shoulder. "You know what, I have the perfect position for you!" She then pointed at the outfield.

Charlene posted the team's positions at the end of the day. I had been relegated to the left field. Kindly, Charlene had also listed me as third-string pitcher. My heart warmed.

༄

Even though meals were served in the school's cafeteria, Mom brought a cooler full of cold cuts, bread and apples.

"Eat before you go," was the refrain we heard each morning. Dutifully we would wander back and grab an apple and half a sandwich before joining our friends.

"Your mom sure yells a lot," Ricky Junior commented one day.

"What are you talking about?"

The members of the File Hills athletic team exchanged looks with one another. It said, "You mean she doesn't know?"

Their awareness switched something on inside me and suddenly I could hear my mom as she shouted at my brother to put his sweater on. Not only was she loud, she was louder than everyone else on the field. This meant she was louder than all the mothers from all the reserves in Saskatchewan. Perhaps natural ability wasn't always such a great thing.

⚘

I had my first race at eight AM. The organizers tried to put the long distance races early in the AM so that the runners wouldn't have to run in the hot sun. Also, so that spectators would not have to suffer through them. Short-distance races like the sexy 100 metres were scheduled at peak hours. "It's not your fault long distance races are so boring," Celeste comforted me.

Everything I knew about running I had learned from a book. My brother, finding the book in the bathroom, scoffed at my methods. "Only a nerd reads about jogging!"

What did he know? He ran on the outside of his feet. Sure he was fast but what about in 20 years when the strain injuries started to show up? What about then, huh!

The book taught me that you must always run, heel-toe, heel-toe. I found this advice very helpful as long as I didn't question it too much. I mean, who really walked toe-heel? It wasn't even possible.

My first race was called the 3000 metres on account of its length. It was 13.25 times around the 400 metre track. In any race, two of the participants would be serious runners, the third would be an okay runner, and the fourth would be some poor schmuck who signed up without knowing how far 3000 metres really was.

However, in this particular race, I decided to challenge myself further. It wasn't intentional. I had been digging through my older sister's closet and had found a pair of blue short-shorts. I put them on and found that they sat easily on my hips. They put little pressure on my tummy and as a result I felt thin when I wore them. The baby blue was also flattering on my legs. And they were short which was always good for running. As I lined up with the other runners, I felt proud knowing that I looked the cutest in my shorts.

The gun went off and the runners hurried to form a line that quickly stretched half way around the track. I was in first place and increasing my lead with every step when I first felt my shorts inch down my waist. It seemed that my shorts were so flattering because they lacked an elastic waistband. And without an elastic band or hips, there was nothing to keep them up. They began to slide down. I grabbed onto them with my right hand and pumped with my left.

It was only the first lap out of thirteen. I realized that I had two choices: one, quit the race and run back to our tent and cry, or two, finish the race and then run back to our tent and cry. I looked behind me; the other runners were far behind. I made my choice. I was going for it.

The race felt very long that day. I had to switch hands every half lap as one arm would get tired. One of the other runners ran up to challenge me and I blocked the challenge by pumping harder with my left hand, which apparently was my better running hand. After the runner backed off, thankfully too winded to comment on my shorts, I kept up the pace. The best way to get this race over with quickly was to run as fast as possible, so that's what I did.

After the race, I walked over to Celeste who sat on a blanket with some of our friends. By this time my shorts were stretched out several sizes too large. No more sexy short-shorts, they were now a blousy wrinkled blue diaper.

"Good race. Congrats."

I nodded. "Did you notice anything?"

"Yeah, those other runners sure were slow."

"Anything else?"

"It looked like you were moving pretty fast."

"Anything else?"

She smiled. It turned into a smirk. "Well, your right hand sure was busy." She stared at my hand still holding onto my shorts.

⚘

The best part of being a long distance runner is that you can eat anything. Every day I ordered a hot dog, fries and a drink. I sat at a picnic table in broad view of everyone and ate it without guilt or shame. I had a gold medal and this meant everything I did must be right. Even my mom agreed. "Get those calories in there. You're gonna need them," she said as she massaged my shoulders. While Mom was never big on encouragement in the early stages of an endeavor, she was a pro at jumping on board when things were going well: she was a good Coattails Mom.

Ricky Senior sat down next to us. "This girl of yours sure is something."

My mom agreed. "She's a natural athlete like her dad. Although I wasn't too bad myself, I mean no one could throw a ball further backwards than I could."

Ricky Senior looked me over like a rancher might examine a steer. "This one is definitely long-winded."

Long-winded? I pondered this as I ate my fries. I supposed that was a good thing.

He added, "She's barrel-chested too. Means she's got big lungs."

I guessed that could be taken as a compliment, if I were a horse.

"Then there's her head. See how round it is — cuts down on wind resistance. It's pretty big, but that's why it's good that her neck is so short and thick."

I walked away before I could hear any more of his "flattering" remarks. I had no doubt that he had compliments a-plenty for other parts of my anatomy. Perhaps my big flat feet, or my tree trunk legs, or my aerodynamic face. In any event, I needed no more praise. It had been confirmed by a source other than my mom, or myself: I was a natural athlete. Take that Mr. Broderick, I said under my breath. Then I finished my coke and went to take a nap.

SECOND BEST FRIEND

ONE YEAR THE INDIAN SUMMER GAMES WERE held in Meadow Lake, a northern reserve about eight hours from ours. Both Celeste and I had made the cut for the File Hills track and field and softball teams — which meant we had written our names down on the sign-up sheet. Our brother couldn't make it because he was in hockey school. For the same reason, my mom couldn't come with us.

"You're going to be okay, right?" Mom said as I packed up my clothes.

"Of course."

"It's only a week and you can call me collect anytime you want."

"Mom, I'm thirteen, I don't get homesick anymore."

Mom raised an eyebrow; there had been an incident only a few weeks before.

"That was different. Someone spilled pop on my sleeping bag, I can't sleep in a wet sleeping bag. I could get double pneumonia."

Celeste, my best friend Samantha and I travelled with the other athletes on a chartered bus from File Hills to the Meadow Lake First Nation. I had been worried about being bored on the eight hour long bus ride even though the bus had a TV that played movies, so I brought a small collection of ten or twelve books.

There was no watching or reading on this trip. The boys made sure of that. They dared each other to flash their dicks or behinds to other cars, to run up and down the aisle and generally make fool of themselves and endanger everyone in the process. Us girls rolled our eyes at them; secretly we adored every stupid thing they did.

I declared that Jared Bighead was the cutest guy that God had ever put on the face of the earth. He had dark black hair and long eyelashes. His eyes were a golden brown that matched his perfect tan. He was a fast runner and an excellent ball player. He was also my third cousin.

"All those Bighead boys are good ball players," Mom had commented when she saw him play, "Just like their dad. My *cousin*." The word was pronounced in bold with italics and double underlined for emphasis but it had no significance to my sister and me. Mom implied that we were related to every boy within a five-hundred-mile radius. We had heard her say, "Too bad he's your cousin," so often we no longer paid attention.

Mom counted cousins up to fifteenth and sixteenth. And, if you called bullshit, she would pull out her family tree that she had painstakingly designed in her Adult Social Studies course and show us the exact relationship.

"It's not like I want kids with him or anything," I said to my sister the night before, as we wrote out our crushes' names three hundred times.

"You do want to marry him, don't you?"

"That's when we're twenty-three years old and he's a banker and I'm a lawyer and we have a house in Hawaii."

"Hey, am I still getting the second biggest bedroom that faces the ocean?"

"Yes. Now stop asking."

Samantha had been my best friend for one whole year. That was a new record for me. It's not that I wasn't a good friend, although I certainly wasn't a great friend. I forgot birthdays and if a friend tried to hug me, I laughed at them. I blamed my lack of friendship skills on my early isolation from normal human beings. For the first ten years of my life, I only hung out with my sister and cousins who indulged my bossiness.

Also, my friendships were of short duration. My buddies were all Aboriginal girls and they had a tendency to relocate in the middle of the year or at the end of each year. Their parents would decide that they were moving to the city or to a new province or that they should put their kids in the local boarding school in order to stop disrupting their academic careers.

My mother had decided early on that we would never switch schools. I appreciated the stability but I disliked the effect on my social life. Whereas my friends were making friends with Native kids from around the province, I was only able to befriend the people who came to Balcarres School.

And unfortunately, the majority of Aboriginal people in the area had declared Balcarres racist. There were only a few Native families who kept their children there. In fact, Edward Pinay was the only Native kid that started with me and graduated with me.

Samantha was an extrovert who loved having lots of friends. She actively kept up friendships when other people might stop. She would write letters to me when she moved to the city and then when she moved back to the reserve and started school at the Peepeekisis School, she called me daily. Samantha would even get her parents to drop her off at our house with a backpack and would spend anywhere from a day to a couple weeks at our house.

Samantha was an athlete. She was built for speed with her muscular body and huge bum. The latter embarrassed her. At pow-wows, boys would run up behind her and pinch it. She told her dad. "Well, if he pinched you anywhere, he'd probably hit that thing," he joked. If my dad had said something like that to me in public, I would have crawled up into a ball and died in the dirt.

Samantha didn't care. She was fearless. I was shy and depended on her for introduction to other kids.

"This is my friend Dawn; she's really smart."

I would make a face as if to say, I'm not really smart. I wouldn't verbally deny it because secretly I believed I had a genius IQ. I used this belief to make myself feel better in times of stress. "The reason why they are calling me names is because they are scared of my intellect." Yes, that was it.

Samantha was not afraid to talk to anyone. Sometimes she didn't know what to say. I always had something to say but didn't have the courage to say it. So we compromised.

"Nice T-shirt, where'd you get it? Your grandma's closet," I mumbled under my breath.

"Hey, Loser, quit robbing your grandma's closet," Samantha said loudly. Everyone laughed and Samantha would wink at me. I would grin back. We were a great team.

Samantha, Celeste and I explored the sports grounds. Meadow Lake was bigger than any reserve we'd been to before. It had two huge gymnasiums and six ball fields. It also had a track and well-stocked band store within walking distance. Even better, less than a kilometre away they had a lake where you could rent motorboats for five bucks and you didn't have to have a license or anything. It was truly a paradise.

There were brown faces everywhere you looked. If you listened, you could hear a variety of languages spoken.

Not everyone was brown. One afternoon, a group of pale-skinned girls strolled past us. There were a few golden-haired blondes and even a redhead in the bunch.

"Why are there white girls here?" I wondered aloud. And not happily either. I had to contend with white girls in school, I didn't want to have to deal with them on my summer vacation.

Samantha laughed. "Those aren't white girls. Those are Bill C-31s."

"Bill what's?"

"You know their moms married white guys."

Bill C-31 had just been passed in Parliament and now its effects were trickling down to us. Before it was passed, the Indian Act narrowly defined who was and was not an Indian. The Indian Act magically turned a Non-Native woman into a Native if she married a Native man. The Indian Act transformed any Native woman who married a non-Native into a non-Native person. It also made her Treaty rights disappear. They should have called it the Houdini Act. Once Bill C-31 was passed, the Native women who had lost their rights got them back.

I was instantly envious of the Bill C-31s. These girls had all the rights of Indians and because they tended to be lighter, they faced less of the racism; it was the perfect deal. Mom had made a similar comment in reference to Valerie, a white woman from our reserve. "That Val's got it made in spades." Valerie was a southern belle from West Virginia. She introduced the reserve to grits, fried chicken and "Y'all." In return, we taught her to fry bannock, make Indian tacos and say "youse."

I showed Jared to Samantha and she agreed that he was cute. "Who do you like?" I asked.

She shrugged. "No one."

"Don't worry we'll find someone for you. Maybe another athlete like yourself," I said helpfully.

From my avid research, I knew that Jared hung out with Mike, who was tall with a face like a horse. Mike had a loud laugh and liked to crack jokes. He always stood a foot behind Jared effectively protecting Jared's perfect skin from the sun.

Their tent was located twenty feet northeast of ours. They didn't have a chaperone because Mike was sixteen years old.

"What events are you in?" Samantha boldly asked them as we walked to breakfast together.

Mike was just there to play baseball he said. Jared was in all of the short distance races and also playing on the baseball team.

"You're really good," I whispered, staring down at the ground.

"I hear you're really good," Samantha said loudly.

Jared smiled, "Thanks."

In the bathroom, Samantha and I discussed the exchange. "Do you think he likes me?" I asked Samantha as I smoothed my hair down in the mirror.

Samantha shrugged. "Why don't you ask him?"

"I can't do that!" That wouldn't be romantic. Jared and I were soul mates and you don't have to ask your soul mate if they like you. You know by looking into their eyes. Unfortunately I was too shy to look into his eyes.

Celeste said that she figured he liked me because he kept looking in my direction. I thanked her with my eyes and silently promised her the biggest bedroom overlooking the ocean.

Charlene Bear was our chaperone and slept at the front of the doorway of our tent.

"Nobody but nobody is getting in trouble on this trip," she said calmly as she laid out her sleeping bag.

"What kind of trouble?"

"Oh, you know."

I don't think we did know. All we knew was that we wanted to get near the boys but we didn't know what we would do with them once we got close. Kiss them? That seemed do-able. And, what about this French-kissing thing kids were talking about? I didn't know if I'd be good at it; they didn't start teaching French at my school until grade nine.

And what was all that first, second and third base stuff? I barely understood when I was supposed to bunt.

And what exactly was "doing it?"

I know this seems incredibly naïve but remember, this was before Discovery channel and the Internet. All I knew about sex I'd heard from listening in to my mom gossip with her friends. Whenever they got to the good parts, they would drop their voices and lean close to one another. I'd have to leave my hiding spot and pretend to walk through the kitchen for some water. "What are you doing? Go play outside!"

NOBODY CRIES AT BINGO

"I'm thirsty."

"Since when are you too good to drink out of the hose? Now, out!"

When I looked at a boy, all I noticed were his facial features. It took only one glance to declare if they were handsome or not. And it took only one more to fall in love. Without their heads, I wouldn't even recognize them. What was the point? What else could possibly be of value beyond a pair of long eyelashes and a sexy smile?

I knew that underneath their clothes boys were different but I didn't know how exactly. I barely understood my own anatomy. I mean, yes I knew that I was flat-footed, barrel chested and longwinded but what did that have to do with anything?

I was clueless and this was evident in my style of flirting. I had discovered that talking to my crush was much too nerve-wracking so I couldn't talk to him directly. Instead I teased his best friend incessantly.

"Hey, Mike, you ever let little kids ride on your back? Yes or neigh?"

Mike laughed and returned the teasing, "Hey, Dawn, did a ball hit you in the face? Oh sorry, you just look that way naturally."

With the friend, I could be bold. With my crush, I was quiet, verging on taciturn. If Charlene had witnessed my flirting style she would have felt more than comfortable moving her sleeping bag to the back of the tent.

Samantha on the other hand had no problem talking to all boys, including Jared. She didn't need to bounce her remarks off Mike to whom she barely paid any attention. She and Jared invented little nicknames between one another. "See ya later Jer." "You too Gonzales."

"Why did he call you Gonzales?"

"Oh you know, speedy Gonzales, after the cartoon. It's stupid."

"It sure is stupid!" I laughed loudly. Anger simmered beneath the surface.

I took a walk to the bathroom with my sister. "I think Samantha likes Jared," I huffed.

"Maybe she just wants to be his friend?" Celeste offered.

I wanted to believe Celeste even though I knew it wasn't so. My friend was betraying me and there wasn't anything I could do about it.

I suppose I could have hung out with other friends but since I didn't have any, that didn't leave me with many options. I decided I would continue our farce of a friendship.

My races became of secondary importance. I even missed one race because I was over at the ball fields watching the boys play.

Charlene took me aside. "What are you here for, Dawn? I mean, really."

I knew immediately what I was there for. I was there to be the third party in the most painful love triangle the world had ever seen. "To have fun?"

"Yes but also to compete. Remember that."

Ah, competition. The answer was right there in front of me. I was not some passive baby; I was a fighter. I was Rocky Balboa in the fifth round, bloody and bruised, with a core of power that was yet untouched.

The next mealtime I purposely sat next to Mike and Jared.

"Hi Jared, how are your games going?"

Jared looked surprised to hear me speaking to him. "Okay. Looks like we're gonna take gold."

I tried to be witty. "My aren't we cocky."

"What?"

"Sorry, didn't mean to insult your immense ego, *Jer*."
Mike laughed.

"Right." Jared looked wary.

My brain screamed, "You're losing him! Abort, abort!"

Instead I said, "You're so pretty Jared, anyone ever mistake
you for a guy?"

Jared picked up his tray and left.

I looked across the cafeteria. I could see Samantha sitting
with a group of girls I had not yet met. After lunch I joined
her. She was cold. "So what did Jared say to you?"

"Nothing."

"I think he likes you."

"Not anymore," I whispered under my breath.

We ran to our ball diamond. Charlene had taped the roster
on the side of the bleachers. Samantha was playing first base. I
was playing right field as usual.

"Ha ha, the outfield is for bad players." Samantha laughed
at her own joke.

"Well, first base is for . . . for . . . show-offs!"

"Dawn, you have spit in the corner of your mouth," Celeste
said helpfully.

I wiped my mouth and turned away from Samantha. I
found another girl to warm up with.

Every one of Samantha's laughs was a knife through my
gut. She. Is. So. Annoying. The ball said as it landed in my
glove. I had never been good at throwing a ball but it became
remarkably easy when I was angry. The other girl throwing
the ball had a worried look on her face, "Not so hard, Dawn.
We're just warming up."

"Yeah, sorry. Don't know my own strength."

I decided I was warm enough and climbed up the bleachers. I was half way to the top when a foul ball strayed from the diamond and struck my shoulder. A hot pain reverberated through my body. I even felt it in my teeth as I crumpled onto the bleachers. I bravely fought the pain with a righteous scream. Soon tears joined the party and I was viewing the world through a blurry mist. The first face I saw was Samantha's.

"What happened?"

"The ball hit me!"

"It's okay. It's not turning blue or anything," she said, as she peeked at my shoulder.

"It still hurts!" I whined.

She sat next to me and rubbed my shoulder. It made the pain worse. I didn't complain because it was the nicest thing a friend had ever done for me.

Our chartered bus left at seven PM on the last night of the summer games. As we left, fireworks lit the sky. Celeste sat in front of me with her best friend and Samantha and I sat behind them.

We compared medals. Samantha had five. She wore them all round her neck. I had two; they were safely stashed in my backpack. We talked about all our fun times. It had been a great two weeks and as the bus pulled onto the highway, I remembered that I had forgotten to call my mom.

I tapped Celeste's shoulder. "Hey, Celeste did you call Mom?"

Celeste shook her head. "I thought you did."

NOBODY CRIES AT BINGO

"Boy is she gonna be mad." As I said it, I secretly marveled at my new independence. I could spend any amount of time away from Mom . . . as long as boys were somehow involved.

Mike walked up to our seat and whispered in Samantha's ear. She looked behind us. Jared waved at her.

"I wonder what he wants?" she asked innocently.

"He probably wants to shine your medals," I offered dryly.

Samantha grinned and went to the back to sit with him. Mike gave me a shy smile.

I slid over. He sat next to me and I noticed that he smelled kind of nice. Perhaps, second best wasn't so bad after all?

Mike talked about their last ball game and then said something that surprised me even though it shouldn't have.

"I was talking to my mom last night and I told her about you."

"Oh." My face turned red as I realized he liked me. Oh yes, he smelled very nice, I thought as I leaned closer.

"Yeah, she said we're cousins. Weird, huh?"

"Nope, not weird at all," I said flatly and slid closer to the window.

Within a few hours, everyone on the bus was asleep, except Samantha and Jared, who joked together the whole ride home. Even though it pained me to hear it, eventually the sound of their laughter lulled me to sleep.

The Conscience

M Y OLDER SISTER TABITHA WAS THE SUPREME ruler of her four younger siblings since the first of us stumbled out of our mother's womb. I'm sure she sighed when she saw my head, "What is this now? I am already so comfortable being an only child. I have my toys, my bedroom, my pet chicken. What am I supposed to do with this round-headed, chubby-cheeked interloper? Must I feed it, must I pet it, must I like it?"

She chose to enslave us. "Go get me a pop." "Open that door." "Close that door." "Hit yourself." No matter what the order was, we would rush to complete it for her, often banging into one another in our haste.

Everything Tabitha did was perfect. She would place her long legs on the walls and shimmy to the top of the hallway in her bare feet. Then she would look down at us with her head resting on the ceiling as we stared up at her, open-mouthed. "How did you do that? Are you magical?" Later, we would try to imitate her but our short legs would not allow it.

Tabitha could take her bunny rabbit T-shirt and make the rabbit hop by tugging on her T-shirt. She could take an ordinary apple, suck on the seeds and pelt them across the room like bullets from a gun. As we danced around trying to avoid the seeds, we wondered: how could one person be so talented?

Tabitha was also our in-house baby-sitter. She made the rules and then broke them depending on her mood. As the next oldest, I was Slave No. 1. Not an exaggerated title — it was a real title, with attendant privileges and obligations. Those privileges included having the choice seat next to the bag of chips and second last cup of pop. And, of course, I had a measure of control over my bedtime. Often I got to stay up later than my other two siblings and keep her company as she waited for our parents to get home from bingo.

Celeste felt this was unfair since I was only one year older than her. She fought this injustice with the determination and persistence of the French resistance. Long after we thought she had gone to bed, I would hear her creeping down the hallway. When she reached the doorway of the living room, I would spot her from my perch on the couch. I mouthed the words, "Get to bed."

"No!" Celeste mouthed back, the word escaping from her lips, making it sound like a petulant ghost haunted the hallway.

Then depending on my annoyance level at her various shenanigans during the day, I let her sit there a few minutes before I ratted her out. It was never a question of IF. I would rat her out. I had to. Staying up late wasn't a privilege if my other two siblings could experience it. Also, if I didn't tell, then I might lose my place as Tabitha's favourite. I had angered Tabitha once and still remember the stinging feeling of seeing my siblings raised to the level of demi-god in my place.

Once caught by Tabitha, Celeste screamed at the top of lungs as we pushed her towards the bedroom. She cried hysterically, "It's not fair! Dawn gets to stay up!"

"Well, you're not Dawn, are you?" Tabitha coolly replied. Her younger siblings never flustered Tabitha. If I yelled that I hated her, she smiled and said, "I love you too." What could you do in the face of such self-possession?

Celeste screamed all the way back to her bedroom. Then as the door was shut and held closed, her screams got momentarily louder until they receded into violent sobs and then, mercifully, turned into grumbles as she made her way back into bed.

Afterwards, Tabitha and I watched TV in the living room. "That kid drives me crazy," Tabitha said, allowing me to see a crack in the wall.

"I know, I know," I murmured comfortingly as I poured more pop into her cup.

People never understand how lonely it is at the top. I understood. After all the kids had gone to bed, Tabitha had no one to talk to and certainly no one to run and get her snacks. I stepped in and filled the void. I would sit next to her on the couch and watch music videos with her and agree with her comments. "Bryan Adams is a babe, I would marry him in a second."

I thought he was gorgeous too. Even if I didn't think so I would never make the mistake of offering a different opinion. The duty of Slave No. 1 was to be agreeable and comfortable company, not unlike the TV itself. I had seen what happened to people who were not agreeable.

During one period, Tabitha and I watched *Rock'n'Roll High School* at least a hundred times. The movie went completely over my head and I couldn't figure out what it was about or why the Ramones were hanging out in some teenage girl's shower. "I wish that was me," Tabitha sighed. I — on the other hand — checked behind the shower curtain every night with some trepidation.

Tabitha who was five years older than me was in high school by the time I reached Junior High. My Judy Blume books warned me that the transition from child to teenager was a precarious business. Tabitha made puberty look easy. She slipped her slender shoulders into a faded denim jacket, and shone. She eased her way down the hallway, a mixture of elegance, grace and confidence . . . surrounded by all the fun people. I squeezed my chubby bum into pink jeans and chased the crowd, always ending up on the fringes. I clung to my friends and they peeled my hands off of their arms. "Be cool, Dawn. Be cool."

I paced in my room and formulated plans for popularity. "If I could just throw a party, I know I could get a lot of friends. Now how do I throw a party? I need beer. How do I get beer? I get fake ID. How do I get ID? I become friends with an older kid. And how do I make friends? I throw a party . . . This is impossible!" I would throw myself face first on the bed.

Celeste listened to my concerns and offered tips of her own. "Maybe you could just serve coke at your party? Most people like coke except for David, he only likes 7-Up. That's why I drink it all up on him."

Tabitha would know how to fix my unpopularity but she was too busy with her friends to pay attention to me. Everything had changed when she reached high school. She had no more need of Slave No. 1 or even a chubby sidekick; she had real friends who had cars and could drive to visit us. I was not pleased to be booted from my lofty position and I made my displeasure known. I played pranks on her, hiding her car keys, hanging up on her friends when they called, and telling on her for not doing her chores. Not surprisingly, I was not her favourite person.

Nothing I did could quell her popularity. Five minutes after our parents went to bingo, her friends arrived at the house. Celeste, David and I would be excited to see all the teenagers in their leather jackets and blue jeans. "Hi, who are you?"

"Where's Tabitha?" they asked without even glancing at our faces.

Our desperation for company could not be easily dissuaded. "What's your name? How old are you? Is that your car? How come you wear only black?"

Tabitha rescued her friends and ushered them past our curious eyes. Her bedroom door shut in our faces.

We stood outside the door listening to the laughter and music. They were having a party right inside our house; this was impressive. We weren't invited; this was disappointing. The three of us retired to the living room and returned to irritating one another as best we could.

When annoying each other became boring, we turned to annoying other people on the reserve. We had a party line on our phone. This invention allowed many families to share the same phone line. Everyone had his or her own special ring and you only answered the phone when you heard your ring. At least you were supposed to. We picked it up whenever it rang and listened to other people's phone calls. Most of them were boring discussions between old people who were dying of something terrible. If you were lucky you might encounter a conversation between two teenagers. Boyfriends and girlfriends were the best. You had to be careful not to giggle. Clark, a fifteen-year-old who lived about twenty minutes from us, had a girlfriend in the city and he was attempting to seduce her from his bedroom on the reserve. Every night he tried to convince her to buy a bus ticket and travel all the way to Balcarres.

"What would I do there?" she would ask smacking her gum.

"There's lots to do," he lied smoothly. I nearly choked on my water.

"I'm not going to have sex with you," she replied sharply.

"I just want to be near you. To hear every breath you take . . . every move you make . . . I'll be watching you."

I made a sound that was a cross between a cough and a snort.

Clark heard this and his tone immediately changed from Sting-inspired wheedling to annoyance. "Who's there?"

I held my breath and went completely still.

"Get off the phone, you fucking creep, before I kick your ass," Clark snarled.

I knew he was bluffing; he didn't know who it was. It could be any kid from any of the ten families on our party line. Still maybe my breath was recognizable! My hand shook as I returned the phone to its cradle. Then I hurried into the living room where I became indistinguishable from my siblings.

While playing with the phone one night, I discovered that if I dialed our number our own phone would ring. Tabitha was having one of her meetings in her bedroom and I decided to bug her. I dialed our number and let the phone ring a couple times. I heard her bedroom door open. She always answered the phone as ninety percent of the time it was for her. As she hurried down the hall, I answered the phone. "Hello? Oh hi, Mom. Tabitha? Oh she's busy right now, she has a bunch of friends in her room so we're looking after ourselves . . . – "

Tabitha wrenched the phone out of my hand. "Hello? Hello?" Her relief immediately turned into annoyance as she realized what I had done.

My brilliance was rewarded with a glare from Tabitha who then dragged the phone all the way into her bedroom where it, too, was locked in. David shook his head at my stupidity. "Clark is calling his girlfriend in ten minutes — tonight he's trying to talk her into sleeping in his bed — and now we're going to miss it. Idiot."

Tabitha and I were further divided by our innate differences. If you put her in a room with a group of people, they would be drawn to her quiet confidence in a matter of minutes. If you put me in a group of people, I would find a book and ignore them, too ashamed of my incredible need to be liked to reach out. If there were no books, I would try to impress them with my knowledge of trivia. Sometimes Tabitha called upon my talents. Once while driving us home from school, she gave a good-looking guy friend a ride home. "Dawn, tell Zach some trivia."

I pushed my glasses up on my nose and they quickly slid back down. "Well, what kind of trivia? Animal, place or thing?"

"Anything!"

Zach turned to me. He had green eyes, dirty blond hair and a huge head. "C'mon little Einstein, teach me something."

"The . . . uh . . . the human head weighs 8 lbs." Though, yours might weigh a lot more I thought to myself.

"That's funny, little Dude." Zach answered. "Do another one."

What was I? A human trivia jukebox? Part of me felt indignant at being displayed for this stoned slacker. The other, more dominant part of me, savoured any attention. I began spitting out facts without pause. "Diamonds can cut glass. The gestation period of an elephant is twenty-two months. The average human eats 100 spiders a year."

When we finally dropped Zach off, I was shaking and sweating from pure effort. My sister bought me a pop.

The phone rang off the hook day and night for Tabitha. It seemed like she was always on her way out the door to a party, a concert, or god knows what type of tomfoolery. I begged my mom to set down some rules or invest in a cattle prod. I felt that my sister was headed for ruin. I'm not sure what kind of ruin — I was relatively ignorant on that subject. There were a few girls in my sister's year that had dropped out due to the size of their bellies. There was a listless shadow of a teenager walking the halls, his personality stolen by drugs. When he walked past, other students whispered, "Burn out." There were students who had run-ins with the law — they got special visits from the police and even free rides up town. There were brutal fights on school property in which girls tore at each other's faces like wild cats and the loser wore the marks for months. I didn't understand the reason behind these things but I knew they must be avoided.

Like most parents, mine had no idea what they were doing. Tabitha was the oldest and the first teenager Mom had to deal with so Mom made up irrational rules. While she was outside hanging the laundry, one of these rules popped into her head. She declared it to us as we sat at the dinner table. "From now on, when Tabitha goes out, she will take Dawn with her."

"And me," added Celeste stubbornly.

"And me!" chimed in David.

Nobody paid any attention to them. Only ten and eleven, they had recently worked together on the theft of seventy-five dollars from Dad's wallet. Everyone knew which side of the trouble they worked on.

I don't know how Mom knew that I was the Jiminy Cricket of no-fun. Perhaps it was the way that I always told on everyone else. Maybe Mom had discovered this fact from viewing the neat placement of all my board games, with all original places still intact, beside my bed. Or maybe it was the time she walked into my room and saw me lecturing to my cousins and younger sister about the proper way to play with Barbie dolls. "Barbie has no desire to kiss Ken. Okay? He and Barbie are just friends. Also, Jolene — this is for you — Barbie does not like walking around wearing only heels, understand? She likes clothes." Somehow Mom sensed — correctly — that I had a special knack for sucking the enjoyment out of any activity.

Tabitha was working her job at the time — a waitress in a pizza restaurant, a licensed restaurant! We had gone to visit her at work and ordered a large pizza. Mom and Dad introduced themselves to Tabitha's boss, a hard-looking woman with thin, sharp lips and generous cleavage. She nodded in acknowledgement of our presence and told us our sister was a hard worker. Then she lit a smoke and went back into the kitchen. Though I admired the woman's glamour, I knew she did not belong within a hundred miles of my sister.

My parents — again — did not know what they were doing. When they looked at my sister, they saw a good teenager, working. Sure the boss woman was a little trashy but she was still white, a business owner, and a respected member of society. Well, maybe not respected, but a business owner. Their daughter had made it over to the other side and that was good enough for my parents.

Tabitha earned enough to buy a car so when she wasn't
working she was driving her friends around. Now her
bedroom was empty and the answer to the question, "Where's
your sister?" was always a sad shrug.

While she was gone, I would rifle through her things
trying to figure out the secret of who she was. Was Tabitha's
confidence bottled up in the perfume? Was the message in her
music? Did it have something to do with the posters on her
wall? I would plead with the picture of Prince, "Help me." He
would stare straight ahead, immersed in rocking out in his
high-waisted, skintight polka dot pants.

At school my popularity had rocketed from two best
friends down to none. I spent my lunch hours standing in the
bathroom slicking my hair down with water. Another quality
that set us apart — Tabitha had great hair. It was light brown
and feathered away from her face in gentle symmetrical waves.
My hair refused to do to anything close to feathering. It chose
to ramble all over my head in a collection of knots and curls,
while spikes of it poked out of my head. We didn't have cable
at our house so I didn't even know what people meant when
they called me Lisa Simpson. "Yeah, right, thanks," I would
say as I headed back to my office in the bathroom.

I was able to control my hair with water — until the water
dried and then the problem was even worse when static was
added to the mix. By the time I was done drenching my head,
everyone would be standing outside the school in the smoking
area. All the students would be lighting up their butts from
the period before as I wandered past with my wet hair.

"Did you just have a shower?" one of the boys would ask
incredulously.

"Uh huh," I would answer unintelligibly looking for a
friendly place to stand. I could usually depend on Trina, a girl

who had once been my best friend, to make room for me. Trina and I had been close until she started going out and now she and I had nothing to talk about. She went to parties and made out with guys; I made popcorn with Celeste and David. Trina pointed at a hickey on her neck. "My boyfriend did this."

"You have a boyfriend? A real one?"

"Well . . . duh. I like told you that last week." It was true she had mentioned a story about a twenty-eight year old who had told her she looked sexy. I had stopped listening because the age twenty-eight was reverberating around my head like a gong. I was the most sexually ignorant person within a mile radius of the high school but even I knew there was something wrong with a man dating a thirteen-year-old girl.

Later that recess I brought up the story to Tabitha. "Yeah, I know," she said, nodding that it was okay for me to leave and go back to my side of the wall.

"What if he — y'know — pressures her to do stuff — like the stuff they told us about in Health class?" My voice dropped to a whisper.

"I know what to do," Tabitha said and turned her back on me.

⁂

"I know." "Yeah, I know." "I said, I know." "I already know that." Tabitha's refrains were slowly driving our family insane. "If you know so much, then why am I lending you gas money?" Mom would argue, as she reached into her pocket for another twenty.

"You don't know everything, you're only seventeen!" I would yell at her through her bedroom door.

Dad tried a different approach. "Tell me this . . . do you know all the names of the Great Lakes? Do you know who all the Cabinet Ministers are?" Dad lost credibility when we discovered he didn't know the answers to his own questions.

One night Tabitha shook me awake. It was after midnight and I thought we were running away from Dad. "Dad's drunk?"

"No. But get up anyway."

I jumped off the bunk bed and combed my hand through my buffalo hair. "What's going on?"

"We're going to the drive-in."

"Why are we going there?"

"Stop asking questions."

I pulled on my jeans and tucked in my sleeping T-shirt. The drive-in? I didn't even know what was playing. And frankly, I was surprised that Tabitha wanted to go; she'd never shown herself to be much of a movie buff, unless the Ramones had a starring role, of course.

Celeste slept on the other side of the room and didn't wake as I crept out. She rolled over and made a noisy grunt in her sleep. I'm sure she sensed the injustice even in her dreams.

I wandered into the bathroom where Tabitha was using her curling iron to feather her hair outwards when it finally clicked. I was going out! I was going to be around the cool teenagers! I was going to be popular!

Here I had been fruitlessly searching for popularity and it had woken me up in the middle of the night. Screw you, Judy Blume; being a teenager was easy.

I followed my sister out the door to her green Ford and climbed into the passenger seat.

"So who is going to be there? Will there be cute boys?" I asked.

"Sit down. Shut up." Tabitha lit a cigarette and turned the music up loud.

We arrived at the drive-in. A party was at full tilt by the time we got there. I had naively thought that drive-ins were for movies and that parties could only be held in houses. How wrong I had been! Teenagers moved from car to car to truck carrying bottles of beer as music blared from their stereos. When they needed mix, someone would wander to the concession stand and buy a pop.

We pulled up next to another car and my sister got out. She leaned against the car and began talking to her friends. I wandered over to where she stood and stared at her with a bewildered look on my face.

"What?"

"I just . . . what am I supposed to do?"

Tabitha glared at me. "Just go. Have fun."

How exactly? How am I supposed to hold my arms? How do I laugh? Which people do I talk to? Should I tell them trivia? Before I could formulate my answer, another teenager wandered over with a twelve of beer under his arm. He handed it out indiscriminately and I was more surprised when my hand found its way around the neck of a bottle. I opened the beer and took a sip. It was bitter and warm. It tasted like apple juice that had been held in someone else's mouth and then spit back into the bottle and left in the sun for a few hours. There was no sweetness to the drink; I could not see the point at all. I spit out my mouthful and kept the bottle as a prop.

My friend Cara stood by an old pickup truck with some other girls. Her parents let her go out with her older brother. They reasoned that she wouldn't sneak out and get into trouble if they allowed her to do whatever she liked. Their rationalization was more proof that parents were improvising as they went along.

"Hey, Cara."

"Hey, Dawn. What are you drinking?"

"Labatts."

"Oh, cool. I've already had two."

"Yeah, this is my fourth."

We talked about school and sipped our beers. Suddenly boring life was interesting. The drive-in took on sepia tones and my friends and I became husky-voiced philosophers.

"Yeah, math tests are way too long."

"If Mrs. King gives me shit one more time, I'm totally gonna walk out."

Trina stumbled into our conversation. Her eyes were streaked with mascara. "My boyfriend broke up with me."

"The twenty-eight year old?"

"Yeah, someone told my brother and he told my parents and my parents told the police."

"Aw, that sucks."

Our drive-in party was over too soon. It seemed we had just started having fun when the last movie finished. Soon the owner of the drive-in would be walking through the crowd with a flashlight telling everyone to get lost before he called the police.

Someone decided that the party would move to the beach. I was not impressed; didn't everyone know that the beach was closed at night? That there was no lifeguard on duty and that public drunkenness was a crime?

"Your little sister is such a drag."

"Get in the car, Dawn."

"There's too many people in the car already. How will I put my seat belt on?"

"Get in or I'm leaving you."

My sister raced down the curvy valley roads. From my seat where I sat pressed up against a window I could see the

DAWN DUMONT

trees blur into one fat green forest. Tabitha had a lead foot and she needed little encouragement to go even faster. Another teenager-driven car passed us. We passed them back. It was three AM and I was in a race. I could hardly contain my delight or the contents of my bowels. I was buried beneath a bunch of bodies and I calmed myself by remembering that I'd be the last one to fly out of the car. The volume on the stereo was maxed out so nobody heard me ask, "Is no one afraid of dying?"

During the race, Tabitha dropped back behind the front driver and turned off her headlights. The road in front of us went suddenly dark. Then we saw the red brake lights of the front car. We crept along the road, only the moonlight lighting up the pavement. The driver and his passengers stood outside of the car, looking over the edge of the ravine. My sister turned on her lights and beeped her horn. They thought we had died! What fun! What amazing, scary, fun.

"Please take me home now," I whispered into the upholstery.

The party had barely begun. By the grace of the overworked and under-appreciated angels that protect teenagers, we reached the beach safely. My half a beer had worn off. I felt tired and cranky.

"So what's the plan?" I said to my sister. Well, that is what I intended to say. Instead it came out as, "I'm tired! I want to go home." Tabitha rolled her eyes at my petulant tone and moved closer to her friends. I sat on the hood of the car and pouted.

"Stupid teenagers," I mumbled under my breath. What fun did they derive from the softening darkness as morning crept up? What was so great about wading into the water and splashing one another? A girl my sister's age took off her clothes and was swimming in her bra and panties. "Idiot," I thought, "she's going to end up getting polio."

If this was cool, I wanted no part of it. I wanted my warm bed and Celeste sleeping across the room. I wanted to wake up to the sound of Mom screaming at us to get up for school.

"I'm only thirteen-years-old, for God's sake. I should not be at a party," I said to myself.

I began to cry into my hands. This was weird to the teenagers. Tears were saved for break-ups and near-suicides. I was an A student, but I could see in their eyes that I was failing partying. What's worse, I didn't care.

My sister walked over to the car. "What's the problem?"

"I hate it here."

"Go sleep in the car."

"I don't like sleeping in cars. It makes my neck sore."

"Quit being such a brat."

"I'm gonna tell Mom."

I was declared hopeless and she walked away. She stood on the pier with her friends and they laughed and joked around. Others swam in the dark waters. I could hear their laughter coming in over the waves. Their fun made me even unhappier. I decided to remind my sister of our curfew, of our obligations to family, of our happy home.

I glumly made my way to the pier. "Tabitha!"

"What do you want?"

"When are you planning on leaving? Because it is already very late. And I know Mom would like us to go to church tomorrow."

Tabitha sighed. She was bending. I could feel it. I pressed my case. "I shouldn't be down here. You know I'm allergic to mosquitoes."

Someone in that crowd must have had a younger sibling for whom they held some resentment deep in their soul. I do not know. All I know is that one second I was standing in front of my sister and the next I was flying into the water. I landed feet first in waist deep water.

"Tabitha!" I yelled. I found her concerned eyes peering over the pier.

"Are you okay?"

"Someone pushed me in!" There is something about stating the obvious that teenagers find hilarious. They broke out into rough laughter on the dock.

Tabitha helped me out. "It's not so bad, you're only half wet."

"I want to go home now!" The water and cold air gave my voice an imperious air, which probably reminded the teenagers of all the oppressive figures in their lives: their parents, their teachers, the police, the guy at the arcade who wouldn't let them drink in the parking lot . . .

This time it was not a gentle shove. This time it was multiple hands on my legs and arms, throwing me off the dock into the water below. "TABITHA!" I yelled on my way down.

I was not the only one thrown into the water as someone else took the opportunity to push his little brother in, too. Our heads popped up at the same time. I was on the verge of crying when suddenly he laughed. And then I laughed.

I got it, finally. "This is what it means not to care," I thought myself. "This is pure unadulterated fun." Fortunately I had enough self-awareness not to utter that phrase aloud.

On the ride home, I sat in the back seat. My sister's best friend sat in front beside her. They discussed their night, its ups and its downs. I can't remember what they talked about, it's not important now, as they've settled into families and careers and wouldn't even remember the boys they laughed about.

Instead, I remember the red cherry of their cigarette as they passed it between one another. I remember their laughter in between the songs on the radio. I see the way their hair moved in the wind, as it dislodged their hairspray and disturbed their feathered bangs. I recall the smell of their smoke, the way it tunneled out the window as we climbed the hill back to the reserve. I can still hear the hum of the car as I laid my head on the seat. I can feel the rough upholstery up against my pimpled cheek and the rocks underneath the car on the gravel road. I remember feeling safe knowing that it was my older sister driving the car and that she would get us home.

THE WAY OF THE SWORD

WHEN I WAS GROWING UP MY HERO was Conan the Barbarian. He wasn't just a comic book character — Conan was a way of life, a very simple way of life. When Conan wanted something, he took it. When someone stood in his way, he slew them. There were no annoying grey areas when you were a barbarian.

Uncle Frank introduced me, my siblings and all my cousins to Conan. He arrived from Manitoba one day with a bag filled with clothes and a box full of comics. I was ten and had no idea who Uncle Frank was. "This is your uncle," Mom said pointing at the thin man with no hair sitting next to her at the table.

"Yeah, hi, okay," I said, breezing by as I polished an apple on my T-shirt.

I would have kept walking had I not overheard the words, "horse ranch." I stopped short, reversed and sat to my uncle's right as he laid out the plans for possibly the greatest single thing that has ever happened to the Okanese reserve — Uncle Frank's ranch.

Frank had no children but his interests in horses, comic books and candies guaranteed that they would always surround him. From the first day he arrived, all the kids within a three-kilometre radius spent all our free time at Uncle Frank's — a fact, which delighted our bingo-addicted mothers to no end. When the horses weren't available, or the weather was inclement or we had stuffed ourselves with too many cookies and potato chips, my cousins and I gathered in Uncle Frank's living room where we would leaf through his Conan collection. Each week, we'd fight over who got to read the latest issue, but it was just as easy to lose yourself in an old comic while a slow reader mumbled his way through the new one.

Uncle Frank had hundreds of Conan comics from various different series. You see, Conan led such a long and complex life that it had to be told from several different angles. There was Conan the Barbarian, Conan the King, Young Conan and the Savage Sword of Conan. The Savage Sword was my favourite because it was more of a graphic magazine than a comic book. On these pages, the artists took extra time and care to bring across Conan's heroic form, stylized muscles and the blood splatters of his foes. These stories were savoured; each word would be read, each panel would be studied, to achieve maximum Conan absorption.

Every time I opened a new comic, I read the italicized print above the first panel that described the world of Conan, "The proudest kingdom of the world was Aquilonia, reigning supreme in the dreaming west. Hither came Conan, the Cimmerian, black-haired, sullen-eyed, sword in hand, a thief, a reaver, a slayer, with gigantic melancholies and gigantic mirth, to tread the jewelled thrones of the Earth under his sandaled feet."

Through these magazines we learned all we needed to know about Conan and his life philosophies. There was a recipe for living in those comics: love those who love you and conquer those who don't. My cousins took this to heart and ran headlong into adventures like chasing down the bantam rooster until he turned on them and flew at their faces with his claws. They emerged from their adventures with bruises, scrapes and confident smiles. I always hung back, afraid of breaking a limb or scratching my smooth, plump skin. I knew I could be like Conan too, but in the distant future, far away from sharp claws and bad tempered chickens.

Part of the reason we loved Conan was we believed he was Native. The story of Conan mirrored the story of Native people. Conan was a descendent of the Cimmerians, a noble warrior people who made swords yet lived peaceably. They were attacked and annihilated by an imperial army who murdered the men and women and enslaved the children. Conan was one of those children and the only one to survive slavery (according to the movie.) He was the last of his kind.

This was exactly like our lives! Well, except for the last of our kind business. We were very much alive and well even though others had made a concerted effort to kill us off. Later, I learned that throughout the world, people thought that Indians had been killed off by war, famine and disease. Chris Rock does a comedy bit about this point, claiming that you will never see an Indian family in a Red Lobster. This is a misconception: my family has gone to Red Lobster many times. (However, we are most comfortable at a Chinese buffet.)

In Saskatchewan, most non-Native people were very much aware that nearly a million Native people still existed, mainly to annoy them and steal their tax dollars.

But someone had tried to annihilate us and that was not something you got over quickly. It was too painful to look at it and accept; it was easier to examine attempted genocide indirectly. We could read about the Cimmerians and feel their pain; we could not acknowledge our own.

Once we had owned all of Canada and now we lived on tiny reserves. While reserves weren't as bad as, say, a slave labour camp run by Stygian priests, sometimes life was reduced to survival. Like Conan, all we had was our swords and our wits. And if we weren't allowed to bring our swords to school, then we would use our fists. There was an unspoken belief among the Native kids that we would fight to defend our people should anyone decide to annihilate us again. As Conan once said as he incited a group of slaves to overthrow their master, "I would rather die on my feet than live on my knees!" I think other people have also said this. Most notably, Mel Gibson in *Braveheart*.

⁊⃥

My sister Celeste and I made swords out of tree branches and practiced our swordplay in the backyard.

"Today I'm Conan," she announced proudly.

"No you're the Evil Wizard," I replied. I refused to be the evil wizard because with my dark hair, brown skin and, well, evil personality, I worried about being typecast.

"You were Conan yesterday."

"That's because I'm bigger."

"No, just fatter."

Thunk! Our swords met and the resulting explosion reverberated up our arms. It did not matter that Conan was a man and we were girls; we were all Conan in spirit.

Besides, in the barbarian world, women were just as good fighters as men. Conan had several female sidekicks who fought alongside him (and who often became his lovers.) These women usually had long hair, feisty spirits and exceptionally large breasts. Perhaps there was a connection between hefting a sword and breast growth?

The women were just as much heroes as the men. There was Valeria, who was Conan's first love. She figured prominently in the Conan the Barbarian movie where her purple prose helped to cover her co-star's poor English skills.

Then there was Red Sonja who could not be beaten by any man. A goddess gave Red Sonja's her fighting powers and attached a powerful price: Red Sonja could never take a man as a lover unless he had bested her in battle first. Needless to say, this was quite a drag on Red Sonja's sex life. Only Conan connoisseurs will remember his lost loves: Tetra and Belit. Tetra made it through a couple of stories before she died and was reborn as an evil witch who tried to kill Conan. Somehow this experience did not sour Conan on women. He later fell in love with the Pirate Queen Belit. Belit had been a princess whose ship went down. She convinced a group of Kush pirates (who looked a lot like Africans) that she was a goddess and became their leader. Unfortunately as a Goddess, it was tough for her to show her affection for Conan in front of her crew, as a goddess does not have "needs." I had such regard for Belit and Tetra that I ended up naming two horses after them.

All of Conan's girlfriends were warriors like him; he had no place in his life for skinny little chicks that didn't know how to defend themselves. Conan was very forward thinking for a man who lived in the time before the oceans swallowed Atlantis.

These warrior women were my role models because they reflected the women in my life. Native women were also warriors though not always by choice. They would show up at the band office on Mondays with black eyes, bruised faces and swollen knuckles and tell stories about heroic battles held the weekend before.

"Thought he could just come in and kick me around. Well, I showed him a thing or two."

"He'll think twice about bringing the party back to the house next time."

"Kicked him in the ass, right between the cheeks. Sure taught him a lesson!"

Then they would throw back their heads and laugh, sometimes stopping to cough up a little blood.

From what I could see, Native women were tough as nails. My mom worked anywhere from two to three jobs while looking after all of us plus whichever friend or cousin was staying with us. She changed her own tires and siphoned her own gas. Mom wasn't much of a warrior in the physical sense. She had a wry sense of humour that evolved from watching conflicts rather than from engaging in them. In her mind, it was better to mock the fools than to be one of them. As long as you could run faster than the fools, that is.

When my dad would come thundering home after a week long drinking binge, Mom would pack up quickly and stealthily escape through the other door. Then again, stealth is also part of being a warrior. Many were the times when Conan had to run away from an irate King after sleeping with the wrong Queen.

At school, Natives were assigned the role as the ass-kickers. Even if you were a girl, you were expected to be as tough as a boy. And if you grew up on a reserve, you were doubly tough. In grade one when the girls in the class decided to punish the boys, they enlisted my help as the only Native girl in the class.

"You're tough, Dawn. Go beat up Matt; he's being mean to us," they cooed into my ear.

How did they know I was tough? I wondered. I'd never fought anyone in the class; I'd never fought anyone outside of my immediate family. Perhaps they could sense the Cimmerian blood pumping through my veins.

Or maybe it was just that they saw the way the older Native girls punished one another in the schoolyard. They would throw down their jackets and pull out their long, dangling earrings, and run at each other with abandon. We'd make a ring around them so that they could have their privacy. Then we'd chant "fight, fight, fight!" so that they had proper motivation. The fighters would punch, pull hair, scratch, whatever it took to get the other girl down to the ground. For boys, that might be enough. For these girls, the loser not only had to fall to the ground, she had to stay down. And unlike the boys, these fights didn't end with good-natured handshakes.

My first fight happened when I was ten years old. I was outside of a bingo hall with my brother and sister and older cousins. We were playing on the playground equipment when a thin Native girl and her thin brother claimed the swings next to us. The two groups warily watched each other, each labeling the other group as outsiders.

My cousins were a few years older than me and a lot more foolish. When the little boy started to throw rocks at us, they devised a special punishment for him. They instigated a fight between his sister and me. I knew that this was not a good idea. The girl had not done anything to me and I had done nothing to her. It offended my barbarian sense of justice.

Darren, my older cousin, took me by the shoulders and explained the reasons why the girl needed to be beat down. "It'll be fun!"

I didn't want to fight, but I had to. As a Cimmerian, you couldn't back down. At that time my motto for life was, "What would Conan do?"

The girl was taller than me and had long legs. I remember this quite clearly because she kicked me in the face about five times in quick succession. *Whomp. Whomp. Whomp. Whomp. Whomp.* Her long legs flashed as they rose up to meet my head.

She did not vanquish me. As she tattooed my face with the bottom of her shoe, I managed to keep moving forward, mostly out of confusion. Once I got close enough, I employed my natural hair-pulling ability. I was the hair-pulling champ of my family and I often bragged that I knew seventy-five different ways to pull hair.

We ended up getting pulled apart by a security guard. I was crying. My opponent was crying, although I couldn't understand why since I had clearly gotten my ass handed to me. I suppose even Conan cried after his first fight.

My cousins hurriedly escorted me to their house. They cheered my exploits and flattered my fighting style in the hopes that I wouldn't tell on them. They didn't have to worry; I had no intention of reliving the battle any time soon. I excused myself to the washroom and examined my battle scars. There was a little blood under my nose and my lip was puffy and had its own heartbeat.

As I washed the blood off my face, my hands shook. Even though I was no longer in danger, the memory of the fight hummed through my body. I could not relax and felt like puking. I never wanted to fight again. That desire was incompatible with my love of Conan and with being a Native woman. By Crom, I'd be coming to this bridge again and next time I would be prepared!

I vowed that from now until my next fight, I would train every day. Like when Conan was kidnapped from Cimmeria and sold as a slave to the gladiators, I would train to be a warrior. Every night, to increase my strength, I would do push-ups, wall-sits and take out the garbage. I would beg my parents to enroll me in martial arts classes where I would find a sensei who would mold me into an unstoppable force. I would watch kung fu movies and practice the moves on my siblings.

Several years passed, in which I did nothing to prepare for my next bloody entanglement except read more Conan magazines. My next fight occurred in the seventh grade. There were many bullies at my school that year: older girls who gave you the mean eye and who looked for reasons to exercise their already honed fighting skills, and younger girls looking to establish themselves as "toughs." There were even aspiring Don Kings who went about their day trying to promote fights among the girls.

One of the tough older girls decided that I had called her a bad name and she stalked me in the hallways for weeks. Her name was Crystal and she was three years older than me. She was a single mom bravely going back to school to make something of herself for her child. She kept getting distracted by her frequent smoke breaks, make out sessions with the bus driver and her love of terrorizing the younger girls.

Crystal wasn't extraordinarily big or muscular but she was rumoured to be a fierce and merciless fighter. She wore a lot of makeup and had a feathery haircut tailored to hide her acne-scarred forehead.

I became aware of her dislike for me gradually. It took me awhile to figure out that someone would distinguish me from my group of shy friends. So Crystal had to make it clear. When

I walked past her and her group leaning against the lockers, she whispered to them and they erupted in laughter. When I offered a nervous smile in their direction, they laughed louder.

When my group walked outside the smoker's door to make our way downtown for lunch, she spit inches from my feet.

In the hallways she stepped past me and pushed me with her shoulder as she did. At first I thought she was just clumsy but when she knocked me into the wall and did not pause to see if I was okay or even say "excuse me," I suspected it was personal.

"Umm . . . Crystal . . . are you angry with me?" I asked her, one afternoon. I was nervous. Still I managed to keep my voice relatively normal. However, I had no idea what to do with my hands. They moved around me as I spoke, settling on my hips for a second before migrating towards my tummy.

Crystal pressed her chest up against mine. I took a step back, partly from fear, partly from a natural aversion to touching boobs with another woman.

"Yeah, I am. Got a problem with that?"

"No. Well, yes. I mean you can have a problem with me if you want to . . . ." Was that my voice sounding like I'd sucked back a litre of helium? I cleared my throat. "I guess I'm just wondering, what did I do?"

"You know," she snarled.

I looked around at the people watching our exchange. A crowd of teenagers had gathered, attracted to the smell of conflict. Everyone seemed to be glaring and shaking his or her head at me. "Yes, she is exactly the type of person who would do something and then pretend like she didn't know," their accusatory eyes said.

I wondered whether or not more questions would help or hinder my case. I decided to try again.

"Don't take this the wrong way but I'm not sure what I did. Or didn't do."

She pressed her face closer to mine. Her nicotine-tinged breath warmed my face. "You. Called. Me. A. Bitch."

There was a collective gasp from the onlookers as well as from myself. Her accusation reminded me of the feeling when I set off shoplifting sensors in the mall — even if I had done nothing, I still felt guilty. I ran through my activities for the past few weeks: had I done it? Had I called her a name and then forgotten?

I wasn't one to censor myself that was true. My friends depended upon my unedited commentary for entertainment, but calling someone a name, particularly someone far stronger and meaner than myself? That seemed out of character for a cowardly type. I shook my head. "You must be mistaken Crystal, I would never do that."

"So now I'm a liar?"

I had fallen down the rabbit hole into the nonsensical land of teenage fighting. There was no getting out now. Still I tried. I apologized. She refused to accept it. I stared at her with soft eyes. She glared at me. I backed away. She gave me the finger. We were enemies and there was nothing I could do about it.

My friends Trina and Lucy and I discussed the situation behind the school. Trina was not helpful. "Did she say if she was mad at me?"

"She was too busy hating me."

"She doesn't hate me, right?" asked Trina.

"I don't know."

"Because I always liked her. Maybe I should pass her a note. Is that Crystal with a C or a K?"

My friend Lucy was no more helpful as she described Crystal's frightening prowess as a fighter. "I hear she grew her nails extra-long so she could scar the faces of the girls she fights," Lucy intoned. "They say that none of the girls she's fought have ever been the same again. One girl nearly lost her eye. Now she has a scar right down the middle of her retina. Eye scars never heal completely. That's what they say."

I shuddered. Although I often cursed my greasy, pimpled skin, I also loved its soft plumpness. I stroked my cheeks protectively. "Nobody will ever hurt you," I promised.

That day we headed downtown for lunch. I had just ordered and paid for the single greatest creation known to man, a peanut buster parfait, when the she-devil strode into the Dairy Queen, smacking her gum and glaring at everyone that stood in her way.

This was one of the moments when Crom separates the girls from the Cimmerians. A true Cimmerian would throw the parfait in her face. Then, while she was blinded by caramel and chocolate sauce, would throw a kick at her abdomen all while uttering the deadliest war cry every known to man.

I chose my plan of action from Column B (B for Bashful). In an attempt to avoid her, I slowed my steps. If this move was done correctly, I could avoid eye contact as well as stop myself from crossing in front of her. My shaking hands betrayed me and instead I dropped the tray in front of her and watched as my parfait scattered across the floor. She smirked and stepped over me.

I had no more money for a new parfait so I sat next to my friends who had witnessed the interaction. They did not mention the incident though neither of them offered me any of their ice cream.

I had to find a non-violent solution to this problem. I turned to Ghandi. Somehow he brought the British to their knees without even skinning a knuckle. This appealed to me.

I dove into his book hoping to find some techniques to use against my violent opponent. After I learned that he had done it mostly through starving himself, I put aside his book. I'd been starving myself since I became a teenager and it hadn't helped me conquer shit.

Out of desperation I turned to my parents. I knew my mom's philosophy about fighting, which consisted of running to my aunt's house in the middle of the night. That technique wasn't going to solve this problem. So I turned to my dad.

I think I have consulted my dad exactly once in my life. And this was that one time. When I approached, he was watching television in the big chair. I sat next to him on the couch and laid out the problem to him during a commercial break. Dad realized the import of the situation and turned down the TV.

He took a deep restful breath as he leaned back in his chair. "When I was at school there was a bully." He smiled as he often did whenever he thought about his childhood. "He was a big guy, a boxer."

My dad had attended a Residential school. He had been raised in it. He had started when he was seven years old and had been accelerated two grades by the time he finished his first year. He graduated at the age of seventeen and went to business college until his grandfather, the chief of the reserve, asked him to come home and manage the band's affairs. We knew this via my mother who always relayed everything about my dad. If we hadn't had her, we would know anything about the dark-haired man who ate all the bacon and insisted that we watch hockey on Saturday nights.

My dad continued his story with a glimmer of excitement in his eye. Though most of us would have dismissed his upbringing in the red-brick boarding school as Dickensian, my dad had enjoyed every minute of it. The friends he made there were still his friends and they still had the power to make his laugh echo through the house when they called.

"This guy had been a provincial champ a few years in a row. He got so good no one wanted to go into the ring with him anymore to practice. Then he started picking on the younger students. Every week he would choose a young kid to jump in the boxing ring with him. He'd beat the hell out of them. One day he came up to me in the hallway. He pointed his finger in my face and told me the date and the time. I looked at my friend Irvin. He'd been in the ring the week before and still had a black eye and a cut lip from the lickin' he got. I knew I had no chance of beating the boxer so I had to be smart about it. When the day came for the fight, I was the first one in the gym."

"I know how you like to be on time," I chimed in. My parents' punctuality was legendary.

"It was more than that. I had to be first in the ring for my plan to work. That day I laced up my gloves as fast as I could. They weren't even completely laced when I saw that the Boxer had climbed into the ring. His friend was still lacing his when I made my move. I ran across that ring, pulled back my arm and punched him right in the nose."

My dad sat back in triumph.

I was confused. "When did you beat him up?"

"I didn't. I threw off my gloves and ran out of the ring. The boxer's nose was bleeding so badly he had to go to the nurse." My dad threw back his head and laughed.

I couldn't help but notice that my dad was no Conan. He wasn't even Red Sonja. "Uh, Dad . . . wasn't that a cowardly thing to do?"

My dad looked not a bit embarrassed. "It's not like I had a chance against him."

"You cheated."

"Let me tell you something. It doesn't matter if you beat a bully, you only have to let them know that you won't go down easily."

Now here was something that made sense. Don't go down easy. That was easier to do than win at all costs. Especially since winning at all costs might scar me for life.

I took my dad's advice to heart and resigned myself to fighting the bully, though not in a fair fight. I walked around with a loonie tucked in my hand and waited for Crystal to approach me and invite me outside. I decided this was very Cimmerian of me. After all Conan would not force an enemy's hand but rather would let the enemy come to him. She never did. I suspect that Crystal got her satisfaction from the peanut buster affair and decided, quite rightly, that I wasn't worth it.

A few years later, my sister and I were outside a bingo hall again when my next battle occurred. We were teenagers and had the teenage ability to walk through the middle of town without supervision, which suited my mom and us just fine. My sister and I had escaped from the front door of the bingo hall as three Native girls were going in. "Excuse me," I said politely.

"Why? Did you fart?" retorted one of the girls. It was an old diss, one that I had even used myself on occasion.

However instead of dismissing it as such, I rose to the bait. "Maybe you're smelling yourself," I shot back and kept walking.

My sister and I thought nothing of the encounter as we returned to our conversation, which I am sure was about boys.

We reached our destination, the local arcade. Celeste set up shop in front of a Pac Man game. Celeste was a better than average player and could spend an hour on a single quarter. I stood beside her; my lack of hand-eye coordination had forced me to give up on video games years before. Kimmy, a friend of ours, jogged over when she saw us. "Your mom at bingo?" she asked.

We nodded.

"Yeah, I've been here since this afternoon — it's laundry day." The laundromat was directly across from the bingo hall.

I made room for Kimmy next to the Pac Man machine. She easily slid between two video games. Like my sister, Kimmy was a long stripe of a girl. When I walked between the two of them, it looked like two giraffes were being taken for a walk by a hobbit. Kimmy and I watched as Celeste decimated the ghost population of the Pac Man game.

Someone tapped me on the shoulder. I turned around and saw a young boy standing there.

"My sister wants to fight you," he pointed over his shoulder at a group of girls. My eyesight wasn't the best especially as I refused to wear glasses in an attempt to make my parents get me contact lenses. As a result, the group of girls could have been anywhere from four to twenty depending on their individual size and breadth. All I knew from gazing at their amorphous hateful mass was that they did not like me.

My heart immediately began to pound. It was the age-old fight or flight response kicking in. In my case, it was more flight than fight. I wanted to run out of the arcade back to the bingo hall and cower next to my mom. My pride and the tightness of my jeans prevented that.

I cleared my throat as it had suddenly become thickened with fear. "Tell her I am not afraid to face her on the field of battle; that I will not lie down and allow her bullish stock to rule the world; that here on earth there remain a precious few who will stand up for what is right, what is strong and what is pure."

He rolled his eyes at the tremor in my voice. "When?"

"Anytime, anyplace."

"Can you pick one?"

"She's the one who wants to fight. She can make the arrangements."

He sighed and returned to his sister's side. I turned back to the Pac Man game and pretended to be calm.

"What was that about?" Celeste asked.

"Some girl wants to fight me," I replied casually as if I fought every day, while inside, my colon and spine were melting. Celeste and Kimmy nodded as if they, too, were approached to fight every day of their lives.

My mind began to analyze the situation with military precision. Numbers? Unknown. Fighting arena? Unknown. Fighting strength? Limited. Courage? Too low to gauge. I looked at my two compatriots. "If this girl doesn't fight fair — and it isn't likely that she will — then I will need one or both of you to step in."

Celeste nodded nonchalantly as her Pac Man feasted on another ghost. Kimmy looked slightly less sure.

"I don't know if my mom would like me to fight."

I ignored this. "Can each of you handle two girls? I mean I can handle three, I'm bigger than you two."

Sure, they nodded. Their body language seemed to say that they were almost insulted to be asked that question. However, their eyes shifted back and forth as if they could escape from their heads and therefore from this situation.

I looked around the arcade. It was filled with fifty or so young people and a harried looking middle-aged man. Like me, he surveyed the youth and looked as though he was seriously reconsidering his life choices. Why an arcade? Why not just sell drugs? He shook his head and returned his gaze back to the TV where nubile women danced through music videos. I looked around at the youth, my colleagues and saw my future. Within this group, my future boyfriend, best friend or enemy could be standing in front of an arcade game. These were my peers and in these last few minutes I realized how lucky I was to have them. Fear had made me sentimental.

The boy returned. "She said she'll meet you outside in ten minutes."

"Whatever," I answered, as my heart rate went from zero to sixty. I looked at my back up.

Kimmy's eyes flashed towards the exit sign. "Maybe we need another person."

"There's no time," I replied. If it were possible to hold onto her sleeve and hold her in place, I would have done so. But experience had taught me that you could not restrain people into being your friends.

"My cousin might be at the laundromat." Then before I could stop her, Kimmy slid away from us and scurried out of the arcade.

My sister dragged her gaze away from the Pac Man game. Our shared glance communicated everything: we were fucked.

It was two against six or seven or even eight. I'd been in one other fight and Celeste had never fought anyone except for our younger brother and me. My hair pulling techniques were effective against my sister but how effective would they be against someone who didn't know the rule about not hitting in the face?

Celeste and I had no way of knowing how this battle might escalate. I knew that even if it was tough we could handle it. Now if only my hands would stop shaking and my bowels would stop gurgling.

Pregnant women have told me that the anticipation of pain is always the worst part. I mentally played out scenes from the Savage Sword of Conan. Conan fought men bigger than him all the time and he was never afraid. He jumped in with both feet and his meaty fists raised. I clenched my own fist. It was not meaty. In fact, I could see the blood vessels below the skin, the outline of my slender bones, and covering it all, my smooth, unscarred skin. Such beautiful skin.

My sister continued playing her game. Her self-possession was to be admired. I stood beside her wracking my brain for some way to fix this problem. I was a nerd in school; surely I could make my brain find a non-violent solution to this problem? My brain seemed to disagree.

Perhaps I could walk outside and juggle a few rocks. This would show them that not only was I talented, I was also funny. If only I'd learned to juggle!

Perhaps I could put my oration skills to the test: "Must we fight, my Native sister, when the world has been fighting us for so long?! I say, let us unite against the world." Somehow I knew that would invite a more vicious beating.

Perhaps I could pretend that I was a felon with dangerous fists. "I can't fight you. If I do, the police will lock me up and throw away the key. I'll kill you and not even notice. My fist is registered as a dangerous weapon on six different reserves. I can't tell you which, otherwise I'd have to kill you."

Ten minutes later, my sister and I looked at each other and walked towards the exit. Let it never be said that the Dumont girls were ever late for a fight. Our residential school grandparents had ingrained punctuality into us. Though they might fight over everything else, my parents were never late for anything.

Celeste and I stood on the sidewalk. My fists were already clenched in anticipation of the brawl. A group of girls stood twenty metres in front of us. I had trouble making out their features in the light cast by the dim neon lights of the arcade.

"How many girls are there? Six?" I asked Celeste, under my breath.

"There's eight," she replied.

"Eight!" my voice squeaked out.

Then one girl stepped out in front of the group. She was little more than a blur to me; I got the sense of long dark hair and square shoulders.

"You ready to fight?" my enemy drawled. Her voice came out loud and brash.

"I'm ready." My voice sounded thin and shaky, like it had been drawn through a hose.

The girl and her friends laughed. "You sound scared. You wanna call this off?"

This was my chance. I could back down now, make a silly joke and walk away as if nothing had ever happened. Yes, people would mock me but who cared what every teenager within a hundred kilometres of my house thought of me. It's not like I was Miss Popular. I could stay inside for the remainder of my teen years and then move to New York City when I turned eighteen where nobody knew that I had cowardly backed down from a fight.

But I couldn't walk away. I had ten years of Conan flowing through my veins. Each comic book, each violent storyline, each panel had laid out my future. I was a fighter and fighters fight.

"I want to fight," I said firmly. My voice was still high and reedy but at least my eyes were not tearing up.

The girl and her back up fighters approached Celeste and me. "Remember," I whispered to Celeste, "you have to let them hit you first otherwise you can be charged with assault." This was an urban legend currently circulating among teenagers.

"Fuck that. I'm kicking them as soon as they get close."

Celeste and I held our ground. If we were American history students, one of us would have whispered, "Not until we see the whites of their eyes." For myself, I was going to wait until the girl was within hair-pulling distance. Hopefully, this one would not know how to kick.

As the girls got closer, my heart rate began to slow as if readying itself for the battle that was ahead of us. It was almost as if my body knew what to do. I can do this, I thought to myself just as a deep voice rang through the air.

"Hey!"

Every eye turned towards the right. In the doorway of the laundromat there stood a tall, dark-haired woman. Her long black hair outlined a tough masculine face — it was as though a Cimmerian woman had been transported through space and time to the streets of this Saskatchewan valley-town.

"You girls want trouble?" She crossed the distance from the laundromat in two steps with her tree trunk legs. I had no idea which side she was on until she came to stand in front of my sister and me. She stared into the face of my enemy. My enemy stared back with widening eyes.

In a low, quiet voice our Cimmerian growled, "Which one of you has a problem with my cousin?"

It might have been the timbre of her voice, the muscles in her biceps or the confidence with which she held herself that made all eight girls take a step backwards.

The lead girl sought to save her dignity. "Not your cousin, just this girl," she said pointing at me. I had no idea what was going on. I wasn't even sure who this barbarian woman was. I hoped we were related.

"They're all my cousins," the Cimmerian shot back.

"Yeah, all right," my enemy nodded as if they had made a deal that was to her liking. She backed away into her crowd. They absorbed her and as a group they went back into the arcade.

My sister and I stared at our unknown hero. Kimmy skipped out of the laundromat. "This is my cousin, Freda."

What do you say to someone who has saved you from a beating? Who has saved your ego, personal dignity and facial skin — three things that are invaluable to teenage girls?

"Hey," I said awkwardly. Celeste hung back shyly.

Freda barely acknowledged us as she gave her cousin a quick lecture. "You girls shouldn't be fighting," she said as she wandered back into the laundromat to finish folding her laundry. I'm sure she had no idea of what she'd done for us. In her eyes, this was a silly, pre-teen drama, one of many that would play themselves out on that street that night.

It was life changing for me. I knew at that moment that I would never be a warrior. If there were girls like Freda out there, my fighting career was over before it had begun. Even having someone like Freda on your side was frightening. Perhaps you could learn to resemble a Cimmerian but that was nothing compared to actually being one.

My sister and I headed back to the bingo hall where we sat beside our mom and harassed her into buying us junk food. We never discussed our adventure. Not because we were secretive — I certainly wasn't. Relating my adventures to my mom was one of the highlights of my day. I couldn't tell her this story because there was no way of telling the story that would make me look good.

Perhaps Conan was not the right hero for me. Perhaps I needed a mentor who offered a peaceful alternative, someone who did not need to prove their worth by separating a man's limbs from his body or a woman's hair from her head. There was one epic character who was currently dominating my thoughts at this time: a man who fought, not with a sword, but with great stick-handling skills; a man who would not be drawn into battle, but would only skate faster than the men who sought to bring him down; a man who defeated his enemy with goals rather than with landed punches. Swiftly my mantra changed from what would Conan do, to what would Wayne Gretzky do? Now all I had to do was learn how to skate.

THE LONG ROAD TO FREEDOM

I REALIZED BY THE AGE OF TEN THAT I could never have a social life if I didn't learn to drive. We lived on the reserve where houses were miles apart and it didn't matter how much you liked walking or how good you were at it, you could not reach a cute guy's house before the coyotes started howling. Our closest neighbours were half a mile away and they were our relatives and worse, not cute guys, just Jolene and Adelle, a pair of sisters about the same age as my sister and me.

We took turns travelling the distance; we walked across the road, down the horse path, into the corral, and then, finally, squeezed ourselves through the electric fence. That last obstacle always put a little spring in your step after the long walk. Once we reached our destination, we lamented about the lack of fun things to do on the reserve. "Someday," I said, "we will have guys coming to OUR houses to pick us up." Nobody believed that, not even me. We would have to learn to drive or else resign ourselves to setting up a sewing circle.

Our driving lessons began with the tractor. Someone had abandoned it in our uncle's field and we claimed it as our first motor vehicle. It was older than all of us put together. Still, it was better than walking. It took five kids to start the grumpy old thing: two of us at the front cranking it, two of us working the sticky gear shift, and one to let out the clutch at the appropriate time. Then the tractor would jump forward and begin rolling. Everyone would climb on and we would enjoy the ride for the entire three minutes that the tractor ran.

Even though the ride was short and had few thrills, driving it taught us the basics of vehicle ownership. For instance, we learned that operating a motor vehicle is often more trouble than it's worth. It took at least half a day of tightening nuts and bolts, pouring diesel over the engine and cranking, to get the tractor started. The ratio of fun to work was around one to three hundred. Despite our dislike of hard work, we persevered, as the ratio of fun to sitting on our butts in front of the television with only two channels was around one to one thousand and one. One channel played only hockey, the other, only Ukrainian programming. By the age of seven, I had seen enough shumka dancing for a lifetime.

The tractor also taught us vehicle safety. Such as you should never put a vehicle into motion until you know exactly where your bratty little brother is. Fortunately for him, David had great reflexes. Every time we nearly ran him over, he threw rocks at us as we bounced to our destination a few feet away. Then we would be forced to jump off the tractor and chase him down and deliver our revenge "charley horses" on him.

We learned to plan ahead. This is an important skill when you are operating a vehicle that eats gasoline like a big butt eats thin sweat pants. In fact, when gas is in short supply, you should know your destination before you leave the yard. Otherwise, you would run out of gas on your own driveway as your drivers argued over whose turn it is to decide where to go.

We abandoned the tractor the day Uncle Johnny started leaving his car keys in the care of his girls. Johnny was a mechanic and let the girls move his cars around the yard. They never hit anything or killed anyone (bigger than a cat) so he entrusted them with the keys when he left for bingo.

Like Celeste and me, they were a sister-sister team but their relationship didn't follow the usual sibling rules. For one thing, Adelle could never lead her sister. Jolene pretty much did whatever she wanted and when Adelle tried to assert herself they would scrap it out. As a big sister, I sympathized with Adelle.

Younger siblings were supposed to respect the older sibling, not bang them over the head with hockey sticks when they weren't looking. I imagined only Napoleon's older brother had it harder than Adelle. She coped by yelling at her sister and when that didn't work, Adelle would throw up her hands in disgust or deliver a stinging pinch. For my part, I tried to keep my sister away from Jolene's influence. Our relationship was delicately balanced, a little in my favour, and I did not need anyone disturbing it.

The sisters would drive over to our house after everyone had left for the bingo hall. Neither girl was sixteen, yet they both felt confident behind the wheel.

"My dad says I should have my license already," Jolene said, "cuz I'm such a good driver."

"He never said that! He said you shouldn't drive off the reserve without a license or else he would kick your ass," Adelle said.

"How come he lets you guys drive without a license?" Celeste asked.

Adelle shrugged. "Prolly cuz he doesn't have one either."

Though we assured her that the girls were competent drivers, Mom banned us from riding with them. Each time she left for bingo, she would threaten us. "If either of you gets in that car with those girls, I will spank your asses red."

My sister Celeste and I were thirteen and fourteen, way past spanking age. We no longer feared our mom in any way. We were pretty scared of our dad. Luckily, he was only around once in a while. He was the wildcard that made us think twice before doing something bad.

"What are the chances of Dad getting home tonight?"

"Maybe one in eight."

"Of him getting home to not getting home? Or the other way?"

"Don't ask me, I hate math."

So whenever Jolene and Adelle came over, we all jumped in the car to head off on a new adventure. Adelle never went over forty kilometres an hour. That was okay because it made the ride seem longer. Jolene always drove fast which made us feel more like adults. Every once in a while a dog or bird or a plane in the sky would distract her. Her attention would drift and the car would follow. One of us would have to yell at her to get her focus. At such moments, us passengers would think that walking might not be so un-cool after all.

Jolene and Adelle drove over one day and told Celeste and me some exciting news: Shane's family had moved back to the File Hills. They had been our best friends for years before family strife had forced them to move away. They had left in the middle of the night without warning and we hadn't heard from them since. We hadn't seen them in over four years.

Normally if we received news like this we would have to wait to tell our mom, then wait for her to ask around and then wait for her to remember to tell us, then wait for her to do something about it. With access to transportation we could cut out the middle-mom. Jolene drove us directly to Shane and Dylan's new house in twenty minutes.

As we pulled up in the yard, my palms began to sweat as they did every time I encountered a new situation. "You're sure this is the place?"

Jolene nodded. "Yup, my dad came here to drop off their new truck. They bought the orange truck off him."

The truck was gone but there was a black car parked in the yard so we decided to try our luck. We got out and walked up to the front steps.

"What do you think they'll say?" I asked Celeste.

"I don't know. Probably they'll just be happy to see us."

I hoped so. We had missed them a lot. Adelle and Jolene were our best cousins but Shane and Dylan were our best friends. After they left, it seemed like the fun had been drained out of our lives.

We knocked on the door. Nobody answered. We tried again with no results. Jolene honked her horn. We looked at the windows. Even if someone didn't want company, a horn usually resulted in a curtain twitch at the very least.

"We can come back later," Jolene said, and revved the motor. She wanted to go to the store.

We jumped back in the car and pulled out of the driveway so fast that gravel spun out from her tires and hit the side of the house.

"Smart'en up, Jolene!" Adelle called from the back seat. Jolene and Adelle could not sit next to one another without fighting so I sat in the front seat instead. I grabbed for my seat belt and tried to find the clasp for it.

We were a few minutes away from the house when we noticed a car following us. From her view in the backseat, Celeste noticed it first. "Hey, that car is moving fast."

I looked in the rearview mirror. "Jolene, did you notice that car?"

Jolene checked her mirror and nearly drove off the road as she did so. "I see dust."

"Uh . . . it's there — don't check! I'll tell you if it gets closer."

It pulled up next to us.

"He's not giving me any room," Jolene complained. She beeped her horn and our car veered off the road again.

"How about I'll control the horn?" I asked as I leaned over and beeped the horn helpfully.

The car continued to move towards us. "What the hell-" Jolene struggled with the wheel as our car swerved in the thick gravel on the side of the road.

"What a dummy! Don't they know there's just a kid driving?" I asked.

Adelle came to the solution quickly. "Brake!"

Jolene sped up.

Adelle got mad. "Brake! You stupid idiot!"

Jolene pressed the pedal harder. She smiled and glanced in the rearview mirror to witness the reddening of her sister's face. I said nothing, as I was too busy watching my rather short life passing before my eyes; I noted that I had spent most of it eating pork chops and sneaking potato chips out of the cupboard.

"Hey, Jolene, how about braking so we can see who it is?" Celeste said.

"Okay!" Jolene stopped the car suddenly.

Adelle bounced forward and hit her sister's seat in front of her because her seat belt no longer worked. "You bastard!"

she yelled and reached for Jolene's arm to pinch her. Jolene dodged her in the front seat.

The other car drove past us. Then it stopped and began to back towards us.

"We're all going to be murdered." Adelle was sure of it. "And then I'm gonna get in shit cuz I'm the oldest."

"Who the fuck is that?" Jolene directed her question at us even though the driver of the other vehicle was standing at her window.

It was Dylan. He was older and had a mustache. Other than that he looked the same, he had not grown much. He was still thin and you could see that he would never be a big man. He peered in the window. Jolene rolled it down so he could get a better look at us.

"Jolene? Dawn? Adelle? Celeste! What are you guys doing here?"

"We came to visit you."

He didn't seem to know what to make of this information. "Well, sorry I ran you off the road."

"Why did you do that?"

"It was a strange car and you were driving all over the place. I thought it was a bunch of drunks." He leaned back on his heels and stared down the road. "You guys should start heading home, it'll get dark soon."

That was it? No invitation to stay and visit with him? No promise to come visit us soon?

"Where's Shane?" I asked.

"He went to town."

"Tell him that we came to see him, okay?" I said.

Dylan nodded and returned to his car.

I glanced at Celeste; she looked puzzled by Dylan as well. Maybe Dylan was so used to leaving people behind that he didn't really care anymore when they were reunited.

Even though we were disappointed by Dylan's reaction, we were still excited by our adventure. We had gone on a mission, faced danger and succeeded. Now we only had to figure out how to bribe our brothers into secrecy.

Our parents didn't understand our desire to see the world. Mom said we should count ourselves lucky because at least we had a TV. "When I was younger, we had nothing to do except chase each other around with a hammer. That was our fun. Nothing but hammer time, day and night."

Dad was no help either; he would only tease us when we complained about our lack of travel. "If you never go anywhere but school, when you do go to school, it's like a treat."

Ha, ha.

So whenever Jolene or Adelle pulled up in the front yard, we immediately reached for our shoes. Because we usually had to baby-sit our brothers, we would take turns going on rides in various permutations of Celeste and Jolene or Adelle and me.

One night I went on the first ride with Jolene as my driver, leaving Adell behind to baby-sit. We had no place to go so we decided to investigate a newly built road. Someone had built their house a few miles from the main road forcing the reserve to construct a road just for them. We had seen the grader going in and out of the driveway for months. It was the longest driveway on the reserve; it wound itself through four kilometres of brush and cropland.

Jolene loved curvy roads. "I feel like a race car driver," she said, as she moved the steering wheel with expert ease.

We felt like grown-ups taking a drive through the countryside as we gossiped about our sisters. The topic then turned to boys. I had not seen a boy in two months so I had little to say on the subject except to reiterate for the 1,008th time that I would probably marry Corey Haim.

Jolene, on the other hand, had ongoing flirtations with several boys from her mother's reserve up north — the infamous — Whitefish Reserve. According to Jolene and Adelle, anything was possible on Whitefish. It was a combination of Las Vegas, New Orleans and New York City, except better because Whitefish also had bush parties. This topic so consumed us that we didn't immediately notice when she began to lose control of the car. It happened slowly and then speeded up quickly. The car swayed way over to the left, so Jolene pulled the wheel way over to the right. The car fought back and we veered left again. The car began to move sideways, and then slowly turn itself around. Jolene made a stuttering sound with her mouth, it sounded like, "whhhhatttt the hellll . . . "

I kept my mouth shut, afraid that even a word could unbalance the car. For a second it seemed she had gained control. It was a short-lived hope and a second later the car was skidding off the road, then over onto its roof where it settled in the ditch.

The accident happened just like in the movies. During the worst part of it, everything moved in slow motion — real slow motion since we were only going about thirty kilometres an hour. My life didn't pass before my eyes, only gravel, dirt and small weeds that pressed against my window.

I had closed my eyes at some point in the accident and when I opened them, I found myself lying on the roof of the

DAWN DUMONT

car, in the back seat. Jolene was at my feet. I nudged her with my knee and her head came up. "What?" she asked.

"I smell gas," I said. If this accident was like the ones in the movies, then, in seconds, flames would consume the car and light up the Saskatchewan night for miles.

Jolene said she didn't smell anything as she felt around the ceiling for her other earring. "Why did my earrings fall out? That's weird."

"Forget your earring. We have to get out before we are burned alive!" I tried to open my car door but the sides of the ditch held it closed. "It won't open! Try yours!"

Jolene yawned and scratched her head. She did not seem to understand the dire nature of our situation, so I took a page from the book of Adelle and pinched her arm. "Ow! You ass!" she cried.

"Open your door!" I commanded.

Jolene made a face at me. She tried her door. It would not open either.

"We're trapped!" I said. "We are trapped in an upside down car and we are going to be burned alive . . . like . . . like . . . h amburgers." It was the best I could come up with under the circumstances.

Jolene was not convinced this was an emergency. She lay back down. "I'm tired."

"Don't fall asleep, you'll die!"

I rummaged through the back seat — now the ceiling of the car — and found a bottle and an old sock. I put the sock on my hand and hit the window with the bottle. The window smashed; I cleared away the glass with the bottle and crawled through. I was proud of my ingenuity and remarked up on it several times during the next half hour.

Jolene followed behind me and said little except, "Why did my earring fall out? That's so weird."

It was a warm night, which was good because we had a long walk to the nearest house. A young man we had not yet met answered the door. His name was Super Dave. He laughed when he heard about the accident. Then he asked if we were okay.

I nodded. "There aren't any visible injuries . . . but there might be internal bleeding. You never know."

He climbed in his truck and drove us home. As we passed the car, he stopped and inspected it. He let out a low whistle. "Did that window break in the roll? You girls are lucky you didn't get cut up."

Jolene pointed at me. "No, she broke it."

"Only because we were trapped inside the car and I could smell gas!" My hysteria returned as I recalled our close call.

"Why didn't you just roll the window down?" Super Dave asked.

It was a simple question. I could not formulate an answer that did not make me seem like a total idiot. Instead I said that my leg hurt and asked him to hurry so I could go put ice on it.

❧

When Super Dave dropped us off at the house, Adelle and Celeste were annoyed that we had taken so long. Their annoyance turned into relief when they heard what had happened.

"I am so glad I didn't go first," Celeste proclaimed. "Because Mom and Dad are going to kill you."

Adelle was upset at Jolene. "We have to go get the car."

"How are we going to do that?"

"We'll walk and then when we get there, we'll tip the car over."

"Can we do that?" I knew Adelle was strong — I had seen her lose her temper when some boys had teased her about her weight — but this was a whole car, not a couple of teenagers.

"Yes, you just tip it. Tip it."

Adelle kept repeating the phrase over and over again. Jolene ignored her and went to watch TV in the living room.

My gut was sore. Not from the accident itself, from the anticipation of all the trouble I was in. If it were only Mom, I would have been fine. She yelled, but her yelling was powerless, and if I pretended my leg hurt, she would calm right down. Unfortunately for me, my dad had recently rejoined the family circle. And like my mom, he was a firm believer that we ought to stay out of cars driven by Adelle and Jolene.

I decided that we should alert Uncle Johnny to the accident. Jolene was against this plan. Adelle was on the fence and Celeste thought it was a good idea because she figured it would be more interesting than anything that was currently on TV.

I shared my rationale. "If Uncle Johnny finds out about the accident at bingo, then he'll have time to get over it. That way he won't be so mad when he gets home."

The girls looked unconvinced. In retrospect, I can see the flaw in my reasoning. Telling our parents at bingo interrupted their good time and also gave their anger more time to grow. I know that now.

We made the phone call to the bingo hall and paged my uncle. By the time he got to the phone, he sounded anxious.

"Who's this? What's going on?"

"Uncle Johnny?"

"Yes. Who's this?"

"It's Dawn. Your niece."

"Right, what's wrong?"

"You see, your car. It's been in an accident." I commended myself on my choice of words. It wasn't anyone's fault, really, rolling over and totaling themselves was just something cars did.

"Was anyone hurt?"

"Well, my leg hurts a little but it's not as bad as the time I got my tonsils out--"

"Let me talk to Adelle."

I handed the phone to Adelle and gave her an apologetic look.

"It's Jolene's fault! She's in the living room. Jolene! Jolene! She's not listening. Because she never listens! I told them not to go! I'm not stupid, you're stupid, Dad!"

Adelle hung up the phone. Now we just had to wait.

When my parents arrived home, I knew I was in big trouble. It was clear from the way my mom rushed into the house before my dad. I could hear his booming laugh on the steps of the porch as he exchanged accident stories with my uncle.

Mom grabbed my arms and pushed me towards my bedroom. "Go to sleep."

"What about Dad?"

"Go to sleep!"

I sat on the edge of my bed in the dark room. This was not going to solve anything. Mom was judging the situation based on what she would do. Her temper was like porridge; it was hot, but if you ignored it, it quickly turned cold. Dad's temper only got hotter and hotter until it was vented.

The next sound I heard was Dad's big booming voice. "Where is Dawn?" I stood up in the dark.

My mom answered for me. "Oh, she's tired."

"Tired from what? Rolling cars! Is that what makes people tired? Accidents?"

My stomach could not take it anymore. I opened the bedroom door and padded into the kitchen. Dad stood by the cupboards and pondered his rhetorical questions at the top of his lungs.

"I'm sorry." I hung my head.

"You should be sorry! You ruined your uncle's car."

"Adelle said she could tip it over?"

"Tip it over! Tip it over!" My dad was incredulous. "Is that your answer for everything?"

This was normal. My dad's temper often grew so hot that it melted his reason. "I did not raise you to tip over cars! We drive cars! That's what we do! Not you. And not your cousins! You don't drive cars! I drive cars!"

"I'm sorry."

"Sorry for what? Sorry that you got caught or sorry that you rolled?"

I wasn't going to take a chance on that one.

Mom decided it was time for a story of woe. Her voice took on the sad tone she normally reserved for discussing the Holocaust. "We pulled up beside the car and your uncle got out and all he could say was 'it's totaled. It's totally totaled.'" As she imitated Uncle Johnny, her voice dropped to a sad whisper.

My dad ignored her. "You could have died! You could have killed someone! And what about your brother and sister, who was watching them?!"

At this point, my brother and sister were standing in the kitchen behind him, each of them leaning against the cupboards counting their lucky blessings that they had decided to wait for the second car ride that night.

The yelling continued for a few minutes longer. I was grounded, which normally had no effect on us except that the next night was Halloween, ironically the only night when we got to leave the house.

I knew I had done wrong and I served my punishment without complaint.

Jolene, on the other hand, went out trick or treating. She came by the house dressed as a raccoon. Adelle was dressed as a clown.

"Wasn't your dad mad?" I asked.

"Yeah. He was really mad." Jolene seemed unconcerned.

I looked to Adelle for comprehension. Adelle rolled her eyes. "She never listens."

"Anyone wanna go for a ride?" Jolene dangled a set of car keys from her finger.

❧

When I was fifteen, my mom took me to Fort Qu'Appelle to write my Learner's test. It was no surprise to my mom when I passed the written portion. "Just like me. I passed on my first time too," Mom crowed.

In our province, the Learner Permit allowed you to drive at any time as long as there was an adult driver next to you. On the reserve, this requirement was pushed to its limit to include situations such as, "permission to drive your mom around after she's had a few," "permission to drive your unlicensed uncles to the store to pick up smokes," and "permission to drive your cousins home after midnight because you're all making too much noise and Mom is too tired to do it."

After six months of supervised practice driving, you were allowed to do the test. To keep my fear at a minimum, Mom described the driving test in detail. "It's the worst half hour of your life. They're gonna make you parallel park and you have to be twelve centimetres from the curb. If you're off by even one centimetre, it's all over."

Mom was in charge of teaching me to drive. She didn't just have the regular class six license; she also had the class eight license. If the class six exam required you to drive to hell and back, the class eight exam made you drive around each of the rings of hell in perfect concentric circles, backwards.

Driving lessons with Mom were perfect training for the test because they were also had the taint of hell on them. Mom was an exacting teacher. If you made a mistake, she bellowed in your ear or sucked in her breath in the manner of someone who had accidentally swallowed a lit cigarette.

I would quickly lose my temper. "What! What did I do?'

"Oh nothing. You only failed to come to a complete stop back there. Do you know what the instructor would do if you made a rolling stop? Do you?"

"Fail me?"

"If you're lucky! And you're not lucky so he'd probably make you get out of the driver's seat and drive you straight back to the test agency and tell you to wait another six months for your license."

"Oh god."

Normally, if you failed your exam, you had to wait two weeks before you could book again. By virtue of her class eight license, Mom claimed internal knowledge of the working of the provincial licensing department.

"And they hate, hate, hate it when people chew gum while they drive. Let me tell you."

"How does gum affect my driving?"

"Can you think and chew and drive all the same time? Who are you Mario Andretti?"

I rolled down the window and spit out my gum.

Mom learned to drive when she was thirty years old. Before then she was completely reliant on others for transportation. With four kids and an errant husband, this meant a lot of weekends stuck at home. A friend laid down the facts for her: she could never leave a man on foot. After a few weeks of instruction on the reserve's grid roads, she went and passed her test.

This is why her teaching style blended instruction with motivational fear tactics. "Do you want to be trapped for the rest of your life? Do you want your grocery shopping to be done at the nearest convenience store? Because I am not going to drive you around like Miss Daisy! No way, Jose. You get your ass into that car and start driving right now."

She taught the basics well. Parallel parking, shoulder checking, awareness of blind spots and signaling — these were tested and retested until I was a highly capable driver. Mom's problem was she always took it one step too far. "When you pass a car, you have to stay exactly two metres from the car. Exactly!"

I got tired of her rules and sought help elsewhere. "Dad, can you teach me? Mom is driving me crazy."

My dad could understand that. She drove him crazy too. He was a confident driver, the type of person who in the case of an accident would assume that the car was at fault, or the dog or the train. He laughed at my frustration. "Just tune her out."

"It's kind of hard when she's sitting right next to you," I whined.

Besides, she wouldn't let me play the radio or daydream. Whenever she saw my eyes glaze over as I contemplated my new life as a licensed driver, Mom would slap my arm and awaken me to reality.

"Oh no, you're not having any fun yet. Not on my watch!" she said.

Without taking his eyes off the TV, Dad reluctantly put on his jacket and threw the car keys at me. "Let's head to the valley. I'll grab a coffee," he said.

Driving with Dad was immediately cooler than with Mom. He didn't wear his seat belt and he didn't expect anyone else to do so either. Instead of critiquing every inch of road driven and smacking his lips against his teeth, Dad stared straight ahead and tuned me out. It was twenty kilometres to Lebret and with each one my confidence grew, perhaps too quickly. I drove down the hill heading towards Lebret and left my foot on the gas. Our speed increased and then doubled, then tripled. The short stubby trees that dotted the hills began to fly by.

"Slow down." The words were delivered in an emotionless monotone. He knew his order made perfect sense and expected it to be carried out immediately.

It was a simple request and normally I would have calmly stepped on the brake. Before I did, I glanced at the speedometer and panicked when I saw the needle was way over the sixty kilometres that I was used to. I stomped on the brake. The car squealed in outrage and we skidded uncomfortably close to the three hundred metre drop on Dad's side of the car.

"What the hell!" My dad jumped back from his window.

The car slowed to a turtle pace. I gave Dad an apologetic smile. "Whoops."

"Why would you do that?" He stared at me as though he had just discovered me.

"I slowed down like you said."

"You stomped on the brake. Why would you stomp?"

I shrugged. "The brakes are touchy."

"You have to be smooth. Do you understand?"

"Should I start again?"

"No. Pull over." He opened his car door and walked around to the driver's side.

"Dad!" It was too late. My dad had retired as a driving instructor and would never be lured out of retirement again.

⁂

The first driver's test did not go as planned. Expectations were high in any event. Not only did I expect to pass; I wanted a perfect score to wave in my mom's face. "See, I AM Mario Andretti. Suck your breath in now!"

The instructor was a masculine-looking woman who simultaneously chewed gum and sucked on her teeth.

"Turn here." *Smack. Sigh. Smack.*

"Turn here." *Smack. Sigh. Smack.*

"How am I doing?"

"No comment." *Smack. Sigh. Smack.* "Pull over a bit, you're too close to the middle of the street."

She directed me out of the city for the two-point turn. I executed it flawlessly and knew my mother would have been proud. Then I turned and drove back towards the city. The instructor asked for another parallel park in front of the motor vehicle department. Parallel parking was my mom's specialty and I almost laughed as I pulled in and turned the wheels perfectly.

She made a notation on her clipboard and told me to follow her in.

I walked in behind her. She went behind the counter. I waited. *Smack. Sigh. Suck.* "Well, you got a perfect score."

"Yes!"

"I had to correct you once and that's an automatic fail."

My eyes began blinking of their own accord. "What?"

"Better luck next time." She turned her attention to her next victim. "Keller? Keller!"

I took my results out to the parking lot where my mom waited.

"Well?"

I could not speak. Mom took the form out of my hand and looked at it. Then she patted me on the shoulder and said nothing.

After two weeks of more lessons, I passed the second test with ease. Everything fell into place. The instructor was a happy looking guy who took pity on my sad eyes and nervous smile. The test was short, only fifteen minutes. Then the instructor shook my hand, "pleasure doing business with you," and handed me my license sheet.

I walked out the door proudly knowing that from now on I was free to go wherever I wanted, to visit whomever I wanted — forever.

I forgot to read the small writing. The cars were my parents' and the keys were often in their pockets, which meant I was still at their mercy.

"Why did I work so hard to get my license if you weren't planning on letting me go anywhere!" I cried in frustration.

"Life is unfair," Mom sang.

"My house, my rules," Dad harmonized behind her.

They were right: life was unfair. Life was also ironic because the last I heard Jolene still did not have her driver's license. And reportedly, she still does not listen.

WE'LL TAKE THE WHITE ONE

M Y MOM WAS THE FAIREST CHILD IN a family of twelve children — a family that large can be legally called a "litter." Mom's hair before it was grey used to be cinnamon coloured and her skin now cinnamon coloured, used to be white. If we were black, she'd be known as the light-skinned one. Being Native, however, she was just called the fair one or the *monias iskwew*, which means white girl in Cree. Her brother, John, was the next fairest kid.

Mom's fair skin made a big difference in her life. When she was in her early twenties, people thought she was white so she didn't have to deal with the racism that was around at the time. She worked a series of jobs in which she sort of spied on the white people around her. She worked for the lawyer who defended the men in the infamous murder of a young Cree woman in The Pas, Manitoba. When we pumped her for inside information, she only commented, "The lawyer was very nice. Loved animals a lot. And he was enormously fat."

She talked about being invited to parties that her Native-looking friends and family would not be invited to. "I never thought it was such a big deal, the racism. I floated back and forth. Never ashamed, mind you. It just wasn't a big deal to me."

Mom's skin also allowed her to date men who were not Native. "I could have married this white RCMP officer, not sure why I didn't," she'd say casting a sidelong glance at our dark-skinned dad lying on the couch.

The story she liked to tell the most happened when she was a child. She was six when a car owned by a white couple drove up her family's long driveway and parked in their yard. (This was unusual: not that white people had cars — at the time *only* white people had cars. I know it sounds crazy, but this was rural Saskatchewan. We only got running water in the late 1970s. Then we lost it in 1985. Then we got it back in 1986, but we couldn't drink it. Hopefully, this problem will be resolved before the end of the twenty-first century.)

The unusual part was that a white couple was even on the reserve. The world was still segregated back then. Whites did not go near the reserve. Indians did not leave. Although the Indians did not have a choice in the matter, it was illegal to leave the reserve without a permit from the local Indian agent until the late 1960s.

According to my mom, Indian agents abused their power. Some would withhold food rations to make people do their bidding. One agent had affairs with Native girls and when he knocked them up, he forced them to marry single dudes on the reserve. Apparently the job description for Indian agents began with the phrase, "Have you always wanted to visit the prairies and be a huge douche bag to Native people?"

So when a Caucasian couple drove to the reserve, it was a big deal. They and their family were not strangers to Native people. They bought hay and produce from enterprising Native businessmen who snuck off the reserve in the middle of the night to sell it to white farmers. The couple had even hired young Native guys to labour on their land. And like everyone else, they had seen the Native families when they came to town, the mothers wearing a tail of children. Perhaps they had seen this particular family and made their decision then.

Finding your way through the reserve is a tricky business. For one thing, there are no road signs and no addresses. People find their way by memory or else with the help of a guide. Directions are no help unless you've been there a few times, because they tend to sound like, "Turn at the hill that looks like a buffalo hump. Then keep driving past Rabbit Hill, take a right at the old Nokusis place and then a left at the new Nokusis place. If you reach the old, old Nokusis place, you've gone too far."

When they arrived, my grandfather's yard was full of activity. The couple must have been momentarily entranced by the chaos: chickens, horses, pigs, goats, dogs, and children running to and fro.

Some of the children were in the midst of chores, others in the midst of avoiding them. The kids pulled away from their activities and picked their way carefully through the various types of animal shit to look at the car and the couple more closely. They ran their hands over the car. They stared at the couple who smiled in a friendly way to them. After a minute or two, the kids grew bold and asked them a few questions, "Would you like to buy some eggs? How about some milk? We got goat and cow milk if you want."

Experience had taught the kids that white people meant money and the kids weren't afraid of money.

The man and woman introduced themselves to the children and began to ask them their various ages. The kids shouted their ages proudly. "Ten" "Nine" "Six" "Twelve" "Four" "Seven!"

About this time my grandfather William made his way out of the barn. He invited them to join him inside the house for tea served by my grandmother, Rose.

Grandma Rose was friendly in a careful way. She washed her hands free from flour and asked them to sit at the table. She was polite to white people but did not trust them. Grandma had attended the Indian Residential School in the valley and still remembered people in white sheets standing outside the school in the middle of the night, their hoods illuminated by the candles they carried.

Then her oldest daughter, Edith, had married a white guy and moved to British Columbia. The man was nice enough; his family was not. In an effort to fit in, Edith was pretending to be Italian. It made Grandma laugh to think of her daughter pulling the wool over her in-laws eyes but it wasn't a happy laugh.

My grandfather knew his way around the white world. He had attended university for a degree in music. He spoke four languages: English, Cree, French and Ukrainian. He felt comfortable sitting in the kitchen of any of the white farmers living around the reserve. It helped that he didn't look like the stereotypical Native: his eyes were grey, his skin was light brown and he often had a full beard courtesy of his Metis ancestors.

My grandfather figured the white people had stopped by to buy some chickens or vegetables from his immense garden. When you have twelve children, you can have a huge garden. And when you have a dozen kids, you probably should have a huge garden.

The couple got right to the point. They wanted to adopt a child. They pointed out the window at a five years old girl playing with her siblings. She was the fairest of my grandparents' children.

"It would be easier for her to fit in," explained the woman.

"We would be able to give her a good home," said the man.

"If you can't part with her," the woman offered, "we could also take one of your boys. That one is also very fair."

I was not there that day (my mom was only five years old after all). I can imagine the look on my grandpa's face (red) and the nature of his language (profane). From the facts available to me, the couple left quickly after making their request, and did not return.

My mom grew up knowing this story and it gave her a sense of importance. She even went so far as to find out where that unlucky couple lived. One day, our family drove by their place on our way to Melville, one of the larger small towns in the area. "That could have been my house," she said, pointing at a large ranch-style house.

The house was impressive. It had four bedrooms (at least), a kitchen, a dining room and a breakfast nook. And could it be? Yes, there was even a pool sparkling in the backyard.

"They're millionaires," she sighed. "Can you imagine how rich I'd be?"

Mom rested her head on her seat and considered her wealth.

This thought was somewhat unsettling to my eight-year-old mind. "What about us? Would you still have had us?"

She looked into the backseat and studied our brown faces and dirty limbs encased in (from what I can tell from the photographs) colourful striped polyester shorts and tops that covered only three quarters of our round bellies.

"How would I know?" she said airily, her voice and diction already whiter.

I looked up at my dad, dark and quiet in the driver's seat. And I wondered, would he have tracked her down to the white people's house? Or would he have found a different Native wife? And would my mom have married a Native, or a white man? And if she'd married a white man, would we be her kids? Or Dad's?

It was a difficult question. Truth be told, I'd have preferred to be my mom's kid swimming in her deliciously cool-looking pool.

Then I looked down at my brown skin and knew that if I'd been in Grandpa's yard I'd have never made the cut. Nor would my little brother, David, who was a tiny, pudgy version of my dad. My sister, Celeste, had fair skin and honey coloured hair — now she stood a chance of being picked. But she was such a mischief, tantrum-thrower and all round wild Indian that any white people unwise enough to have picked her would have surely brought her back the next day.

By the time I finished considering this, we were safely back on the reserve where we belonged.

When it came time to pick a high school, my parents had a choice of sending us to an all-Native boarding school or to a mainstream school about half an hour away.

The boarding school was one of those "Indian Residential" Schools that had a terrible reputation for abusing Aboriginal people for decades, though my parents didn't quite understand why.

My dad had attended a red-bricked Residential school from ages seven to seventeen and my mom for two years when she was a teenager. Neither of them had any complaints. "Just a school like any else," Mom would say, "I don't see what the big deal is about them."

A year after he was enrolled at the school, the nuns and priests at the school decided that my dad's last name, "Day Walker," was too Native-sounding and changed it to "Walker."

Mom figured they meant well. "They knew he'd have an easier time fitting in if he didn't have a damned Native name ruining his chances for jobs and whatnot." I looked over at my dad's dark skin, raven black hair and hawk nose and wondered how the priests and nuns planned on hiding that from future employers.

When she was in the mood, Mom would share her Residential School experience with us. She had watched as two girls were beaten with a strap in front of her for trying to escape one night. "I was so glad I didn't go with them," laughed my mom. "That could have been me!"

Mom told us about always being hungry. "My stomach would hurt but that's only because I was used to eating so much more at my mom and dad's. Sure it bothered me that the nuns and priests ate better than we did. That was to be expected, they're God's helpers." Her off-hand manner was confusing; it was wrong to hurt children but how come Mom and Dad weren't mad about what happened to them?

My dad had been bullied by older kids and narrowly escaped a beating at the hands of one of these bullies but that, too, was all in a day's fun. "Oh, the good times we used to have, running away from the big guys. You'd be surprised how long you can hide in a broom closet."

Listening to their stories, I would wonder what they would consider abuse: hot pokers? dog attacks? waterboarding?

If you have followed the history of residential schools, you know that Native people sued the residential schools and their organizers: the United Church, the Catholic Church and the Canadian Government. The lawsuits alleged physical, emotional and sexual abuses at the hands of the people who ran these schools. After years of litigation, the Canadian government settled with the Aboriginal people who attended the schools and paid out money to everyone who had attended. The payments were called, "The Common Experience" payments because the students had the same common experience that residential schools sucked.

To my parents the schools were tough, yes. Abusive? No. Even when I would argue that the rational behind the schools was inherently racist and say, "They wanted to beat the Indian out of you."

My parents disagreed.

"You can't make someone not Native. Either you are or you aren't."

My parents did not deny that some children who attended these schools were abused. "Well, yes there's always some of that everywhere you go."

"And you don't think these schools left children particularly defenseless?"

"Well, of course. No one meant anything bad by it." They were always hopeful, always optimistic about the intentions of others. I could never get my parents to admit that the residential schools were a terrible thing.

"I had a good time. Maybe not everyone else did, but I did. And the schools prepared you for life — you know, for the real world," Mom said.

"Yeah, if the real world is the Jerry Springer show."

"Oh go on! It wasn't that bad."

As time went on, their tune began to change. When the first lawsuits were being litigated, my parents moved onto the fence. "I suppose it was bad for that person but I don't remember any abuse like that. Still, that sounds really awful . . . "

After hundreds more people had received their money, "Now that I think of it, they were pretty mean at those schools and they didn't need to be. We were just kids."

Then finally when Canada announced the Common Experience payouts, my parents printed off their forms and dutifully listed the years they attended the schools. We knew our parents deserved the money. Still we teased them about their hypocrisy.

"I thought you said it wasn't that bad," I commented.

Mom gave me a hurt look. "I did go hungry and my parents could only visit once a year."

My dad added, "I didn't get to speak my language. I missed that."

Mom agreed. "Honestly, I'd love your father more if he could speak Cree. A lot more."

In the early Eighties, a Native band near us came into a lot of money and bought the local Residential school. They removed the Catholic component and replaced it with a curriculum based on sports and being cool. At least that's how it seemed to my sister and me. Our cousin Rachel went there. Her enrollment guaranteed that for the rest of her life no matter where she went in Western Canada, she always knew where the best party was. Only the most socially progressive Native teenagers in the province attended it: the girls with the best hair and clothes and the guys with the widest smiles and the deepest dimples.

I saw one of the Lebret girls in our town one afternoon — Stacey Littlechild. She was famous for being beautiful and dating one of the hot Gambler boys. She stood in the dingy foyer between the restaurant and the bar. Her hair was straight and sleek, a black sheet that floated down her back, as she got up to look out the window for the Greyhound bus. I walked past her and ate her outfit with my eyes in the three seconds that you are allowed to stare before you're marked as a creepy weirdo. Sadly I knew that even if I had the money to shop in the stores she frequented, I would never, ever put together an outfit that was so stylish and casual and cool. Stacey was in my town, standing in my bus depot and yet it was like she owned everything. Simply by passing through, she put her mark on the place.

Rachel knew girls like Stacey (or Stace as you called her if you knew her.) Her stories were coloured with their names; Rachel wasn't bragging about knowing Native celebrities, she simply knew them. And we didn't.

Celeste and I were jealous. We asked our parents to let us switch schools. They wouldn't budge. Mom preferred to keep her children where she could see them. Dad had a different reason; the residential schools were segregated and Dad believed in integration. Whenever my sister and I would bring up the idea of moving to the Residential school, he would say, "You might as well learn how to get along with *them* now."

I complained to my parents. "It's racist at our school. Everybody knows that."

Mom disagreed, "Just be yourself and people will want to be your friend."

At school a veil of air separated the Natives and whites. You could be standing right beside a white person and it was as though you were invisible. They would stick their arm up and address the teacher. "I don't have a partner!"

"Dawn doesn't have a partner."

"Oh right. Dawn?" I would nod and internally roll my eyes. I didn't dare reject my partner as it meant another class sitting alone in the back. By the way, doodling for entire class isn't as fun as it sounds.

Celeste was fearless and outgoing so I always figured she had it easier than me. One day she came home seriously pissed off. "You will never believe what Sandy said to me!" Sandy was a chubby, dark haired white girl in Celeste's class.

I knew who Sandy was; I had tutored her in math the year before. She was nice even if she did tell me that my chapped lips looked gross one day. She was right; they did look disgusting.

"Was it something about your lips?" I asked.

"No. She told me that if I wanted to, then I could be white."

I wasn't exactly stunned. I knew that my sister was fairer than the rest of our family. In fact, she was the blondest person on the reserve (other than Valerie, our resident southern belle.)

"Why would you want to be white?" I asked.

"That's the whole point. Sandy assumed that everyone would want to be white, if they had a choice."

"Why would she assume that?"

"Because she thinks we're ashamed of being Native!"

Sandy was wrong on both points. Nobody could choose to be white at our school. Even if your looks allowed you to jump over the first barrier, how would you explain what bus you got off of each morning? How would you explain your cousins, your brother or your sister? These weren't decision that you could make or unmake. Despite her hair colour, Celeste was

First Nations. She lived on the reserve, she ate Indian foods and went to pow-wows. She said, "as if" and "Ch." She played "boys chase the girls" and "girls chase the boys" at recess.

Sandy was wrong about the second point as well. While we didn't wear our pride on our sleeves, we didn't want to be any other race. I wanted to make sure that Celeste was on the same page, so I asked her, "Do you want to be white?"

Celeste looked at me as if I had grown horns out of my head. "Of course not," she huffed.

I was relieved. The white girls already had everything; they couldn't have my sister too.

"So what did you tell her?"

"I asked her why would I want to be white? And she said, 'how rude Celeste!' I told her if she mentioned it again, I would punch her in the mouth." My sister smiled at her own viciousness.

I felt sorry for Sandy. I'm sure she was surprised to find out that even though the whites considered us inferior, we did not.

The white kids dominated the school while the First Nations kids pretended they didn't care. But they did care, and they showed how much by dropping out. When I started junior high, there had been at least fifteen reserve-raised girls in my class. By the time I graduated, there were none left. The others had transferred to city schools where they fit in better, where there were more Native students, more guys to crush on, more parties to attend. There were more races in the city too, so racists had to split their attention among Asian, Black, Aboriginal and immigrant students.

My old best friend, Trina explained, "In the country I'm an Indian. Up here, I'm a minority. You know?" I missed my friends but I understood their reasons for transferring schools.

I was lonely, but I knew things weren't going to change any time soon. I consoled myself that there were only three more years to go. I could deal with having one friend in some of my classes and blending into the wall in my other ones. There was always recess when I could detach myself from my classmates and join the small group of Native and Metis kids hanging out at our table in the library. We would survive.

⁂

While becoming invisible at school was a natural choice for me and my introverted siblings, this strategy wouldn't work for the brash and confident. When my aunt Beth had trouble with her two oldest sons in The Pas, Manitoba, she decided to send them to our school. One of them, seventeen year old Malcolm, had gotten into trouble with gangs in the area. They had offered him a choice between joining the gang or getting beat up. Malcolm chose to beat up the guy sent to beat him up. Though Malcolm had no fear of repercussions, his mom was scared for him and his younger brother Nathan — and drove them five hours south in the middle of the night.

They stayed across the road from us at Uncle Frank's. For my siblings and me, it was like we had been in a coma and now someone had brought us back to life with a shot of adrenaline straight to our hearts. From the day they arrived, Celeste, Dave and I were hanging out at Frank's. We loved being with our cousins who had lost none of their enthusiasm for everything mischievous. We watched as they transferred a tractor motor into a truck frame in order to make the world's first "truck-tor."

"So are you coming to our school?" I asked.

"No, the goat is going to home school us," Malcolm replied. "Boy, you ask a lot of dumb questions for someone who's supposed to be smart." Malcolm was still as charming as ever.

"What's the school like?" Nathan asked, "Are there lots of pretty girls?"

"You're gonna have trouble — they don't like Natives at our school."

Malcolm shrugged. "Where do they?"

A thrill went down my spine. My cousins weren't scared; they were big and bold. They had faced down violent, drug-crazed gangs; the spoiled white kids would be no match for them.

Nathan was in my year and I couldn't have been happier. Our first class together was math. I felt so proud seeing him walk in wearing his black jeans, ripped jean jacket and leather vest. I smiled at him and called his name. Every head in the class turned towards me; the other students had forgotten the sound of my voice. Now with the support of a cousin who HAD to be friendly with me, my voice was already louder and more confident.

Nathan sat behind me and tapped me on the shoulder to borrow a pen, then a piece of paper. Then he tapped me again. He handed me the piece of paper that read: "Where are all the Indians?"

I wrote, "This is all there is." And handed it back. He read it nodding. Then he stared out the window for the rest of the class.

At lunchtime, instead of eating my lunch alone in front of my locker, I went to look for Nathan. I wanted to explain to him that it wouldn't be so bad, that he and I could have lots of fun even if no one ever talked to us. "We can study and we can write papers together and in science class, we can even share a microscope!"

By the time I found him, he had already found his friends. The school had built a place for students like Malcolm and Nathan. Half school, half detention centre — Remedial — was the holding cell for students who could not make it anywhere else. There were a lot of Native students in Remedial.

"You guys don't belong here," I argued. "You both have good grades."

"Nope. We failed our placement test," Nathan said. He described how they had fooled around during the test period.

My self-esteem depended completely on my grades so I could not understand how someone would want others to think they were stupid. Nathan and Malcolm believed that the sacrifice was worth it; now they could hang out with the only other Native students in the school and do less homework.

I chided them for taking the easy path even as I inwardly congratulated them for finding a way out of the jail I'd been sentenced to. They rejoined their motley crew. These were students who had been sidelined early in their academic careers. All boys — they came from the poorest families on the reserve.

I recognized some of them. David had been in my class until grade four when he got stuck on math. Then there was Everett, who often switched schools three or four times a year, depending on which relative was keeping him. There was Jack — nobody knew what was wrong with him — but he had never been in regular classes. All of them had an unfit, unkempt look about them as if they had been looking after themselves since they were small children. They were the lost boys, and Malcolm and Nathan were their Peter Pan and Tinkerbell.

One of the lost boys was a white kid known as Samuel. He was mentally disabled. I don't know how the remedial students treated him. I knew that the mainstream students treated Samuel poorly. On a bus ride to a track meet, a few of the white boys had made him sit on the floor of the bus. I wanted to speak up but making a big fuss out of a terrible situation can sometimes make it worse, so I didn't. (Also, I am a coward.)

My cousins adopted Samuel into their gang along with the other lost boys. They walked downtown together and hung out in front of the ice cream store. Malcolm and Nathan would flirt with girls and the lost boys would stand in the background and grin. Then they would wander back to the school at their leisure. After school, Malcolm and Nathan bid Samuel adieu, piled the rest of the Native boys into their truck-tor and drove everyone home. It had been two days and my cousins already had a better social life than I'd ever dreamed of.

Two new students — even Native ones — in the middle of the year did not go unnoticed by my schoolmates. The white guys noted their proud posture and their large muscles and decided to ignore them. The white girls kept looking and some went even further. Ginnie was a tall blonde in my sister's class. In the morning biology class, she whispered to my sister that she was interested in Malcolm and by afternoon's English class they were a couple.

"I like dating a Native guy," she cooed to her friends as Celeste and I walked by. "He's a bad boy."

Celeste rolled her eyes. "I hate that. Just cuz he's Native, she assumes he's wild and crazy."

It would have been insulting except that Malcolm WAS wild and crazy. If he auditioned for a high school production of *Rebel Without a Cause*, Malcolm would have been the first person cast. His clothing, demeanor, language and even his walk screamed bad boy. I wasn't surprised that Ginnie was excited about him. They were a good match. Ginnie was also something of a bad girl; rumor had it that she had had intimate relations with a vegetable. It was also rumored that she had started this rumor herself.

Their romance became the talk of the school. Heads turned as they walked past. Both Malcolm and Ginnie found the interest exciting. It made me nervous. Before Malcolm and Nathan came along, Natives were disliked but generally ignored. Now, our dark skin was attracting attention.

A group of boys called out Malcolm and Nathan about a week after the relationship with Ginnie started. They told Ginnie that she had to break up with Malcolm or else they would fight him. Ginnie told the white boys, "I can see whoever I want! Nobody owns me! I may be a beautiful white woman but I am not a prize to be fought over!" The boys ignored her hysterics and told her the time and place.

Malcolm and Nathan gathered up their lost boys a few minutes before the fight. Celeste and I hovered near them.

Everything I knew about fighting I learned from watching movies. "Don't worry, it'll be over before you know it. Float like a butterfly, sting like a bee. Eye of the Tiger. Kumité," I said, as I bounced around them, my anxiety making me bouncy.

Malcolm smirked. "Has anyone ever told you how much you resemble a chipmunk?"

Just him. Many times. I covered up my cheeks defensively. "I'm worried, that's all. I don't want you guys to get hurt."

Malcolm laughed. "We won't even fight. You'll see."

The white guys had not expected them to show up; this was apparent in the nervous smiles that crept across their faces.

Nathan wore a confident smile that comes from knowing that you will not be beaten.

Malcolm wore the stoic expression of someone who approaches violence as though it is work. And, not hard work, more like distasteful work, like taking out the garbage. The rest of the lost boys looked bewildered. This was more attention than anyone had shown them in their lives so far.

As the lost boys fanned out behind him, Malcolm walked forward and told the group of pale guys in front of him that he was ready.

Celeste and I stood on the sidelines. Ginnie hurried over to join us. "Today, I am a Native," she said bravely and put her arms around Celeste and me. I was grateful that she had not found a feather to wear in her hair.

The white boys began the process of backing down. A young diplomat — I think he was on the student government — stepped forward and told Malcolm that it was all a big misunderstanding, "Nobody wants any trouble. It's just that . . . "

"What?" Malcolm asked.

"That you guys think you can run this school or something." The guy said it apologetically.

"Who says we don't?" Nathan asked. He laughed, which took the sting out of it.

A few others joined in the laughter and Malcolm allowed himself a faint smile.

It looked like the fight was unraveling until one guy — a known bully — yelled, "Samuel!"

Samuel stood in the centre of the lost boys; his height making him stand out like an oak among the willows. Slowly he turned his attention to the bully.

The bully gave him a charming smile, "Samuel, what are you doing with these guys? We're your friends."

Samuel was confused.

"Whose side are you on Samuel? You're not an Indian, you're white!" the bully yelled.

Malcolm looked at Samuel. Samuel looked at the group of white boys and he broke free of the lost boys to join them.

"They made you sit on the floor," I wanted to remind him. "They treated you like crap."

Malcolm turned his lost boys around and walked away.

Later that week, Mom went to her monthly school board meeting. Mom was the first person ever appointed to the school board from the reserve and she took her duties very seriously. She wanted to ensure that we had the best education possible. It also gave the inside track on the best school gossip.

That night, Mom returned later than usual. She hurried into the living room and asked Celeste and me about the near-fight between Malcolm and the white guys. We told her what we had seen.

"The school board wanted to kick Malcolm out," Mom told us.

"He never fought anyone!" I protested.

"The fight is just an excuse. It's because of that white girl. I set them straight," Mom said, congratulating herself on her assertiveness as she nervously sucked on her cigarette. "I told them, this isn't the 1950's. No way, Jose. This is the twentieth century and he can date who-ever the hell he wants. This is what those black people were fighting for down south — you know with the bridge and the hoses and the water truck — for the dream or whatever that was — just like that I stood up to them, and told them all off — you bet your ass!"

Confrontation was as natural to Mom as a savings account and I knew we'd be hearing about this one for a few years at least. She retold her story several times, adding and refining her speech until it sounded like she had delivered Martin Luther King's "I have a Dream" speech to the school board.

Finally the adrenaline wore off and she became calm. Then a thoughtful look crossed her face. "Doesn't Malcolm have a girlfriend back home?"

He did. And when she found out about the white girl, Malcolm was ordered home. He left that weekend, deciding that pissed off gang-bangers were not as scary as a pissed off girlfriend.

Nathan hung on to finish the school year with the lost boys. While he lacked Malcolm's leadership skills, he had enough charm to seduce every Aboriginal girl within fifty miles. The lost boys followed in his wake; proximity to girls is more than enough reason to follow a leader.

Fun dominated their school schedules and I watched them frolic in the parking lot from my classroom window. They teased each other and play wrestled under the spring sun. I also noticed the tall, pale lost boy playing along with them, too slow to remember that he did not belong with them or wise enough to know that it didn't matter.

The Reserve vs. Satan's Brides

GROWING UP THE QUESTION, "WHAT ARE YOU going to be?" never baffled me. A movie, *And Justice for All*, had sealed my fate. So when the question was asked, my answer was given without a moment's hesitation, "A lawyer, of course." No one ever asked the follow-up question, "What does a lawyer do?"

Because if they had asked, my answer would have been revealing: "They wear pretty suits with high heels that clack smartly down the hallways of justice."

When I went home after my first year of law school, my relatives had their legal questions ready for me. They sat across from me as I ate my cereal and laid out their legal dilemmas:

"Now let's say I punched a cop in the face . . . no, no, hear me out . . . you haven't heard the whole story . . . if I punched him right in the kisser after he accused me of stealing a car and everyone knows it was my brother, and not me . . . my question is: do I have a case for mistaken identity?"

"So I was coming out of the grocery store and the clerk stopped me and found three cartons of smokes . . . and this is the tricky part . . . the cartons were stuffed in my two-year-old's backpack. Even I know that two-year-old's can't be prosecuted so why am I getting charged?"

"Okay, so I stole a doctor's prescription pad and wrote myself a prescription — only so I could get some painkillers cuz my hand was killing me after punching out that cop. Isn't that self-defense or something?"

The cases were dazzling in their complexity. I pondered each question carefully, then applied my legal knowledge to the facts, formulated my answer and delivered it. This process took about twenty seconds. Then, I would accept my payment: a look of awe.

It's probably this appetite for approval that got me into trouble. I was at my parent's house on summer vacation when my older sister Tabitha called one night. In clipped words she asked to speak to Mom. I knew her tone. It could mean only one thing: trouble.

I told her Mom was busy and pressed the phone closer to my ear; my toe tapped on the floor as my body eagerly responded to the drama of the situation.

"I need you and Mom to come to my reserve immediately. They are charging our baby-sister with witchcraft," Tabitha said.

"Sorry? Did you say . . . witchcraft?"

Tabitha gave a frustrated sigh, which I took as a sign to quit being a smart ass. She explained that her husband's reserve, the White Lake Nation had charged our youngest sister Pammy with four counts of witchcraft. (White Lake is a pseudonym to protect my family from further witchcraft-related accusations. Also, to protect the real reserve from ridicule, because accusing people of witchcraft in the twenty-first century is some crazy shit.)

The White Lake Band Council had summoned fifteen-year-old Pammy to face the charges against her. They had apparently arisen from her last visit with Tabitha a few months before.

"Wow that's so cool. You're going to a witch trial!" I said, enjoying her obvious annoyance. "Make sure to tell us all about it."

"I'm not going. I have to work. You and Mom are going."

"Sorry, I skipped the class on witchcraft law."

"It doesn't matter if you believe or not, you have to take it seriously." Tabitha knew she wasn't dealing with rational types. She had accepted that when she moved onto her husband's reserve. His community was different from ours, some might say backwards. But it was also rich, much wealthier than ours. They had money; we had science. It's hard to say who had it better.

Unlike my sister, I was not prepared to be diplomatic. I had inherited my mom's impatience and I dismissed people who believed in ghosts, aliens and witches with rolled eyes and a contemptuous shake of the head. I did not listen to them, question them, or worse, drive six hours out of my way to spend a day with them.

Tabitha believed that ignoring the witch hunters would make the problem worse. "If no one shows up, they can just ban our baby sister from the reserve. Forever. And then who will baby-sit for me?"

I told her that my only travel plans were a trip to the beach followed by a quick jaunt to the local Dairy Queen.

Tabitha turned on the big guns. "I thought you were training to be a lawyer or something. Don't lawyers protect people from persecution?"

"Yeah, in a big city where people will notice."

"Don't you want to show people who know you — like your cousins and your ex-boyfriend — what a great lawyer you are?"

Tabitha knew which buttons to press. Of course, I only had one button, labelled, "Ego."

The next day Mom and I drove to my sister's reserve. We had so many questions on the way there such as, what would a witch trial look like? Why Pam? And, of course, who the hell still believes in witches?

Pam was guilty of many things but witchcraft was not one of them. If this crucible was prosecuting her for crimes against pairs of jeans, I could understand. She had a tendency to wear them so tight that their seams screamed for mercy — then again so did any Native girl under the age of forty.

If she were being prosecuted for delivering smartass remarks and being a general spoiled little shit, then that would also be more believable. Even if they had to invent a new charge for her say—"Assault against the English language," then I would nod my head and say, "Yes, I can understand why you created a law in order to punish my sister for saying things like, 'un-fucking-butt-ass believable.'"

As the baby of the family, Pammy was a little wild. The last five years had more than proven that to all of us. When she was a baby, we would stand over her bassinet and imagine her future. Would she be a lawyer? A doctor? A teacher?

"I want to be a stripper," she baldly declared these days to anyone who listened. "Cuz they get to wear cool clothes and have fake tits."

Where we once cheered every time she spoke, now we listened to her stories in open-mouthed horror. The same parents, who used to scream at us for being irresponsible and whiny, now hugged us close whenever we visited. "You're great kids. We didn't know. We swear, we didn't know."

We watched her apply makeup thick enough to protect her against radiation poisoning and squeeze into tops that fit her when she was two. Then when Pammy was sixteen, she got a tattoo of a rose wrapped in barbed wire on her breast. "Like it? My friends say it's the sexiest fuckin' thing ever."

"Are your friends the band Poison?"

"Who the fuck is Poison?"

That barbed wire tittie tattoo was the trashiest thing I'd ever seen until the next year when she followed it up with a tat on her arm that read, "Love 69."

Word of the tattoo spread like wildfire over the phone lines. Celeste saw it first, and then she called Tabitha, who called me. Then I called home, asked my mom about it, who asked my brother David — who didn't know it existed and just said, "What the fuck?" Then the phone was passed to the Wild One herself who proudly described it to me. "My friends think it's fucking awesome."

"Who are your friends, the cast of *Debbie Does Dallas*?"

"You're jealous cuz you don't have the balls."

She bravely went against any notion of class or elegance and we had no idea why. Like conservative pundits, we blamed rap music, her friends, TV, cigarettes, and pizza pops for her behavior but never blamed ourselves. Although in our case, we were right. Nobody else in the family had turned out like Pam. It was like she had emerged fully formed from a mound of cigarette ashes.

But a witch? That was impossible. It was like we had fallen into a low budget horror flick. Except in that case, Pammy would turn out to be a witch and then would destroy the small reserve of White Pine with her powers. Not a bad movie idea really.

When I told her about the witchcraft charges, Pammy laughed raucously and started packing. As she threw her smokes and tube tops into her backpack, she said, "I can't want to hear their charges. I'm gonna laugh right in their stupid fuckin' faces. And then I'm gonna kick the shit outta the bitch who accused me."

Mom was too scared to let Pammy speak on her own behalf. Give Pammy the floor and she would use it to rant for hours, probably implicating herself in a thousand other real crimes in the process. Also, what if this thing were for real? Real witch trials never had happy endings. We knew enough New England history to know that.

After Mom and I arrived at Tabitha's house, we spent five hours discussing everything related to the trial. I have no idea why it took that long since my older sister knew nothing. It was the reserve's first witchcraft proceeding and the particulars had not yet been set down. The trial was scheduled for the next day and over three hundred people planned to be there. "Maybe more, people always turn out for these things," Tabitha said.

I asked her if by "these things" she meant other "witch-related hearings."

She was referring to a half dozen inquiries held in the past year into aliens, werewolves and Sasquatch.

"Is this a reserve or an asylum for mental patients?" I asked.

Tabitha glared at me. "You have to take this seriously!"

I shouldn't have laughed. After all, Mom was a wreck. She sat on my sister's deck and chain-smoked. I couldn't put my finger on the source of her worries. I knew she was scared of speaking in public. It was also possible that she was scared of encountering a real witch at the trial as my sister was not the only girl being charged. I blamed Catholicism. If you believed that wine could be turned into blood, it wasn't so far a leap to believe that a broom could make you fly.

We drove to the White Lake Band hall the next day. It was a low building, hardly impressive enough to serve the needs of such a huge and financially successful band. That's because it wasn't, Mom explained. Down the road was the real hall, a huge modern building with a café on the ground floor.

This was the old band hall and had been left standing to serve the needs of the supernatural believers. Mom added that as a leader you were obligated to respect everyone's beliefs. "When your dad was chief, believe me, I had to deal with a lot of these assholes. In a respectful way, of course."

When we got out of the car, people stared at us. We didn't take that personally because people always stared in White Lake. They recognized as non-band members and had to sift through their files of family trees to put us in the right place. We were related to two large families on the reserve so we were tolerated and received a modicum of politeness. Someone handed Mom a coffee and she gratefully slurped it in the cold morning air.

People were tense. I listened as some people tried to drive away their fear by pretending to be rational. "This is silly. These girls aren't witches. There's no such thing as witches." The warble in their voices gave away their true conviction. I tried to empathize. If I believed in witches, then I suppose prosecuting (persecuting?) them would be a rather scary enterprise. Perhaps my hands would also be shaking and I would also feel the frequent need to urinate.

At every sound, people looked around themselves defensively as if they expected one of the teenage witches to fly in on a broom. If only Hollywood were around, they could have organized a group of young girls to march up the street with cats on their shoulders and black make up around their eyes! I looked at the road wistfully; no witches materialized. Instead, a black car pulled up and a priest, an Elder and a rotund Native man stepped out of it. It was either the set up to an old joke or our judges had arrived.

Three other families had been notified of the charges against their daughters. We were the only ones who showed up. Once again we had bucked the trends. I grabbed Mom's arm. "Let's just go." But Mom worried that the real consequences of this fake trial would follow us out of the building and shook off my hand. "We're gonna see this through," she murmured.

We sat at a table in front of the witch panel. The panel was made up of respected leaders both political and spiritual. On the far right was a councillor for the band. He was a large, red-faced Native man with stubby facial features. He looked exactly like a bear. Next to him sat a Native Elder, who looked like he would rather be on a horse than sitting on a chair, who introduced himself simply as Eddie. Next to him was a middle-aged white priest who called himself "Father Martin." They would serve as the judges, jury and if need be, witch-dunkers.

As we took our seats, everyone's attention turned to us. I could hear the excitement rise in the room. Everyone now had a witch to focus on. I met all their eyes disdainfully, as I imagined a witch might, and thought about the spells I would cast.

Councillor Bear opened the proceedings with a speech about the nature of evil, which I think was basically an excuse to re-tell the entire *Exorcist* movie. Then he explained that the chief could not attend because of his daughter's birthday party. At the mention of the chief's name, everyone started clapping. By the time the applause stopped, Councillor Bear looked annoyed.

Councilor Bear asked us our names and we told him. Mom's voice shook as she spoke out loud. I stated my name, loud enough for the people at the back to hear. I am not my sister, is what my tone said, and I am not ashamed of her, my stiff posture added.

The latter was kind of true. When I first heard about my sister's tattoos, I immediately thought of trailer trash or rezzed out chicks. Because we were poor, all of my siblings had tried to be better than that. When I left the reserve, I stopped saying, "Aaaahhh" and "ch." I stopped wearing sneakers with my jeans and hardly ever wore my AC/DC T-shirt out of the house. When the muffler on my car fell off, I replaced it. I wanted to be known as a person of status, not a status Indian.

Pam had no such desire. She immersed herself in rez culture: the accent, the clothes, the obsession with American rap and hip-hop. And she did so without one iota of shame. Because I had tried to hide everything that connected me to the reserve, I was in awe of her choice to do the opposite.

"We are entering a plea of Not Guilty," I pronounced. These superstitious yokels were no match for me, I was going to beat this rap and then I was going to counter-sue. I would bankrupt the band to punish them for attacking my sister. They would rue the day they ever messed with my family; oh yes, they would be up to their eyeballs in rue.

Now, being only a second year law student, I hadn't participated in a real court yet. But I had watched many episodes of *Law and Order* with my mom, so I felt confident.

Councillor Bear looked at me as if I were a dime that he found on the floor of a casino, pathetic but somewhat useful. When he spoke, Councillor Bear stared at a point above my head as he spoke. "This is not a trial. This is an investigation into the accusations made against your sister."

He then launched into a description of those accusations. He read from a page of lined paper:

Pam had been seen setting fires in the woods, then dancing around those fires while singing songs about the devil.

Pam had threatened other girls with curses.

Pam had made them have nightmares.

The Councillor called a young girl as a witness. The girl was skinny with heavily eye-lined eyes and purple streaks of dye in her hair. She refused to leave her mother's side no matter how much her beefy mom pushed her. "Go on!"

"No!"

"Get up there."

"No!"

"Go!"

"Nooooo!"

The investigation stalled there. Not one to give up easily, the Councillor decided to give evidence himself. Not about my sister, but about witches in general.

He launched into a thirty-minute speech about his twelve-year-old foster child who had turned out to be a witch. With her knowledge of the dark arts, she had almost ruined his life. Because of her spells, he had trouble at work, gained sixty pounds and his marriage was threatened. Everything returned to normal after he got rid of the foster child.

"Got rid of?" asked Eddie the Elder, looking a trifle worried.

"Sent her back, y'know. To the orphanage-thingie." Recognizing that he was losing his sympathy vote, the Councillor yelled, "She was a Satan-worshiper!"

Father Martin looked up as if someone had just called his name. "Satan?"

"Yes. She was a bride of Beelzebub!" The Councillor then explained that devil worshipers and witches were one and the same because in order to get their power, the witches had to marry Satan. This marriage could only take place after their menses had begun. His explanation sounded a lot like the plot for the movie *The Craft*.

Even though Councillor Bear was doing his best to entertain, his audience was beginning to get restless. Mercifully, he called for a coffee break.

"Can we leave now?" I asked Mom.

"No, I want to see what will happen." Mom smiled politely at everyone who passed as if to say, "See, I'm nice. I'm not the mother of a witch."

Once we got outside, she pulled a smoke out of her pack. I noticed that her hands were shaking. "What's wrong?"

Mom took a drag of her smoke and then exhaled. "What if it's true, what if she is a witch?"

I laughed. "C'mon, Pam?" I knew my sister. She didn't have the energy to be a witch. Being evil takes motivation; some get up and go. You can't be a witch and be good at video games. You can't spend twelve hours a day watching TV and be an honest to goodness bride of the devil.

Witch life was an active life. Witches went out into the wood and collected bat wings and goat's blood — that took effort. Pam thought microwaving pizza pops was too labour intensive and ate them straight out of the box.

She was not the type to talk around with powerful spiritual beings even if she did have a talent for chatting with her friends for hours. I doubted that spirits wanted to talk about kicking the shit out of the girl who kept stealing other girls' boyfriends. I didn't know any spirits personally but I hoped their interests were a little less prosaic.

But the idea had been planted in Mom's head and she wasn't ready to let it go. "What about that tattoo on her arm? That Love 69, isn't that the devil's number?'

I stared into her eyes and saw real fear there. Her question told me that I had underestimated her fear of the supernatural . . . and also that she had never watched a porno.

"That's not the devil's number," I said carefully. "The devil's number is 666. Remember when we watched *The Omen*?"

"Oh, I never watch those kinds of movies, those devil-movies."

"Well, I have and trust me, 666 was the number behind little Damian's ear."

"Then what does 69 — "

"Oh look! Breaks over, we have to go back inside!" My mom was an innocent and I wanted to keep her that way.

⁊ᕽ

For the next part of the hearing, Councillor Bear pushed a podium into the centre of the room and told people to come and give evidence against the witches. Nobody got up. Then he plugged in a microphone and placed it on the podium. Suddenly a line-up formed around the room.

Surprisingly, few people were interested in the topic of witches. Many of them seized their moment in the sun to talk about everything that bothered them. We heard about garbage collection problems and mischievous teens that broke windows indiscriminately; we heard tales of huge potholes that were destroying cars and people who never looked after their animals. An individual would reach the pulpit and speak and speak and speak until they ran out of words. Then they would stop, without wrapping up or explaining how their point related to witchcraft. There would be silence as everyone acknowledged that they had spoken and then another individual take the podium and begin their speech.

The mother of the shy witness and also my sister's primary accuser, rose unsteadily to her feet. As she waddled to the podium, her head and body shape reminded me of two conjoined potatoes. She introduced herself as "Edna, a single mother." Edna held a Kleenex to her face to capture the tears already dripping from her eyes. I was immediately impressed; now this was someone who understood drama!

Edna said she understood how kids could get sucked into witchcraft, there was so little to do on the reserve. I nodded in agreement. It was the same on my reserve. However, despite our boredom, we had never considered witchcraft. True, we did tear up a playing card outside the house at night and chanted, "Bloody Mary, Bloody Mary" in order to see a ghost. But that wasn't witchcraft that was a scientific experiment. (We didn't see a ghost. Probably this was because as soon as we finished chanting, we started screaming and jostling with one another to get back into the safety of the house.)

Edna said that she wished the chief and council would take pity on the poor children and their poor mothers. Then she finished by telling the audience that she loved her children. She closed her show by dissolving into loud wet sobs. It was the highlight of the afternoon.

⟡

I fell asleep for a few minutes around three PM. It wasn't my fault, I have low blood sugar and the early afternoon is the worst time for me. It didn't help that Councillor Bear had decided to re-tell his story about his evil foster child one more time. In the retelling, the girl had gotten even more evil and had somehow caused him to gain even more weight. I stared at his belly as he told his story. Perhaps it was the rhythmic movements of his belly swaying back and forth, up and down, like a bulbous pendulum that led me to close my eyes.

When I woke up the Priest was talking. Father Martin spoke about the church's involvement in the community and avoided any reference to supernatural topics. He said nothing about my sister or any of the accused. He had a benign smile that expressed none of his views on witchcraft.

I had been raised Catholic but had left the church when I moved to the city and found that waking early on Sundays clashed with my other religion: partying. I had good memories about being a Catholic. Our reserve parish had been progressive. They were one of the first churches to incorporate Aboriginal spirituality into their services with sweet grass smudging. Our Priest even wore beaded vestments.

The parish's progressive nature was also apparent in the way they answered our questions about God and religion. Sister Bernadette, the presiding nun and who always seemed to be thirty-five- years-old, taught catechism. She could take scripture, and wring all traces of sexism, racism and supernatural mumbo jumbo out of it, leaving behind only fresh-smelling goodness.

In an effort to appear more intelligent, I had once asked her, "What about where it says that God created the world in seven days? How does that make sense when our teacher tells us that the world is millions of years old?"

Sister Bernadette smiled and replied that time was much different to God who had lived forever. I accepted her answer because it made sense or because I was too lazy to ask any more questions.

Her answer helped kick-start my legal mind. Suddenly, I knew how to destroy this mockery of a trial. I raised my hand. The panel ignored it although the Priest did speak louder.

I put my hand down self-consciously. Then when Father Martin paused, I raised it again.

"Father," I said before anyone could interrupt me. "Isn't it true that the modern Catholic Church recognizes the devil as an idea rather than as a being?"

I had him by the balls. He knew it, I knew it, and the crowd knew it. Hell, even the devil knew it.

The Priest tilted his head and looked me in the eye with his steel grey eyes and replied, "The devil is real and he walks among us."

A woman in the crowd gave a little shriek, a baby began to cry and Councillor Bear went pale.

I sighed. With a single sentence, the Priest had unraveled my argument. My only effort had achieved nothing, except making my mom and the crowd full of believers more nervous. The protestant and non-Christians were shifting uncomfortably. Father Martin had confirmed their worst nightmares and I anticipated that many of them were going to have difficulty sleeping for many moons.

The only good part was Councillor Bear was speechless. He rose suddenly and quickly walked out of the room. Nobody asked where he was going. I knew. He was hurrying down to the local casino where the slot machines would gently lull his heart rate back to normal.

The Councillor's departure, ironically, removed all order and sense from the proceedings. The crowd took out their cell phones and called their kids and asked where they were. They made plans for dinner. They drifted in and out of the room. Mom and I gossiped with Janet, one of my cousins. Janet had poked her head into the proceedings, saw us and scurried over midway through the trial.

"So Tabitha told you about the trial?" I asked.

"Nah, I saw a bunch of cars and got nosy. What kind of trial?'

"Oh you know, witchcraft." My mom was already blasé about the experience. Her husband was an alcoholic, her youngest daughter was a witch, her second oldest was in law school and still useless; there was nothing that could upset her now.

The priest and elder sat next to each other and said nothing. They still held a romantic illusion that order would be restored and that the "investigation" would continue. They had not yet accepted that fear no longer had the hold over people that it used to have. With the Internet, computer games and HD TV fighting over their souls, people don't have the time to worry about the devil and his shenanigans.

Mom and I drove to Janet's house and discussed the day's activities. My cousin had married onto the reserve about a decade before my sister. She felt no need to feign respect for the membership. She laughed at Mom's impression of Edna.

Janet gave us the inside information: Edna's kids were in and out of foster care because of her gambling addiction. Mom raised her hand to her heart, as if to say, "Oh, what a terrible woman." Even though, of course, Mom would be in the casino that very evening.

I stood by my earlier decision to like the woman. Yes, she had accused my sister of a terrible crime, but it was the reserve that had chosen to take her seriously. They were just as guilty as she was. Besides, I admired her creativity — she could have accused my sister of anything — she chose witchcraft. That took imagination and balls.

Tabitha joined us at Janet's. "What did they decide?" she asked with her usual clarity.

Mom and I scratched our heads. There had been no outcome as far as we knew. Other than the devil being identified as a real being, no other conclusive statements had been made, I explained.

"Is Pam banned or what?" Tabitha asked.

"I don't know," I replied lamely.

We called the band office the next day. Councillor Bear informed us that Pam was indeed banned. Forever.

Then forever was lowered to a month and now she lives there.

As for the Love 69 tattoo, Mom paid to have it changed to a blue orchid that wound its way down her shoulder. It still looks trashy but doesn't have the same demonic connotations in her mind.

I graduated from law school but never practiced. And despite what my mom thinks, I came to this decision of my own free will, and was not influenced by Edna's "evil eye," "bad medicine," or "ancient Indian curse", although, I would like to speak to her about a recurring rash of warts.